PRAISE FOR GRACE'S BOOKS

Love the beach and Coastal Carolina? Consider reading the two series set in Emerald Isle, NC because ~ *It's always a good time for a love story and a trip to the beach!* ~

THE EMERALD ISLE, NC STORIES SERIES begins with the award-winning debut novel, *Beach Rental*, an RT Book Reviews TOP PICK. Here's what the reviewer wrote:

> "No author can come close to capturing the awe-inspiring essence of the North Carolina coast like Greene. Her debut novel seamlessly combines hope, love and faith, like the female equivalent of Nicholas Sparks. Her writing is meticulous and so finely detailed you'll hear the gulls overhead and the waves crashing onto shore. Grab a hanky, bury your toes in the sand and get ready to be swept away with this unforgettable beach read."

Or visit Emerald Isle, NC i[illegible] S SERIES that begins with *A B*[illegible] a woman from the rural town [illegible] a accepts a temporary job that ta[illegible] — and discovers it may not be so easy to go home again.

Regarding Cub Creek, Virginia—a rural area *in the heart of Virginia, where the forests hide secrets and the creeks run strong and deep*—where Libbie (in *Cub Creek*) goes to hide from a world where she doesn't fit in…and finds her life. Or where Hannah (in *The Memory of Butterflies*) keeps a devastating secret to protect her loved ones. Or where Kara (in *Wildflower Heart*) finds healing from old wounds and heartbreak. Or where Jaynie (in *A Light Last Seen*) finds that you can—and should—go home again.

A Light Last Seen and A Reader's View of Cub Creek

From a reader about Cub Creek and A Light Last Seen: "'In the heart of Virginia, where the forests hide secrets and the creeks run strong and deep,' is a place called Cub Creek. A place that has meadows filled with colorful flowers and butterflies to chase, and dirt roads and Cub Creek to jump over and disappear into the woods. A living and rural place that draws the reader to the setting and the characters who have stories to tell. A place with light and darkness and as unique as the characters who live there. When I opened the beautiful cover of this book, I stepped into the Cub Creek world and met the main character, Jaynie Highsmith. This is her story."—*Reader/Reviewer, February 2020*

BOOKS BY GRACE GREENE

Emerald Isle, North Carolina Series

Beach Rental *(Book 1)*

Beach Winds *(Book 2)*

Beach Wedding *(Book 3)*

"Beach Towel" (A Short Story)

Beach Walk *(Christmas Novella)*

Barefoot Tides Two-Book Series

A Barefoot Tide *(Book 1)*

A Dancing Tide *(Book 2)*

Beach Single-Title Novellas

Beach Christmas *(Christmas Novella)*

Clair *(Beach Brides Novella Series)*

Cub Creek Novels ~ Series and Single Titles

Cub Creek *(Cub Creek Series, Book 1)*

Leaving Cub Creek *(Cub Creek Series, Book 2)*

The Happiness In Between

The Memory of Butterflies

A Light Last Seen

The Wildflower House Novels

Wildflower Heart *(Book 1)*

Wildflower Hope *(Book 2)*

Wildflower Christmas *(A Wildflower House Novella, Bk 3)*

Wildflower Wedding *(A Wildflower House Novella, Bk 4)*

Virginia Country Roads

Kincaid's Hope

A Stranger in Wynnedower

www.GraceGreene.com

Beach Heart

By

Grace Greene

Large Print Edition

This is a work of fiction. Names, characters, organizations, places, events, and incidents are either products of the author's imagination or are used fictitiously. Any resemblance to actual persons, living or dead, or actual events is purely coincidental.

Published by Grace Greene and Kersey Creek Books

ISBN-13: 979-8-9856778-5-0 (eBook)
ISBN-13: 979-8-9862394-0-8 (Print)
ISBN-13: 979-8-9862394-1-5 (Large Print)
ISBN-13: 979-8-9862394-2-2 (Case Laminate)

Cover design by Grace Greene
Printed in the United States of America

Dedication

Beach Heart is dedicated to all lovers of the beach, of nature, and to all those who struggle to do the right thing and feel like they fail, who suffer loss, grief, and trauma and have trouble moving beyond it, but who know there is a better future ahead if they can reach for it ~ even if they must reach more than once ~ as well as to those who offer a helping hand. We are all works in progress.

Beach Heart is also dedicated to our furry friends, our fur babies, our comfort givers, and sometimes our protectors, who greet us with joy and forgive us for falling short, and are always ready to engage with life. They are, in many cases, our best examples of how to live.

Beach Heart

by Grace Greene

Large Print Edition

Kersey Creek Books

Beach Heart

Prologue

The day I moved out of my home in Raleigh was surely the lowest point in my life.

My husband and I had lived in this house since we'd married thirteen years before, but what had begun so happily had ended badly. Very badly. Moving day, and the many difficult days that led up to it, had left me emotionally and physically exhausted. I sat in the last chair in the empty, echoey house, now a widow, feeling much older than my actual age of thirty-seven.

In the waning light of that March afternoon, and with my back turned toward the emptiness, I focused on the view through the tall front windows of my living room—*correction: used-to-be-my living room*. In the yard, the abelias were about to leaf out and blossoms would soon follow. The hummingbirds and honeybees had always loved them. Beyond the abelias, the tall, lush Carolina pines cast large swaths of shade across the lawn that made the grass look so green it squeezed my heart painfully in remembrance.

I'd loved this view in every season for all our years here. As I stared, memorizing the beauty, and the happy moments, the laughter—along with the *feels* that came with the memories—wanting to capture them and take them with me, a small delivery van pulled up to the curb.

A man exited the vehicle carrying a large white envelope, the kind that usually contained official or legal documents. The sight of it dashed what little good I'd been managing to pull out of this awful day, yet the man kept coming up the walk, headed to my front door.

Now what?

I'd taken care of everything pertaining to Gregory and the estate. The loose, frayed ends of our lives had been searched out and tied up, including the claims Macon had made on his father's estate. A few debts remained, but they'd have to wait for payment for the time being.

"No more, please," I whispered. I was supposed to be free now.

But the habit of courtesy prevailed. When he rang the bell, I answered the door, signed the handheld scanner's small window with a scrawl, and accepted the envelope.

Standing in the light of the front windows, I held the envelope close, squinting to make out the return address. A lawyer's office.

My heart sank and my stomach clenched in what had become an automatic reaction to almost everything—or even to nothing at all—in a reflex I couldn't seem to stop.

In my current life, the only *good* news was *no* news.

Bad news didn't improve with age, or with being ignored—I'd learned that—so I opened the envelope, glanced at the enclosed pages in the fading light and my eyes caught on the words, *Beach Heart*.

My knees went weak. The chair caught me.

Beach Heart. My *own* heart beat more strongly responding to the memories the words called up and, in that moment, proving time and logic did not exist in the part of the brain where those elements lived because images of a long-ago beach strand, of endless blue skies and the ocean's infinite moods, instantly swept me back to Emerald Isle and my great aunt Eva—to the years when only good things were expected to happen and life had been full of hopeful tomorrows.

Chapter One

When I was a child, I asked my great-aunt Eva why she loved the beach so much. It made perfect sense to me that everyone *should* love it—running in the waves, hunting shells, and building sandcastles, with no one fussing at you if you were wet or tracked sand into the house. What was there *not* to love? But that kind of fun was for kids. My mom said so.

Every summer and for most school breaks, Mom packed me off to Aunt Eva. My mother rarely came to the beach with me because she was a hardworking single parent. I'd been visiting Aunt Eva for longer than I could remember, so Beach Heart was my home, too. I was happy to go. Plus, Aunt Eva's beach house was a duplex and the people staying in the other half often had kids. Some were fun, some weren't, but each summer, there was almost a never-ending supply of potential playmates. Each time new guests arrived for the east-side unit, I'd watch for them to arrive, just in case. Aunt Eva would laugh and say that I'd never met a stranger. That I'd talk to anyone.

Oh yes, those were great times.

Aunt Eva's hair was threaded with gray. She complained about her back and her joints, but age didn't stop her from enjoying twice-daily walks on the beach. I would run ahead and behind and around her like a manic whirligig as she kept up her steady pace. She'd pause to pick up a shell, examine it, and either return it to the sand and sea, or drop it into a small net shoulder bag that she wore across her body. When the bag was full enough to sag, I'd offer to carry it for her and she always allowed it, expressing her thanks.

Other than the walks, she liked to sit on the porch, either silent or telling me stories about her childhood. On the downside, she expected me to help with the vacuuming and dishwashing. When I complained that there were better things to do than cleaning house, Aunt Eva admonished that there was joy to be had in everyday chores, too.

I made a rude noise to express my doubts about that.

Aunt Eva leveled her gaze at me and said, "One day you'll understand the pleasure to be found in your home and in simple, ordinary tasks. In terms of our days spent on earth, that's where many of the greatest joys can be found." She fixed her blue eyes on me and added, "Joy should be found wherever you find yourself."

Then she smiled and winked, saying, "But everything is better at the beach."

We agreed on that, for sure. From the ocean to the shore to the white rockers on her porch, and even when the gusty winds wrapped around the house and whispered in the eaves—my heart and the ocean recognized each other. We moved to the same rhythm.

On one of those hot, summer-lazy evenings as Aunt Eva and I were chilling in the white rockers on the porch, I gave her a long, searching look. She stared back, frowned, and asked, "Why are you squinting at me? You shouldn't do that. You'll get wrinkles."

When I didn't answer, she asked again, "What?"

"You aren't a kid," I said, touching my flyaway blond hair up near the temple, the area where her gray was the heaviest.

"Very true."

"But you always want to be here and nowhere else."

My aunt smiled in an aunty kind of way—sharp, yet indulgent at the same time. If Mom had been there, she would've shushed me, saying Aunt Eva wasn't old and it was rude of me to imply such.

She fixed me with a stern gaze. "How old are you now, Emma?"

As if she doesn't already know, I thought. But I answered anyway, "Ten."

"Then you're old enough to be clear and specific in your question. Are you referring to my being at the beach generally? Or specifically here at this beach house?"

"Both. They're the same, aren't they? Kind of like . . ." I twisted my fingers together as if explaining my meaning, then shook my head, giving up on getting it right. "I don't know the word."

"Meshed," she said. "Interwoven."

"Meshed." I repeated it after her, testing the sound and feel of the word.

She said, "My dear Emma, there's no mystery in it. The reason is as simple as life itself. When you find the place that's right for you, the place you can always come to—come *home* to when stuff goes wrong . . ." She paused to clear her throat and took a sip of tea. She shook her finger at me. "You watch too much, always trying to anticipate everyone else's wants and troubles, but no one can be prepared for every event—not you or them. It's better to simply live your life, and then you'll be all the more ready to roll, react, or help when those times come."

I knew she wasn't done speaking by how she leaned slightly forward and toward me, and in the way her voice had been rising when she stopped.

After a long sigh, she resumed. "When life gets rough, Emma, home is the place that anchors you to your best self, and after a while you never want to leave again." She pressed the cool, wet side of her tea glass to her cheek. "Everybody needs a place like that . . . like Beach Heart is for me."

But she did leave. I was in my late teens by then and busy with high school and my friends back home. Aunt Eva turned her side of the beach house into a rental and moved inland. At the time, Mom said Eva moved due to health issues. She required more care and was not able to manage alone. For her beloved home, Beach Heart, Eva had followed the owner's path. She changed the furnishings to be more rental-friendly and reserved a week out of the rental calendar here and there. On some of those weeks, I joined her for a few days, but it was never the same, especially after I left for college. It seemed that as my horizons were broadening, my aunt's were shrinking. Even she, herself, seemed to shrink. Mom blamed the health problems, but I was sure it was due to not being where she most wanted to be, enriched by the fresh salt air, the heartbeat of the waves, and the world she loved. Then soon after graduation, I started a full-time job and met Gregory Dance.

I took Gregory to Rocky Mount to introduce him to Aunt Eva at her assisted living apartment. She was noticeably less taken by his charm than I. True, he was older than me, but he was young at heart combined with being well established in his career—stability with a zest for life—whereas I had always been something of an old soul. I believed we were well-matched despite the fifteen years between us.

Gregory and I went to visit her again, and though he tried to get to know her, she wasn't receptive. After that, when I visited her, I went alone. Even between the two of us, she refused to criticize him outright, but our conversations tiptoed around cryptic remarks about people who married for security, or young women drawn to father figures—neither of which was true of me. I refused to take the bait.

She'd asked me, "How do his ex-wife and their son feel about this? You're getting a ready-made family."

"Not really. His son, Macon, mostly lives with his mother, though they share custody. He's a good kid."

"He's only ten years younger than you."

"More like a younger brother than a stepson, true, but he already has a mother, and I've never had a little brother, so this is a good match."

My aunt didn't like that Gregory had already had one marriage that ended in divorce. Aunt Eva was important to me. I wanted to please her, but if I couldn't, I would not disrespect her by arguing with her.

Everyone, including me, believed Aunt Eva was leaving Beach Heart to me in her will. Even Gregory had heard it from Mom or someone, and he told me that when the time came, and it was mine, that I should convert it to cash.

"Sell it?" I'd asked, stunned. I insisted that Beach Heart was more than an asset that could be sold to please a balance sheet. It was one of the few times we'd argued, at least until the last three years of our marriage when *everything* became a dreadful struggle. In the end, the argument about Beach Heart was pointless, because when Aunt Eva died, we all learned she'd changed her will. She'd left Beach Heart to her long-deceased husband's relative. I was hurt, yes, but also relieved *not* to have the property as a point of contention between Gregory and me. But my mother took Aunt Eva's decision personally.

"He's a stranger, Emma. Not even family. A distant in-law."

"Aunt Eva's family by marriage. It was her choice, Mom."

"But it doesn't make sense. She was leaving the house to *you*. Everyone knew that. You two were . . ." She groaned in frustration. "She went to the trouble and expense of changing her will. And kept it secret. Why would she do such a thing?"

I could've said she might've changed it because she didn't like Gregory, or maybe she'd felt neglected by me in recent years—which, frankly, I couldn't blame her for. But any resentment or regret was pointless.

"It was her choice, Mom. Her decision. She didn't discuss it with me, but I'm okay with it. Gregory and I have our own home and our own life. We don't have time for weeks at the beach anyway."

Mom made another noise, but I ignored it. I wasn't getting dragged into one of her long, chewing-it-over sessions.

I didn't say this to Mom because she would shift the blame to Gregory, but he didn't enjoy the beach. He preferred to travel and vacation in other places. I enjoyed doing those things too. There were seasons in life, I told myself. My season at the beach had been during my childhood. Now I led a different life.

Mom stayed on topic. Doggedly. Sullenly. She said, "Nice that you can be so sanguine about it. She did leave you some personal items, no more than trinkets. It's all packed in boxes. Dusty boxes. She must've packed those things up back when she moved away from the beach and then held onto them until she passed. The attorney gave the boxes to me to pass on to you."

"Yes, he informed me he had them. I asked him to pass them to you. Can you hold on to them for me for now?"

"Of course. Also—and don't get angry—I mentioned to him, the attorney, that we might contest the will. After all, Warren's relative likely exerted undue influence at a time in Eva's life when she was lonely and in failing health."

Shame on us for letting her be lonely.

"No, Mom. We aren't contesting the will."

She gave a combined groan and sigh. "I knew you'd say that. Have you discussed it with Gregory?"

"No. I can make up my own mind about such things."

"How is he, by the way? You two owe me a visit. Or Ross and I can drive over and visit you. It's been ages."

"It hasn't been ages, but it has been a while. Gregory works, as you two do, and we all have commitments. But you're right about getting together. Time has a way of vanishing. Why don't Gregory and I drive up on Saturday for a day visit?"

We went on to set up the plans, and we did visit, and it was fine, but we *were* all busy. Days—and opportunities—passed in the blink of an eye, in part because we thought we had forever. And Aunt Eva's boxes continued sitting in Mom's house for a few more years, almost forgotten.

The tenth wedding anniversary is traditionally represented by tin, a metal that isn't sexy but is resilient, doesn't rust or corrode. Tin represents steadfastness.

But not for Gregory and me. Ten years into our marriage, things started going wrong.

I wasn't suspicious at first, but once the idea that he was lying to me, perhaps cheating on me, had wormed its way into my brain, I couldn't shake it.

Illogically, his poor choices felt to me like *my* failure—that I was somehow responsible or unworthy—so I kept my worries to myself for too long. I tried to ask Gregory subtle questions, to discreetly check his pockets, scroll through the call history on his phone. At first, he seemed dismissive of my questions, and then he became short with me, rebuffing my concerns which ultimately reinforced my fear that he was, indeed, hiding things from me. The more I asked, eavesdropped, or otherwise watched him, the more annoyed and withdrawn he became. I was so distracted by the obvious answer offered by my brain—that of infidelity—that I missed the truth. By the time I was able to drag him to see a doctor, it was too late to slow the deterioration that was destroying his brain. The doctor said it would not have mattered in Gregory's case anyway, but if I'd known, understood sooner, perhaps much of the damage he'd done to our lives could've been averted or managed. We could all have been better prepared to help him, and each other, through to the inevitable.

Those last few years with Gregory were especially tough. My emotional bandwidth was overwhelmed with his doctors, creditors, attorneys, and even Macon—now a grown man who found it easier to blame me than to accept his father's changed situation. Macon argued about everything, from the care his father needed, to understanding that his father, who'd been a source of strength and surety for both of us, had squandered money—monies that Gregory couldn't tell us why or what he'd done with it.

How could a son blame his dying father? Macon couldn't. I understood that. But I thought he would understand the truth of our situation when he knew the full extent of his father's actions, and what that meant to my current reality and to his inheritance. Instead, Macon was angry and I was the only safe target. He said awful things. As for me, I didn't have the physical energy or mental peace to spare for anyone. I shut everyone out of my life, including my mother.

I did what I had to do, and I promised myself that when it was done—when the end was finally the end—I'd sit in a corner and do nothing but rest. I'd find peace. I repeated that promise to myself over and over through the last weeks of losing Gregory, and in the days leading up to his funeral, through the arguments with Macon, and despite the realization that I was worse than broke.

Bottom line—the house was in my name and my name was also attached to many of the bills incurred on my husband's behalf. Our home had to be sold. Even so, it wouldn't cover all the bills, but what remained would be more manageable after I found a job.

Preparing to vacate the house, I'd already

moved a few items into a storage unit. The sad truth was that I no longer trusted my stepson not to act out of greed, grief, or spite. He was an adult and should be able to understand what must be done. If he wouldn't help, then he needed to take what he wanted and get out of my way. As a final ultimatum—no more debate allowed—I'd told Macon, "I've taken what's most important to me or otherwise marked what I'm keeping. You must do the same and arrange for it to be moved prior to the sale closing."

Now, on the day the movers arrived to clear what was left from the house, I should've been seeing a fresh start ahead, but I didn't feel free—not even close to it. How did one shake off those ghostly weights of regret and exhaustion?

Macon was there on moving day. He looked past or through me most of the time. Even the unspoken blame he threw my way was palpable. As the movers closed the van door and locked it, Macon stood in the foyer of the two-story brick Colonial that had been our family home, his sandy hair shaggier than usual and his eyes looking angry and haunted—much like mine, I was sure. Our last blowup had happened no more than ten minutes earlier over a stupid chair. A chair I didn't want, yet I'd stood over it, my hands gripping the top as if prepared to guard it with my life.

There was no logic in the act. The chair, unremarkable in its worn, green-blue striped upholstery, was only still there because I hadn't cared enough about it to move it to the storage unit. That morning, I'd left my jacket, tote, and purse on it, and the movers had worked around it. When they finally came for it, I'd told them not to take it. I was embarrassed and confused by my reaction, yet I doubled down on my insistence. I was nearly in tears by the time Macon told the moving men to forget it.

They all left, including Macon. He departed without a goodbye or even an insult. I didn't try to call him back.

Standing beside that chair, alone in the empty house that would officially belong to someone else as of tomorrow, I wished the new owners better luck. The good fortune of our early days here, perhaps. As for me, I was fresh out of luck, hope . . . whatever you called it. I'd become a thin, empty person. *Lank*, my brain said. Like my long blond—now lank—hair, maybe? Washed out.

Lifeless. Empty. Colorless. Drawn out to nothingness.

I told myself to leave too. Go to the hotel here in town where I could hide and hopefully find some sleep. That was the plan. I needed rest. But instead of leaving, I released my grip on that last chair and sat in it, unmoving, as the afternoon light softened and the shadows deepened inside the house.

Gregory, my charming, optimistic husband—the one person (other than Aunt Eva) I'd unconditionally trusted and relied on before he'd changed—had once said to me that negative never begets positive. That was back when our relationship was growing and glowing and I was upset over something so small I no longer recalled what it was. Gregory had lifted my hand and kissed the soft flesh of my wrist. He'd smiled gently and said, "A negative impetus cannot yield a positive result. Find a better starting point, Emma. Rethink, rephrase, and revisualize."

Gregory had been an optimist. But Gregory was gone. The *who* of who he was had been gone even longer. My well of optimism had run dry, and no one was holding my hand today.

When I saw that delivery van, my first thought was that if not for the chair, I would've missed the arrival altogether. Part of me wished I *had* missed it. But bad news didn't improve with time or pretending, so I groaned and accepted the envelope and slid the papers out. And saw the words *Beach Heart*.

Moving closer to the window for better light, I peered more closely at the return address. Yes, a lawyer's office—but the firm's name, the Smithson Group, sounded vaguely familiar. The same firm in Morehead City who'd handled Aunt Eva's estate more than ten years ago? It must be.

This could have nothing to do with Gregory or the financial mess he'd made that I'd nearly lost my mind and health trying to clean up.

But Beach Heart? What was this about? And why now?

The attorney wrote that he was sending the enclosed information for me to review. He asked me to call his office to arrange a meeting to finalize the transfer of the property to me per his client's wishes.

My knees weakened. I stumbled back to the chair and sat abruptly.

Eva had been my great-aunt on my mother's side. Her husband had died when I was young, and I didn't remember him. But she and I were very close for so many years that everyone had expected Aunt Eva to bequeath Beach Heart to me. When it turned out she hadn't, it had caused upset among the family, especially since Beach Heart had been regarded almost as a family property. Not me, though. I wasn't upset. I was married to Gregory and we were busy with life, with travel, and each other. By then, Macon was in his teens and was all but living with us full time with the blessing of his mother who'd also remarried. We were a little family, happy together, and enjoying ourselves.

In honesty, I'd been surprised that Aunt Eva had left Beach Heart to someone else, and maybe even a little disappointed, but not upset because it was her property and her right to make that decision.

Part of me had been relieved. Gregory didn't like the beach. Never had. So not inheriting Beach Heart, had removed it as a point of contention between us.

Was the distant relative now giving it to me?

Why?

Before the doubts, the fears, the expectation that everything I touched was rotten or soon would be, could swamp me and paralyze me, I grabbed my cell phone from my tote and dialed the number.

Chapter Two

Before receiving Mr. Smithson's letter, I'd planned to stay at a hotel in Raleigh overnight and drive to Mom's house in Greenville in the morning. I dreaded seeing her because she'd want to discuss Gregory and Macon and all that had happened from years ago, to the myriad *what-might-have-beens* in the future *if only* things had been done differently, and on and on. She would question and suggest and conjecture, endlessly reviewing the details. She meant well. I understood it was how she processed information, but I wasn't ready for that.

The attorney's office was in Morehead City, about a three-hour drive from where I lived in the outskirts of Raleigh. It would be a longish drive after an exhausting day. His receptionist had offered an appointment for tomorrow morning, but to be there—and in time to get some rest tonight—I'd have to leave for Morehead City soon. I glanced toward the window. The afternoon was passing quickly. Evening was ready to roll in. If I left now, I could at least get a hotel closer to

Morehead before I called it a day and tried to sleep.

At least I'd have a goal. Plus, this stirring of curiosity inside me shouldn't be denied because curiosity, as opposed to apprehension, was a positive feeling. I wanted to grab hold of it like a lifeline. Of course, driving straight to Morehead City meant bypassing Greenville, but Mom wasn't expecting me until tomorrow anyway.

I decided not to call her until after I met with the attorney and knew more. I didn't want to bring up Beach Heart to her again after all these years until I understood what was truly going on. If I called her now, I'd likely blurt it all out despite myself, and she'd start with the questions and gnawing over details and possibilities . . . So not yet.

Stashing the papers in my tote, I picked up my jacket and gave a long, last look at the keys in my hand—the house keys already detached from my key ring to leave on the kitchen counter for the new owner.

Yes, this hurt.

At the front door, as I was about to cross the threshold for the last time, I stopped and looked back, a nagging feeling pulling at me. Was I forgetting something?

The only item remaining was that daggone chair.

My SUV was already quite full, as was the small storage unit I'd rented. I had no home, and thus I had no use for that chair.

Macon and I had argued over it, but our anger hadn't really been about the chair.

Yet if not for that chair, I would've been long gone before receiving the delivery . . .

ꕥ

The next morning, I drove to attorney Alan Smithson's office address and found a solitary brick building in a quiet corner of a commercial area of Morehead City. The parking lot was nearly empty, only two cars plus mine. The building struck me as small, but the exterior was neat and looked respectable.

Stay cool, I cautioned myself. *Be calm and smart about this.*

I'd know more when I went inside.

The foyer had all the usual business equipment, the expected leather chairs and gleaming wood desks and tables, but nothing extra. Lean, I thought. A motherly looking gray-haired woman was seated at a desk working, and she greeted me pleasantly, but the rooms had a quiet feel—that of being generally unoccupied, as if the office was more often empty than in use.

It made me uneasy. *But face it,* I cautioned myself, *this whole thing seems suspect, so be careful.*

Beyond the woman at her desk, a door was open to an office and Mr. Smithson was already walking out to greet me. His hair was gray and his posture perfect. He wore a suit (no tie), but it was apparent that he'd only just donned the jacket because as I followed him into the meeting room, he was still tugging the sleeves into place. I guessed he was in his sixties, but he looked tanned and fit. I suspected he spent more time on a boat than in this wood-paneled place. And yet, when he grasped my hand and spoke in welcome, he seemed trustworthy. Just regular. Legit.

I cautioned myself against giving in to that impulsive judgment. *Be polite but businesslike, Emma.*

He nodded at the envelope I was holding. "I

imagine you were surprised."

"It was pure chance that I hadn't already left home. I nearly missed receiving your letter altogether."

He smiled. "No worries. The courier would've kept at it until he found you."

Until he found me? Really?

"Mr. Smithson, I appreciate that . . . *I think.*" I gave him a sharp look. "I've read your letter several times. I don't understand."

"You are familiar with the property in Emerald Isle named Beach Heart?"

"Of course."

"My client received that property from Eva Douglas ten years ago, per her will, and wishes to convey that property to you now."

"Why? It's a valuable property . . . or used to be."

"It still is. My client is in poor health and is sorting out his affairs. To that end, he has chosen to divest himself of this property, but he didn't want to sell it away from the family. He wished to honor the spirit in which it was given to him."

What did that mean? It sounded odd.

I said, "I must tell you upfront that I'm not in

a position to purchase it. I've just come through a difficult time."

"There is no exchange of monies involved. If, however, you don't wish to assume ownership of the property called Beach Heart, then please say so. We'll make other arrangements."

I gasped, saying, "No, I'd love to own Beach Heart, but I want to be clear about my circumstances."

"I appreciate your candor. The property taxes and insurance are currently paid through the remainder of the year, and the property has been maintained, and . . ."

He kept talking for a while, here and there taking documents from a folder and laying them on the table in front of me.

"It's a quitclaim—a transfer of ownership between parties. There are no encumbrances or liens of any kind on the property, but the nature of this transaction is such that anything that comes along later will be solely your responsibility. You should be aware of that."

Alarm hit me. Okay, so this must be the catch.

"Exactly *what* might come along later?"

He raised his eyebrows and fixed me with his

gaze. "I suppose it could be anything that home ownership opens one up to."

"Oh, I see. But that would be the case anyway, right?"

He nodded. "You'll want to discuss this with your accountant, of course, because there will be taxes to consider for the coming year. As you noted, it's a valuable gift."

How could it be this simple? I distrusted it. But I wanted it.

"I need to know who to thank. Who is my benefactor? I never met the relative my great- aunt gave the property to. I presume I owe my thanks to him?"

Mr. Smithson didn't answer right away, and I felt a moment of blankness. There were questions I should ask, but I hesitated. Why? Because I wanted this to happen. I wanted to believe in it.

I pushed myself to ask, "Why would someone give away a property like this?"

"As I explained, his health is failing and he's getting his affairs in order. If this seems sudden, that's the reason. I'll file the change of deed with the county office in Carteret. As for my client, his name is on the transfer—Charles Grimes."

"Grimes? I understood he was related to my great-uncle, Warren Douglas. Maybe his brother? No?"

"Charles Grimes was married to your great-uncle's sister. So, his brother-in-law."

"Oh. I'd still like to express my appreciation to him."

"I'll convey your thanks." Mr. Smithson paused, and his tone grew solemn. "While I understand your wish to speak with him, to thank him directly, he prefers to only see his immediate family at this time."

"I understand."

"Any questions?"

I shook my head. "I'm sure I should have some. I imagine that I will after I'm past the shock."

"If you are comfortable with proceeding, Ms. Carroll is a notary. She can witness the signature for the deed." He passed me the papers he'd taken from the folder. "These are informational—utilities providers, tax information, property insurance carrier, along with receipts. All that good stuff you'll need. As I said, everything is paid through the end of the year. We have initiated the process of changing these various accounts to your name, but you'll need to call the entities to finish the transfer. If you run into any difficulties with it, give Ms. Carroll a call. Her business card is here too."

He continued, "A management company has been handling the rental units. We paused reservations for the west unit, but the other side has active commitments made, so if you'd like to stop taking reservations, tell the management company immediately. The intent was to give you the chance to decide how you wish to handle the property without disrupting your income from the east unit. You should contact the management company as soon as possible and let them know either way." He dropped a key ring with several keys atop the folder and then slid the works across the table to me. "Spare copies of the documents are in the folder."

"So . . ." I stared at the keys. "I can go over there. *Be there now?* Do with it, and the contents, as I see fit?" I fixed my gaze on his face, hoping to detect any underlying motives, as I said, "Is that what I'm hearing from you?"

"Yes, Mrs. Dance." He smiled, and his

manner seemed reassuring. "Other than honoring the current rental agreements that have already been made for the east unit, that's exactly the case."

ଔ

outside of Mr. Smithson's office, I sat in the car, the keys to Beach Heart in my hand and the folder on the seat beside me. I had a choice. Drive to Emerald Isle, which would take maybe thirty minutes, and see Beach Heart—a place of my childhood that I hadn't visited in many years. Or drive an hour and a half north to visit my mother first, and then another hour and a half back, likely with her in the passenger seat speculating about all this or giving me lots of advice.

But I had to tell her *something*.

The oceanfront was just across the sound, on the far side of the island. Either of the two bridges, one at each end of the island, would get me to Emerald Isle. The easternmost bridge would take me to the island via Atlantic Beach, but then I'd have to drive the length of the island. My best guess was that the westernmost bridge in

Swansboro would be a little quicker.

However improbable this whole thing was, regardless of *why* Beach Heart had been dropped into my lap like an oversized gift with only a big fancy bow missing. Regardless of how or why, I knew it was true by the keys, now tightly clenched in my hand. This was real. Mr. Smithson had not been an illusion created by my need or my imagination. I hadn't misunderstood his letter.

I wanted to see and feel this for myself, in person, to experience the sand beneath my feet or a salt breeze fresh from the ocean. Maybe this was exactly what I needed to get myself moving forward again, and toward the future that I'd promised myself. That better future was out there; I just had to find it.

I dialed my phone. Mom answered right away.

"Are you on your way? Almost here, I hope. The lasagna is put together and ready for the oven. How long before you arrive?"

"Something happened . . ."

"Happened? What do you mean? An accident? Are you okay?"

"No, I'm tired but fine. Something came up unexpectedly."

"So when will you be here?"

I did a quick calculation. Better to save the explanations until I knew more. "Tomorrow."

"I know this is difficult for you. I understand. But, Emma—"

"It's okay, Mom. All the negative stuff is behind me, and I'd like to keep it that way." I knew in that moment I'd have to tell her now whether I wanted to or not because I couldn't leave her hanging like this. "In fact, I have news—possibly very good news—but I don't fully understand it yet, so *please* don't tell anyone. This is between you and me for now, okay?"

"I promise. You know I try to respect your privacy." She sounded wounded.

"This is different, Mom. This is . . . unexpected."

"As you said. What's this about?"

"Remember Uncle Warren's relative that Aunt Eva left Beach Heart to?"

"Of course. Or rather, I remember she left it *to* him. I never actually met the man. You said you didn't want to contest the will and asked me to let the whole subject drop."

"Mom, respecting her wishes was the right

thing to do, so it's all good. This is the thing: I was contacted by an attorney from the same firm that represented Aunt Eva back then. The relative, apparently elderly and in poor health, has deeded the property to me."

There was silence on the phone. I couldn't hear her breathing.

I asked, "Mom, did you know anything about this? Have any inkling?"

"No. Nothing. I don't understand. Why would anyone give away a beach house? Is there a catch? Does he want money from you?"

"Apparently not. I have the keys and the paperwork. The attorney will file the change of deed."

"I don't know what to think. I'm glad, and I think they're doing the right thing—that property should always have gone to you—but I don't understand. Makes it hard to trust."

In my head, I echoed her words. *Hard to trust. Yes.*

"I'm feeling some of that myself, Mom. Trust comes harder for me now than it used to. The attorney is here in Morehead City. I wanted to find out more before I called you, so I came to his office directly. Being so close to the beach now, I want to drive over and see the house for myself. Make sure that it's not termite-ridden about to fall into the Atlantic or such."

"I don't blame you, but I wish you weren't doing it alone."

"I'll be fine, Mom." I started the car and pulled carefully out of the attorney's parking lot and onto the main road. "I'm heading there now, and you'll know where I am. But don't tell anyone please. Remember your promise."

"Of course, but all this unsettles me. Emma. I'll keep quiet about this until you're ready to share the news, but you must promise me you'll keep your phone close in case of trouble and call me when you get there."

଼

It was often awkward between us. Mom wanted me to be the child I'd never really been with her. Most of my early, close bonding had formed between me and Aunt Eva. It wasn't Mom's fault. Not Eva's. Not even mine. Those days and weeks and even months at the beach with Aunt Eva over the years had wired our relationship in a way that sort of short-circuited around my mother. I told myself that love was always welcome, and Mom and I did love each other, but trust and intimacy didn't come easily or naturally. When I started high school, I became involved in more activities and the trips to Emerald Isle became more difficult. I was home more, but by then Mom had remarried and was busy with her new husband, Ross. He was a nice enough man and he made Mom happy, so I was glad of that, but . . .

Even if it wasn't anyone's fault, sometimes I felt our relationship issues were one more failure on my part.

But I remembered those halcyon days lived at Beach Heart, and here I was today, so many years later, driving over the bridge to the island with white clouds sailing by overhead and the blue sky peeking out between them like a promise, so for a short while I gave myself permission to put all the negatives out of my mind as I headed toward the Atlantic Ocean and Beach Heart.

ଔଔ

The Swansboro bridge delivered me directly into Emerald Isle. I was surprised how well I remembered that sweeping view of the sparkling water and tall swaying grasses below as the bridge arced over Bogue Sound.

I remembered Emerald Isle, too, but from a different perspective—that of a much younger person who'd had little responsibility and hadn't seen the sights from a driver's point of view. Some landmarks looked familiar, even unchanged, but not all. As I turned east to follow Emerald Drive, I knew I should prepare for the worst. My memories were so clear, made pristine in the way that only the passage of time can accomplish. How could Beach Heart live up to them? Impossible.

But when I turned off the main road, headed toward the dunes, and then took a left, it was almost like my aunt's hands were guiding that steering wheel. And then, there it was. Beach Heart. The house was situated about midway along this row of tall, wide homes, mostly rental properties. It was still painted a strong, lovely shade of French blue with white trim and looked every bit as good as my memories had billed it. Perhaps even better.

Beach Heart was a three-story beach house—a duplex—with an open, ground-level parking area below the main floor. On the street side, stairs went up to the front porch shared by both units. On the beach side, stairs went up from the parking area to the wooden dunes crossover and the back porch.

The house wasn't falling into the ocean, nor was it being swallowed by monster dunes. Even the concrete drive and parking area under the house had very few cracks, and those had been well sealed. From this vantage point, the house and lot looked great.

I didn't understand this. Any of it.

Chaotic thoughts were buzzing in my head and beginning to vibrate in my chest. This was real. I hadn't believed in this . . . Not at all, I realized.

My nerves were too sensitive these days. Everything and nothing caused worry, and I felt that worry coursing through me now. I pressed my hand over my heart and continued sitting in the car. I closed my eyes and paced my breathing, slow and deep, focused on refusing the panic attack. No breakdowns were allowed.

When I felt calmer, I opened my eyes slowly

and tried again. This time, I managed to exit the car.

Both sides of the house seemed vacant. It was hard to tell for sure, but I saw no other cars were parked here. I squeezed the keys again. Still real. As real as the salt breeze whipping around the house and finding me despite the solid protection of the building. It was chilly but not uncomfortable.

This was March, and any kind of weather was possible.

This was a place to heal. Hadn't Aunt Eva said that?

I was still one big, nasty ball of guilt and regret, and that darkness inside me too quickly welcomed other dark thoughts. Yet I remembered when that attitude hadn't been second nature to me. I wanted that time back.

In a rush, not willing to allow the regrets and unresolved anger to catch up to me again, I grabbed my tote and my water bottle. Sooner or later, I'd track down my benefactor to thank him—or discover the truth—but for now, I was eager to get inside the house to discover what memories remained from the past to greet me, and then I'd go outside again to stand on the deck of the back porch. To stand at the railing and feel the ocean.

The ocean would be unchanged, of course, and I wanted that.

As I stood there on the porch, the air seemed to change. My flesh tingled. I looked up and saw darker clouds edging in. Weather could change quickly on the ocean.

Time to test the key.

It worked.

I passed from the small entry hall and into the dining and living rooms and paused to drop my tote onto the kitchen counter. None of Aunt Eva's furnishings remained. She'd moved them out when she'd turned it into a rental. I'd known that, of course, and yet that was the memory that had stuck in my head through the years. But even so, those furnishings had been changed yet again—presumably by Mr. Grimes after he'd inherited the house from my aunt, so none of this was familiar in any way.

In the living room, the white rattan sofa with its orange and turquoise cushions, and the huge dolphin wall art hanging above it was touristy and fun—the stuff of weekly beachy rentals. Nothing was as I remembered it.

In truth, what I craved lay beyond the walls—the changing blues of the ocean, the energy, the peace, with a brilliant sky above it. My skin tingled as I remembered the electric energy of the ceaseless waves. I paused at the French doors that fronted on the ocean eager to breathe in the sea-salt air and recapture . . . Recapture what? An unsullied time?

I flipped the locks, opened the left-hand door wide and stepped out to the porch—and was slammed by the wind.

The gust pushed me backward, whipping my long hair around my face, blinding me. I grabbed the doorframe and found myself in a funnel of sorts, holding on, eyes closed, hearing the clatter of knickknacks being blown to the floor, and perhaps some larger items, too, and ignoring it. I was strangely content to be swept by the wind as it rushed in from the ocean and up the shore, fresh with the taste of sea salt, dunes grasses, and the spices of unknown places.

It was cold, but the gust blew itself out quickly. My hair was now a tangled mess, and my skin was covered in fine grit. Sand or salt? I didn't care. It felt glorious. This was the beach. This had been Aunt Eva's kingdom. She'd made the rules here, and as far as I was concerned, her rules were still in effect. Rule number one was that if your hair was too perfect, then you weren't doing the beach right and your priorities were askew. In my mind, I heard her laughter and saw her fierce, pretend-mad frown. I wanted to reach out to her, to claim one of her beloved hugs.

I stepped out and crossed to the porch railing. Houses, porch after porch and crossover after crossover, stretched away in both directions. I stood there, focused on the ocean before me, taking in the roar of the waves and the rhythm of their movement. Immediately before me lay the mounded dunes covered in shrubby, scrubby greenery, and the long wooden walkway crossed over them, beginning at the porch, at the privacy panel where the duplexes met, and ending at the stairs that went down to the wide expanse of sand and the ocean beyond. The water was far out, so the tide must be about to turn, ready to roll back in.

A few people were walking along the beach, but not in the water. A kite sailed high overhead, its tail dancing in the winds high above, accented by moving clouds and blue sky. Darker clouds were moving in fast, perhaps associated with that gust. I followed the angle of the twine back to earth and saw the kite's pilot a far distance down the beach. More directly in front of me, near the water, a young boy was building a sandcastle.

Surely it was too cool today to be playing in the water and sandcastle building, but then I'd built a few of my own back in the day and hadn't minded the weather. For a moment I lost myself in watching him.

The boy's light, tousled hair fell forward obscuring his face. I watched him build, focused and industrious, his fingers fast and sure as he shaped towers, turrets, and crenelated walls. His plastic bucket, bright red in a land of beige sand and blue sky, lay as if cast aside and forgotten. The wind jostled it, pushing it ever nearer the ocean. The boy was maybe ten years old, give or take a year, about that same age as Macon back when I'd first met him, two years before I married his father. So long ago now.

This bit of heaven along the Crystal Coast might have changed over the years but not much. The interior of Beach Heart was *very* different—

beachy anonymous—but the landscape looked essentially the same as if it had had nothing better to do than to wait until the little girl returned—the child who'd believed the world revolved around her, that tears or a pout could solve a dispute, and that every problem had a happy ending. A girl who often danced on the beach, pirouetting in sheer joy at being alive. A girl, now a woman with sorrows weighing her down, who'd finally returned to where she once belonged. Probably no pirouettes were in my future. But rest, yes. And maybe peace.

A distant rumble startled me.

Weather conditions at the beach could change quickly. As a child, I'd been caught out more than a few times with my aunt yelling at me to get out of the water and come inside—*Right this instant, Emma!* For now, there were still patches of blue between the cloud banks passing overhead but darker clouds threatened, and the water was taking on a steely shade as if already accepting what was coming.

But the boy was still there in the sand, alone, with a bucket near at hand. He was totally focused on his project. I cast another look at the sky. The storm could pass us by. Some wary mom or dad would be calling out to him as my aunt had done for me. Meanwhile, he was oblivious to all but his task.

The boy moved his hands to shape a turret and enlarge a wall. His shorts looked damp and sandy, but the windbreaker over his shirt appeared dry. His T-shirt sagged, also drenched. As I watched, a stronger wind moved the bucket, shifting it closer to the water and the waves. One more gust and it would set sail.

I called out, "Hey! Boy!" But my voice was lost to the fitful breezes. I scanned the beach and it struck me that maybe he was *truly* alone. There was no one in sight along the stretch of oceanfront. Somehow, I felt responsible for him. Why? Because he was a kid and I was the only adult out here?

Pulled as if by a magnet, I left the porch and walked toward the crossover—the long wooden walkway that was shared by both sides of the duplex and connected the house to the beach and helped protect the dunes. I'd only moved a few feet along the walkway when the boy scrambled toward the water. In one fluid movement, he snagged his bucket before it reached the ocean, scooped up wet sand, and headed back to his castle.

I saw no one—no parent, not even an older sibling—in sight.

What sort of caregiver would leave a young boy to his own devices on a beach?

Those incoming waves were building, rushing in now. Not that the boy was in immediate danger . . . but he was so intent on building the walls and towers higher that he was paying no heed to the water. He and his castle were safe for a while yet, but for how long? I felt that dreaded rush of panic pushing in again. Everything triggered anxiety in me now.

From the crossover, my view was better of the houses to the east and west of us. In fact, looking back, both porches of Beach Heart were fully in view. I scanned the neighboring houses too, taking in the gaily painted houses with their porches and rockers, and saw no one, but as I turned back toward the sand and water and the boy, my peripheral vision caught movement. I swung fully around and saw a large golden retriever dashing across the sand—fur gleaming amber- gold and red in the wind and sun, mouth open and ears blown back—as it raced full-out toward the boy who was turned away and totally unaware of the animal about to barrel right into him.

Chapter Three

At the last instant, the dog slowed, suddenly but gracefully, and greeted the boy by moving close to him and standing there, panting. The boy merely placed his hand briefly on the dog's side. It was an unequal interaction, yes, but they seemed companionable, so I stopped worrying. Whoever was watching out for the boy must've sent the dog to join the child. But where had the dog come from?

Curious, I scanned the beach and houses again.

This time I spied a man three houses down. He was on the porch of a pink house, his arms resting on the railing as he leaned forward—much as I was doing here on the crossover. And he was staring at me staring at him. And he waved.

How long had he been watching me?

I looked away quickly. Clearly, the boy wasn't alone and unmonitored, and so this was no longer my business. In fact, the man might've noticed me watching his son so closely, grown concerned, and had thus sent the dog over.

Or more likely I was making a big deal out of nothing. That had become my style in recent months.

The man was still looking this way. I turned directly toward him and raised my hand in a small wave to show him all was good, that I'd been concerned, but that concern had now been addressed and I was getting on with my day.

He waved back. Trying to move casually, I returned to the porch and moved out of view.

When I reached the shelter of the porch, I sagged against the privacy panel, trying to reduce the feeling of rising panic.

A stranger. He was just a stranger, as was I. Everyone here was a stranger and no one was judging me.

No history. No obligation.

That was a good thing.

I pressed my hand to my chest to will my heart to slow to its regular rhythm.

Past unpleasantness did not belong here, not in this time or in this place. Not at the ocean. Not at Aunt Eva's beach house. Aunt Eva had set the rules here. Rule number two had been that outside troubles weren't allowed at the beach. Only beachy troubles, like underinflated floats when no one could find the air pump. It certainly did not allow for the intrusion of heartbreak over marriages gone wrong or broken families or thoughtless friends. I'd liked that rule because it gave me permission to have fun and not worry.

I'd always tended to worry over stuff I couldn't help or fix. Aunt Eva had understood that.

My phone rang. Mom.

I said, "Hi."

"Emma?"

"It's me."

"You okay?"

"Of course."

"You didn't call. How's the house?"

"Looks great." Another gust blew in and I rested my hand on the back of the rocker.

"Are you outside? Is that the ocean I'm hearing?"

"It is. And the wind." In fact, the clouds were thicker and darker now.

"Hold on, Mom. Looks like weather's moving in." I turned my back on the ocean and stepped into the house. "Okay, I'm inside now."

"Emma?"

"It looks very different in here than I remembered. I expected it to, of course. It's been a rental for a long time. Just seems strange."

"Well, Emmy, as you said, it's a beach rental. That's how they're supposed to look. Something different, you know. People don't pay good money to bring the family to a place that looks like the home they just left." She paused for breath and then started up again. "It has to be practical. Easy care. Folks at a beach don't want to—"

I interrupted. "Got it, Mom. I know all that."

Her voice had lost enthusiasm as she said, "I have those boxes from Eva. Would you like me to bring them down to you?"

"No." I spoke too abruptly. I heard the sharpness in my tone and knew Mom had too. I wished I could take it back, but I didn't know how.

After a long moment, she said, "I understand you don't want to talk about things, though I think it would help, but that's how you're feeling just now, and I respect that. I still want to see you."

I heard the hurt in Mom's voice. The table by the front window had a smattering of sand on it. A lamp had fallen, and a few items were scattered on the floor from when I'd first opened the door. It distracted me, mesmerizing me for the moment.

Mom added, "I get it that things went wrong in your life, Em."

Not going there, I thought.

"I worry that you're punishing yourself, honey. We all make mistakes. We all have regrets. It would do you a world of good to talk about it."

"I'm sorry, Mom, but I'm not ready to do that."

Wind hit the house. A huge gust. The windows shuddered as one vast lightning bolt reached from a black cloud and down to the water. Thunder began ripping before the strike was done. Then nature's switch flipped, and an instant deluge fell in a sheet. *A squall*, I thought.

What about the boy?

It was a gray world outside the windows. The porch railing aligned with the edge of the roof above and was like a line of demarcation where the rain, the ocean, and the sky all merged into one. I couldn't see him—or anything—through the downpour.

"I'll call you back," I said, and tossed the phone aside.

The boy . . . had he made it under cover?

Panic propelled me senselessly out the door. Within a few steps, the rain, now being blown into the porch and wetting the floors, beat at me, and the drops hitting the floor planks shot back up like little slaps against my legs. With my arms over my head, I rushed to the railing and into the sheet of water—and then, as I reached it, the switch flipped again. The rain stopped.

My arms still raised and shielding my head, I waited. Was that it? Slowly, I lowered my arms and saw the rain clouds moving off as fast as they'd arrived, and one last, huge raindrop smacked my already-wet nose.

The boy was gone. The child hadn't had far to run. If unable to make it to the house, he could've sheltered under the stairs at the end of the crossovers. Regardless, his father had been nearby and watching out for him. It wasn't my worry.

And I was drenched.

What was wrong with me? Why hadn't I thought of the good outcomes instead of immediately imagining the worst and rushing out, foolishly thinking I could rescue someone, anyone?

My clothing was plastered to my skin.

Shivering, I plucked at my sleeve. I squeezed water from my shirt, my hair, then stopped, admitting the futility of it, and I laughed out loud. For the first time in years.

Aunt Eva might've said I was doing the beach life right by not stopping to consider before I rushed out into the storm. Or she might've asked me why I didn't have sense enough to stay out of the deluge. I had no answer, either way.

Trying to not drip too badly on the floors, I hurried through the house, grabbing my keys as I went, heading straight out to my car where I grabbed my overnight bag from the front floorboard. Back in the house, I shed my wet clothing on the tile floor of the kitchen and then tossed it into the washing machine in the alcove opposite. A quick unzip of the overnight case gave me a fresh, dry change of clothing. I checked the heat, hoping to warm things up a bit while I dried my hair. I had the essentials but was wishing for a few more of my toiletries that were still out in the car in my larger suitcase. And with that thought, I paused.

I'd stayed in a hotel last night, as planned, though it was a different hotel in a different town.

As for tonight, the original plan had been for me to be at Mom's house in Greenville. Mom and my stepfather had offered to put me up for the foreseeable future while I found a job and got my finances in order.

Could Beach Heart be my "hotel" for the night before moving on to Greenville? Or maybe two nights? Why not? What about a longer stay?

Whoa, Emma. Think this through.

Okay, so tonight made sense. But staying longer? How much longer? I needed a good paying job. Could I find that here? Maybe during the summer season, but what about year-round?

No, I didn't see that working. But hanging out here for a few days? Yes. Except I'd need more from the car, as well as some supplies from the store.

The idea of still felt too new.

And yet, I didn't have to decide today, did I? I'd promised myself no obligations and no accusations. No guilt allowed. I didn't pretend that refusing to deal with all that had happened over the last few years meant the scars would simply go away, but I needed a break from blaming myself for any and all things.

In a way, the beachy rental décor was a blessing because it didn't feel like I was trying to go back to a place and time that no longer existed. Instead, a beachy house meant a vacation, right? A break from responsibility and from the failure of civility in an impossible situation. Just *being* instead of always trying. Maybe that dolphin over the sofa had a purpose, after all.

I dialed Mom again. "Me again. I'm tired. I'm going to stay here tonight."

"I'm not surprised." In a lower voice, she added, "I already put the lasagna back in the fridge."

"I promise I'll drive up to Greenville tomorrow."

"Really?" She sounded doubtful.

"I will," I repeated. "I promise." And I meant it. Sort of.

ꕥ

If I was staying one night or even a few, I'd need some things. Food, of course. My appetite had vanished over the last two years, but the body still needed fuel. Something easy, maybe, like from a salad bar or something microwaveable. Food for today and through lunch tomorrow. Laundry supplies were on the shelf above the washer. I was surprised to see the fabric softener and detergent. They weren't mine. Or were they?

A quick trip to the grocery store would fix the food issue. As for toiletries and other personal items, I couldn't justify buying more when I already owned them. They were down there in my SUV. But accessing my packed bags was a lot trickier since I'd rearranged and jammed things in in to accommodate the chair.

That chair was heavy and awkward. Getting it out of the house and into the bed of the SUV had been a bear. Getting it out wouldn't be any easier, and then what would I do with it? Wrestle it back in all over again? Along with whatever else I took out of the vehicle. No, thank you.

Maybe I'd leave the chair out by the road? With a *Free to Good Home* sign sitting in it?

Grocery store first, and then I'd figure out the rest.

When I returned, I carried my grocery bags up to the porch and into the house, then went back down the stairs. I spent the next thirty minutes in frustration, squirreling my arms around in the chaos of my packed car. I was able to pull out a few more things for the night, and then, exhausted, I carried my bits and pieces up the stairs and into the house. Leaving the foodstuffs on the kitchen counter—and determined to get this over with—I carried my overnight case upstairs.

But I hesitated on the threshold of my old room.

There were four bedrooms on this floor, two front and two back. My interest was in the two large oceanfront rooms with wide, sliding glass doors fronting on a shared balcony with an expansive view of the Atlantic. The smaller of the two—the room I'd used when visiting Aunt Eva had been decorated for a young girl—by Aunt Eva for me. As far as I knew, no one else had ever used it during those years. Now there was a queen-size bed and generic furnishings.

The larger en suite bedroom that fronted on the ocean had been Aunt Eva's room. It had a king-sized bed and an inviting overstuffed chair in the corner with a lovely round glass table next to it. There were no memories here. Only those I carried in my heart. Which made me glad.

This room would do. I set my bag on the floor. Enough for now.

The afternoon was half gone. I assembled a light meal of salad and fruit, and settled in a porch rocker to eat. The rain clouds were long gone, and the sunshine played tag with fluffy white clouds as I watched the ocean. Without the breeze, it was much milder now. The rhythm of the waves was calming and soothing. I nearly dozed off with the last bites of food still on the plate.

There were things to be done, but I didn't want to do any of them. Mom would advise me to sleep on it.

So tonight, I'd sleep, and give my brain a chance to absorb all that had happened yesterday and today. Tomorrow, I'd have a fresher take on my options. I'd also call the utility and management companies.

For this afternoon? I'd throw the rest of my dirty laundry in with the wet clothing, and while that was washing, I'd take a long, lazy walk on the beach.

Expecting it to be cooler down by the water, I carried a jacket with me.

The sand at the base of the steps was dry,

mounded, and shifty beneath my feet. Nearer the water, where the tide was going out, the wet sand was easier to walk on. There were only a few people out for a stroll. I stood there as a couple passed and we nodded, and I realized my jacket was unnecessary. As were my shoes. I tied the sleeves of the jacket around my waist and carried my shoes.

I'd do the beach walk better—less encumbered—next time. Even so, this one was pretty good.

There weren't many shells, mostly just bits and pieces. When wet and shiny, the colors seemed to have jewel-like depths, but when I picked them up and the wet dried as they lay on my palms, they became only dull, broken shells again. I dropped them, brushing the bits of sand from my fingers.

Aunt Eva had collected shells, even the fragments. She'd pushed clay into wooden frames and then pressed shells into the clay, like a mosaic. They were fragile creations and hadn't held up well. Like so much else that we'd lost through the years, I'd forgotten about them until this moment. The next fragments I picked up, instead of tossing them back into the ocean, I put them in my pocket.

Back at the crossover, I rinsed my sandy feet under the spigot, shivering at the sudden shock of the cold water, and then stopped at the area of built-in benches. I should use them. They were inviting. Everything here was. And I owned this? The thought still sent a bit of a reality shock through me.

Back inside, I tossed the washed laundry into the dryer and dozed off on the sofa to the gentle, repetitive sounds of the clothing being warmed and fluffed.

The afternoon was shifting into early evening when I finally accepted the invitation the benches had offered. As the sun approached the horizon on the sunset end of the island, the ocean chill drew in again. Now I would need that jacket, for sure. I grabbed it and went down the crosswalk to the benches.

Using the bench seat as a step, and hugging my jacket around me, I perched on the railing and watched the day give way to night in striking shades of pink and lilac which grew in intensity until the fading began. Swiftly, the colors dimmed into darker, grayer tones which were then extinguished. The first stars popped out and the vastness of the night surrounded me. Beach Heart was only one of many dwellings facing the ocean. It wasn't the grandest, nor the most humble, but knowing it stood tall behind me—and was mine—anchored me. I felt as though I belonged here as much as the stars or the grains of sand.

It was a big roomy house. Ridiculous for one person, right? But for one night of rest? Or even two?

I'd be foolish not to take advantage of the opportunity. And let tomorrow take care of itself.

☙❧

After the fresh air and exercise, and now lost in a silence disturbed only by the muted, rhythmic sound of the ocean, I slumped, exhausted. I double-checked that the doors and windows downstairs were locked and the outside lights were switched on. Satisfied, I carried a tall glass of water up, along with a soothing cup of tea, and set them on the bedside table. I thought I might turn on the TV in the bedroom for something light and inane while I settled into bed, but I didn't. Instead, I found myself listening to the silence.

It felt odd being in a hotel room that wasn't a hotel. Kind of like having the whole hotel to oneself. Yeah, a little creepy.

Also, either the rental management company performed above and beyond expectations, or someone had taken extra trouble to make sure this place was comfy and welcoming. Rose-scented bars of soap and luxury bath salts were in the bathroom. Were they among the usual items furnished for guests? I felt a little spoiled and certainly appreciative.

During the last year especially, caring for Gregory had been more intense and had included tasks like constantly watching him to prevent him from wandering off into the night, or intervening in case he decided to cook at three a.m. and set fire to the kitchen, or to guard the thermostat if he decided he was cold because he'd dial up the thermostat and turned the house itself into an oven.

How many times had he started water running in the tub or sink only to leave it and forget it?

Trying to watch over him by myself had been foolish and dangerous, but the truth was that Gregory had so totally screwed up our finances that I couldn't afford a memory care facility, yet on paper we were still worth too much to qualify for any kind of financial help. Sometimes I'd been able to squeeze money out of the house equity to hire help to watch him; sometimes it was all on me. There were so many late nights—and a few all-night stints—with the television playing mindlessly in front of me like a lifeline to other lives which, however fake, were at least diverting and could be turned on and off at will.

But I couldn't say most of that to our friends and neighbors and acquaintances. They wanted to offer sympathy and then return to their lives. When I came close to putting my feelings into words, I saw the shocked expressions on their faces, so I kept my reality to myself when they visited. Our real life resumed when they left.

I'd cared for my husband to the best of my ability, even to the point of losing everything and more.

My hands were shaking again. My heart was shaking, too. Guilt? Anger? So much was tangled up inside me, that I didn't know where to begin unraveling it. I feared that trying to would overwhelm me.

ଓଃ୨୦

I donned a long white T-shirt that I wore as a nightgown, then opened the blinds and curtains wide. The night was now well-entrenched, and full of stars and a moon whose light reflected in the curling, foaming waves far below.

Up this high and facing the ocean, my privacy was pretty much guaranteed even with the lights blazing.

Today, I'd walked on the beach. I'd eaten a meal on the porch. I'd watched the sunset from the crossover bench.

Aunt Eva, I'm here. I'm back.

I slid the balcony door open a few inches to test the air. Not too chilly. No wind. I stepped out onto the balcony to observe the night. I breathed in the ocean air and felt it fill me.

That night, when I was ready to crawl into bed, I left the vertical blinds wide open and lay on my side in the bed so that I could see the stars. I recited the well-loved *Star light, star bright, first star I see tonight.* It was no more than an old rhyme but wishing on stars surely long predated any written language. To it, I added a heartfelt prayer.

I didn't know what to ask for, so I let the words be ones of gratitude for this soft bed and sound roof, and a hoped-for, peaceful night's sleep.

ꟹ

The first night back at Beach Heart—no longer a child and without Aunt Eva nearby—was still a gift. I felt a tiny bit blessed, if not with success in love and marriage or finances—at least I had a haven safe from the chaos for a night, or two.

I woke during the night as if from a pleasant dream, but with those thoughts in my mind. Simple. Uncomplicated. I lay there on my side, the night beyond the sliding glass doors, starry but dark, and remembered Mr. Smithson saying that no rentals had been scheduled for this side of the duplex. I had to believe that my benefactor had had the idea that I might want to . . .

. . . to stay here for a while. And that would only require one unit. This one.

If I was very careful about purchases, I could hang around for a week or two. Or longer. I needed money, and thus a job. Rental income from the other unit would help, but I had a few debts left to be paid and no resources. Living at the beach, with maintenance and all that—was surely expensive. And there were always the unexpected bills. Oh, you knew they'd come, but only when you least expected them. The when, for what, and for how much was the unexpected part.

But if I stayed—stayed somewhere long enough and somewhere that fed my healing—maybe it wasn't too far-fetched to believe that hope could find me again.

Hope.

I'd been happy long ago. I could almost remember how that had felt.

Maybe hiding was okay if it meant you were staying put long enough for the good things to catch up and find you again?

I thought that might be true. I closed my eyes and next thing I knew it was morning.

ন্ধ

The first tentative rays of dawn lightened the sky beyond the sliding doors of the balcony. The change outside was small, but enough to bring me closer to waking. When I finally gave in and opened my eyes, the sky was being brushed with the first soft colors of dawn. I felt more rested than I had in years.

I stepped out to the balcony to greet the day. The ocean, the beach—the beauty nearly stole my breath. The sky, in the dawning light, was a changing mix of clouds, mist, and sky. The air was fresh and fair. Below, in the lingering soft light of leftover night, a few folks strolled along the beach. Their eyes were trained on the sand, shell hunting, and they didn't notice me up above, hair unbrushed and with my nightshirt flapping around my thighs.

I wanted to be down there by the water, too.

Running a brush through my hair to tame the night tangles, I gathered the length of it back into a low ponytail, then pulled on shorts and a loose T-shirt. They were good enough for an anonymous early morning walk and perfect for dawn at the beach. *Always remember Aunt Eva's rule # 1.*

I'd grab a shower afterward and then drive up to Mom's house.

At the end of the crossover, I kicked off my sandals and descended the steps. I trudged through the small, dry mounds of sand to reach the firmer, more walkable surface near the water.

A couple of men, nondescript in the early morning mist, were minding their fishing poles and ignored me as I walked past. I gave them a wide berth to avoid tangling in their lines. Except for looking down on occasion to spot sharp-edged shells before treading on them, I kept my eyes on the changing sky. When the sea birds flew in groups skimming the water on the hunt for breakfast, I stopped to admire them. Beyond them, the clouds were highlighted, backlit by the rising sun which gave the scene a dramatic, awe-inducing appearance, and as I stood, transfixed, the sun continued to rise and gilded the tops of the clouds until its rays flowed over them.

Once upon a time, I'd raced and danced along this beach in that soft band of sand left by a receding tide. Running and twirling, my arms wide, then crossed, and my bare feet skimming the sand, had felt like flying.

This morning, I felt as new as the day. Now fully here—both me and the day. I forgot my adult dignity and took several swift running strides forward and then, like an ice-skater digging the point of the blade into the ice, I did the same with my toes and launched into what, in my mind, was supposed to be a graceful pirouette. Any question of gracefulness aside, in that moment, as I landed on my feet, I considered my move successful because I didn't crash or injure myself. I felt silly, yet also elated.

But in that instant of landing, my arms still held wide like a gymnast nailing a landing, and with thoughts of freedom and options flitting through my head in a nanosecond, I heard heavy breathing and wet sand splattered on the calves of my legs as a slim leather leash caught around my ankles and tightened.

A large dog was circling me, seeming both excited and confused, the leash catching my legs even more tightly as it moved.

In reflex, I twisted away and raised my hands, but the dog wasn't interested in my surrender. It wanted a greeting. Perhaps even a scratch on the head. And to that end, it tried to get closer to my hands by jumping up and placing its paws on my stomach. Trying to avoid that panting tongue, I moved to step back, but my legs were hobbled, and as I felt myself going down and my arms flailed in the air seeking balance, a hand grabbed me.

Chapter Four

In that flurry of movement—the dog jumping up and me struggling and falling—the man reached to steady me with one hand as he caught the dog by the collar with his other, all of it done in one coordinated movement as he said, "I'm sorry. Really sorry. Star doesn't usually do this."

Still gripping the dog's collar, he let go of me to reach the dog's leash. "Stop, Starfish. Sit."

And I sat. Gravity had its way. My butt hit the wet sand and the dog immediately did the same, plopping down next to me, almost on top of me. Judging by the fidgeting, any moment now the animal was going to spring back into action. I wanted out of this fiasco.

The stranger helped me to my feet. His hair was red—not bright, but an auburn red—and considering what else was going on, I didn't know why that caught my attention and held it, but it did.

He was saying, "I don't understand what happened. We were walking on the beach…half-walking, half-running, when she spotted you. She jumped forward and I lost the leash. Even so, she's usually fine off-leash."

The dog moved, and the man admonished her, "Stay, Star," then looked back at me. "It's like she recognized you, but I don't see how." For a moment, during which everything seemed to pause, he fixed his eyes on my face and asked, "I don't think we've met, have we?"

His eyes were blue-hazel. Gray? He looked concerned but was also smiling, and he seemed to expect an answer.

Great, I thought. *Fabulous.* I was getting hit on by this stranger in a really corny way and this . . . person . . . was using his untrained, out-of-control dog to facilitate it. But, hey, I knew his hair and eye color. Leave it to me to get the unimportant parts right.

"No," I said curtly and started to walk away. The dog was instantly back up on its feet ignoring the man's repeated instructions to stay.

"Sorry," he said to me. He put his hand on the dog's back, saying, "Star, heel."

He waited and she settled next to his foot, not quite "heeling" but no longer moving around us, and then he turned back to me again. "If that sounded like a bad line, it wasn't. I wasn't trying to . . . you know . . . but only to apologize."

I risked a longer look. I had an unfortunate and distracting personal flaw of getting caught in details. Of noticing everything. Aside from the hair and eyes, I noted that this man looked like he'd rolled out of bed and onto the beach with little effort in between. A lot like me. But he also looked reasonable. Not risky. Nice eyes. Kind, I thought. His T-shirt had a washed-out college logo on it. He'd been out of college for a while at least—again like me.

With deliberate effort, I pushed all that aside. I needed to move on. Plus, that dog . . . a golden retriever . . .

Suddenly, it struck me. The dog. The boy. This man was probably the boy's father. My defenses fell a bit. So, a stranger, but not quite. We'd exchanged waves, right?

I asked, "You aren't trying to hit on me?"

"No. Well, I might, I guess. But I hope I could come up with a better line than that if I put my mind to it."

"Well, don't. I'm visiting. I'm not looking for companionship."

"No worries. I'm sorry Star and I disturbed

your walk."

A moment of dignity on my part could end this nicely and restore my morning mood despite the damp, sandy shorts. Summoning what I remembered of courtesy, I asked, "Her name is Star?"

He nodded, still clutching the leash. The beautiful animal with the glossy, burnished coat looked up at me with brown, liquid eyes.

I touched the top of her head. Her fur was silky. She closed her eyes as if holding her breath and waiting for more. I finished with a quick scratch and a gentle pat.

He said, "Her name is Star f-i-s-h actually. But we only say the full name when she's in serious trouble."

I didn't mean to, but the word came out anyway—like I was competing in a grammar school spelling bee. "Starfish?"

Star pulled back, her eyes suddenly wide and worried, and one paw came up to rest on her muzzle. Almost like she was hiding her eyes.

Seriously? Was I a monster? I hurried to give her a quick scratch and an apology. "Good dog," I said. To the guy, I said, "Sorry."

"Don't worry about it. Everyone does that. Like an automatic response." He knelt and gave her a quick rub around her neck and made nice noises.

"And yet you continue to spell it out anyway? Why?"

He shrugged. "Not sure. Maybe another human response?" He laughed. "But you know what, in thinking about it, maybe when you did that jumping and twirling, maybe she thought you were playing."

My face heated up, and I turned away.

"Sorry," he said. "I've offended. Didn't mean to." A quick smile lit his face. "I'm thinking you're a dancer? You move gracefully, like someone with that kind of training."

It was his attempt at a save—perhaps trying to help *me* save face? I reined in the sharp words I'd almost spoken. "No worries," I said. "No harm done. Nice to meet you and Star. I'll be on my way."

"It's a beautiful morning for a beach walk. Would you like some company?"

"Appreciate the offer, but no thanks. Feeling solitary. Have a good day." And I walked off, moving briskly and determined. With some distance between us, I settled back into my normal pace.

Have a good day. Had I really said that?

Yeah, I did. And right after telling him, in effect, to get lost. How stupid was that?

But it served my goal, right? I didn't want to impress or encourage him. He'd leave me alone now. I wanted them all—everyone—to do exactly that, at least for a while.

ॐ

After showering and dressing, I was ready to tackle the drive to Greenville. I grabbed my tote bag and was on my way out, but when I opened the door, Mom was there, standing on the porch, holding a casserole dish and a bag of salad.

"You should see your face," she admonished, with a gentle laugh. "It shows everything you're thinking. Always did." She shook her head and held the casserole dish toward me. "Here, take this please. I'll go back for the boxes."

"Boxes? What? I mean, what are you doing here? I was just leaving to drive up to see you."

The casserole dish was now in my hands. It was heavy.

"Don't worry. I can't stay long. Just through lunch."

"No, I mean, yes, that's fine, but I told you I was coming to Greenville to see you." I saw impatience in her posture and curiosity in the eyes that looked past me, wanting in. I asked, "You didn't believe I'd come today, did you?"

"Yes and no. What I *didn't* want was to spend the day wondering if you'd show up. So here I am. Besides, you look exhausted and very thin. You need rest and nourishment." She gestured toward the dish. "Take that inside and set it on the counter, please. Preheat your oven to 325 degrees." She hooked the bag of salad over my finger. "I'll be right in. You go ahead." She waved me toward the door and went back down the steps to her car.

Mom wasn't frail, but she was almost sixty and those stairs were steepish. I called after her, "Need help? I'll be right down."

She waved at me to go inside. "I've got it."

I put the casserole dish and salad on the counter as instructed, set the oven to preheat, then went back outside to offer help because those stairs *were* challenging. Mom was halfway up. She had both arms around a box, and it was in front of her face blocking her view.

"Wait. Stop, Mom. You're going to fall." I took the box.

She protested, "How is that better? Now *you* might fall."

In a joking tone, I responded, "Then walk behind me. You can catch me if I miss my footing."

She said, with a softer tone, "Will do."

The box was awkward in size, but not terribly heavy, so we made it into the house, and I set it on the floor near the sofa. Meanwhile, I heard cabinet doors being opened and closed. Mom was in the kitchen, checking the cupboards, above and below.

"Are you looking for something?"

"*Somethings*. *Lots* of somethings. I'm checking to see what you have here and what you might need." She was still moving. "Dishes. Pots and pans." She opened a drawer and lifted a spoon up to view. "And utensils." She turned it in the light. "And they look reasonably clean." She turned to look at me. "But it might be a good idea to run them all through the dishwasher first, just to be sure, you know?"

"Mom, it's all good. The unit is well stocked except for groceries and toiletries." I moved closer to her. "I'm not staying long. A few days. Maybe a week."

"Why?"

"Because it costs to live here. I need a job. A good one. This is a beach community. Seasonal work mostly, I'd think. I don't see a lot of year-round job potential here."

Shrugging off my words, she said, "I'm sure there are jobs. It's just in how you look for them and what you are open to."

I wasn't emotionally fit for reasonable, rational employment yet, but I didn't want to say that to her, so when she suggested, "I'll give you a hand unloading your car," I answered, "No, it's all good. The SUV is packed tight, and I'm not bringing up most of that stuff anyway. I don't need those things right now."

She stopped cold. "You're serious about not staying?"

"This can't be permanent, Mom. Even if it's legit."

"Why not? Whether it's permanent or semipermanent, if you're here and there is something screwy going on, it will be harder to oust you. What do they say? Possession is—"

"Stop. Please." That familiar panic was building inside me. I crossed my arms tightly to keep it in. I shook my head. The idea of going through a scandal, another tug-of-war over money and possessions, of losing trust—it made my head feel like it was going to blow up and scatter into a million fragments. "No."

"Sit down, Emmy. Sit down and breathe deeply." She took me by my arms, still crossed, and gently tugged me toward the sofa. "Sit. Please, sit. I'm sorry. It's my fault. I'm much more practical than you ever were. Maybe because I had to be." She sat next to me and patted my leg. "But it's your fault, too, because if I understood more about what's been happening in your life over the last several years, I'd have a better understanding of what I can do to help."

I refused to be drawn in. I covered my face with my hands.

"You are always welcome to talk to me, I hope you know that." After a brief pause, she added, "Remember, I've had my challenges, too, with heartbreak and loss thrown in for good measure." Her voice faded away as she spoke the last words. Then, she shook herself, and said in a brighter tone, "So I have a small idea of what you're going through. And even amid the things that went wrong, there was always you—the bright spot in my life. The reason I kept going." She grunted and changed her tone. "I want to see the house. Both sides of the duplex. You said the other side is empty of guests, right? Great. I want to see exactly how you're fixed here."

I dropped my hands away from my face. "Fixed? Why?"

"Why? I'll tell you why. Because you are too thin. Like flesh over bones. Your eyes . . . they look like you're expecting to be attacked at any moment . . . haunted. Hunted. This isn't who you are. You need to rest and there's no reason you can't do it here." She did a 360 in the middle of the living space. "Personally, I think you'll recover more quickly here, in a place you loved. At least it's livable. We just need to figure out what's needed to make it more like home."

"No. I . . ." I had to say the words. "I can't afford to redecorate or spend unwisely. I need to get a job and that will probably mean moving inland."

"Maybe, but not yet."

"Also, any changes I make here will have to be undone and this furniture put back when it goes back to being a rental."

"I'm talking about small things, Em. Practical things. Like do you have your own bedding? You'll want your own things. A few familiar items, that's all."

What she was saying wasn't unreasonable. But each thing, however small, would add to what must be undone when I had to move again.

"No need to figure it out this minute." Mom brushed at her blouse, presumably smoothing out the nonexistent wrinkles. "I want to see the other side." She dropped her voice into a lower range and said, "The alternate universe." Then she giggled, nearly unnerving me.

I stared.

"Come on. A small adventure. And, remember Emma, it belongs to you, just as this side does. You have the key, right?"

"I do."

She walked to the porch door. "Well, then,

let's go." She grinned. "The sooner I satisfy my curiosity, the sooner I'll get out of your hair and leave you to your rest and recovery."

ଔଌ

The eastern side of the Beach Heart duplex was a mirror image of the west side, my side. This was the east side, and it was as if, when shopping for furnishings for Beach Heart, someone had said of each purchase, "I'll take two, thanks." There were small differences. Perhaps things had been damaged and replaced over the years. But it was eerily the same. Mom might've been onto something with the alternate universe remark.

The furnishings on both sides hadn't been the same when I'd visited Aunt Eva years ago because she'd lived here year-round. My aunt had refurnished both duplex units when she'd turned her side into a fulltime rental. I presumed the new owner had redone the units again after Aunt Eva passed.

Mom hardly spoke as we toured Beach Heart East. Her curiosity seemed more businesslike than personal. Other than a few grunts as she peeked into bedrooms and bathrooms, she didn't have much to say. When she was satisfied, she smiled and said thanks. Oddly, out of nowhere, she said, "The light is better on the sunset side."

Aunt Eva had always called the units sunrise and sunset instead of the official business designation of east and west.

As we returned to my side, Mom went to the oven to check the lasagna, then said, "I'm going to get a few things from the car that you can use."

"Really, Mom. I have what I need."

"Are you going to continue with the cleaning service on this side? If not, you'll need a vacuum, a broom, and a mop."

"I haven't talked to the management company yet. I left them a message. There's a closet with some basic housekeeping equipment, so I'm sure I have whatever is needed."

She ignored what I said about already having the basic equipment. "I brought some extra supplies from home. We've got a few minutes yet before lunch is ready. Give me a hand?"

While the lasagna was baking and beginning to fill the air with delicious aromas, I hesitated. Perhaps feeling resistance, too, to falling in with her plan. She went without me. Within moments, Mom was yelling up the front stairs, “Is that a chair in your car, Emma?”

Oh goodness. The whole neighborhood would hear her.

Hoping I could better contain her actions by being with her, I hurried after her. While she was rummaging in her car, I took time to find the bedspread and sheets I’d stashed in my own car. My favorite pillows were stowed on the back seat in plastic bags. I grabbed a few other small items I touched and with my arms full, I climbed the front steps carefully. What harm could it do to have a few things of my own, especially if I kept it light and simple? Light and simple had been the intention, not the actual outcome.

From the hallway, I heard a clunk. Startled, I dropped the bags and rushed back out to the front. Mom was trying to maneuver a vacuum up the steps while balancing a broom and mop under her other arm.

“Hang on. Just stand there.”

I hurried down and was trying to disengage the vacuum handle from her grasp, when a voice behind me said, “Hi. Need a hand?” I heard the scrabbling sound of a dog's paws on the wooden steps and the man added in a louder voice, "Sit, Star. Stay."

ഩ

Mom had a bright smile growing on her face as she turned toward him.

I said loudly, "No thanks. We can handle it."

Mom switched her attention to me. "But Emma, this nice man, your neighbor, is offering his help."

"Mom, we're good. We don't need help." I faced my neighbor with a polite smile and repeated, "Thank you, but we can manage."

Near us, Star whined. She sounded pleading and anticipatory at the same time.

Mom said, "What a beautiful animal."

The redheaded man smiled at Mom and nodded. "She is." He nodded again, this time toward me. "I don't mind helping. We were just on our way to the mailbox."

"Thanks anyway."

He nodded. "Understood. We'll move along."

As he left us, Mom turned to me with an

expression of bemused amazement. "What was that about? He could've carried Aunt Eva's boxes up for us."

"Not now," I half whispered. I succeeded in taking the vacuum from her and toted it straight up the stairs and into the house.

Mom followed, saying, "This one's our spare. It still works well." She put the broom and mop in the laundry closet. "What was that about out there? That man was nice looking and well spoken. Polite. I'm telling you, Emma, some of those boxes are heavy."

"He lives in the neighborhood. He has intruded twice now. I don't want to encourage him."

"Maybe he's being neighborly?"

"Maybe, but I'm not ready for chummy neighbors." I shook my head. "I live alone. I must be careful staying in a place where I don't know anyone," I said. By now, we were back out by the vehicles, and when I lifted the lid of the next box to be carried up, I groaned. Dishes. Heavy.

Mom went silent. She was staring beyond me.

I turned. Jake and Star were coming back this way with the mail folded and tucked under his arm.

I gave her a look and said, "Stay here. I'm going to chat with him."

He was still a few yards away when I reached him. I tried to speak with dignity. "I apologize for dismissing your offer of help. Please understand my caution. I don't even know your name."

"Jake."

"What?"

"Jake Harris. Pleased to make your acquaintance."

He was extending his hand. As if I might accept it and shake it. So, of course, I did.

A man with a companion like Starfish had a sort of automatic badge of *SAFE*, but of course that was illogical. He was also a bit of a bumbler, awkward and saying all the wrong things. Harmless, I thought. And his style—or lack thereof—made me feel a little less awkward with my own bumbling. I did wonder where his son was today, but I didn't ask because I didn't want to encourage conversation or details about his personal life. He wanted to help carry up the bags. I'd let him do that—accepting his help as far as the porch and then I'd say a sincere thank-you and a firm goodbye.

"If your offer is still open, there are a couple of heavy boxes. If you would carry them up to the porch, I can move them into the house from there."

"Always happy to help. Anytime. I'm usually around, and Star makes sure I get out a lot."

"You aren't vacationing here?"

He grinned. "Me? No. I'm here for a while helping someone out."

I thought of that big house. On the ocean, no less. "Nice that you could help someone and enjoy that beautiful pink house too."

He looked confused, and then his expression cleared. "The pink house?"

"Yes? I saw you there."

"I was just hanging out on the porch."

I struggled to process that. "Oh?"

He said, "Yeah, that house is vacant right now. A lot of them are this week. That'll change soon. Meanwhile, I was putting the oceanfront porch to use."

Hmm, well, no harm in that, right? I'd made assumptions. It seemed the reality was that he was hanging out on a stranger's porch watching his kid play on the beach for hours and hours. Was that creepy or practical? I couldn't decide. I settled for saying, "I'll bet your son loves it."

"My son? You mean the kid on the beach? The architect?" Now he looked confused. "Not mine."

"But Star . . .," I faded off gesturing toward the dog. "Star seemed happy to see him."

"Star is a lover of all kind souls."

I blinked. Such odd phrasing.

"A golden, you know. Hearts of gold. They are like that." He smiled. "As you discovered this morning. We apologize again for that."

"So the boy was alone out there?"

He shrugged. "I haven't seen anyone with him. No one that seemed connected to him except you. I was wondering too, until I saw you keeping an eye on him that day, so I thought he was with you."

"Apparently, he doesn't belong to either of us. Who, then?"

"I'm sure someone is watching out for him."

"Of course. There must be a parent in one of these houses."

"Yes. We just weren't looking in the right direction at the right time."

"Sure."

He was grinning again.

"Well, then . . ."

"Where are those boxes? In this SUV?"

"No, that's mine. The boxes are in my mother's van."

"Is that a chair in there?" He was peering into the side window. "Why don't I carry that up for you too?"

"Thanks, but no. I'm not unpacking all that stuff."

"Well, but you can't, can you, with that chair blocking it all in? I can take the chair out, and that'll give you room to work."

"True," I said but then was cut off as Jake, my oh-so-friendly neighbor, waved at another neighbor who happened to be outside, and the next thing I knew both men were carrying the boxes up from Mom's car and when Jake would've set them down on the porch per *my* instructions, Mom was at the door inviting them the rest of the way in.

I hurried up after them, asking them to set the boxes in the first room on the right, the only bedroom on the main floor. Eight boxes in all. I was surprised there were so many. I was trying to shift the stacks, and the next thing I knew, I realized Mom had gone outside and was chatting with our helpers. Thanking them.

Well, someone *should* thank them. I'd been as sociable as I could, but I should do better. I walked back out to the porch, seeking to offer a little more sociability—our helpers deserved that at least—but Mom was waving as the men, along with Star, turned and walked away.

Mom climbed the stairs up to the front porch. She saw me and laughed. "What nice neighbors you have, Emma."

My privacy wall felt rather diminished, but since I wasn't staying here long, did it really matter?

When I walked back into the house with Mom, I saw the chair.

Mom caught my look. "Oh, I told them to go ahead and bring it in."

"I told them not to."

"Sorry, sweetheart, but you need to rework how the car is packed. You can't leave all that stuff crammed in the vehicle for even a few days. I'm happy to help you, but no one can do anything with it so long as that chair is blocking everything." She walked away, saying, "You must've wanted the chair very much, and I'm glad you were able to keep it, but . . ."

Obviously, Mom didn't require an answer.

ଔଓ

While I was occupied with tossing the salad and setting the table, Mom brought in a few more odds and ends. She placed those items on the counter between the kitchen and the living/dining area. When I turned, I saw the frames . . . the faces of Mom and my stepfather, Ross and a few others. Of Mom and me with Aunt Eva. Of my maternal grandparents, neither of whom I remembered.

I looked at Mom. She was watching my face. When I didn't speak, she said, "You have family. Some are gone but a few of us are still alive and kicking. Let us in."

Without answering, I turned away and resumed getting the meal on the table.

We sat at the table to eat and had barely begun when she asked, "How is Macon doing?"

My fork paused en route to my mouth. I stared at it silently.

Mom cleared her throat, speaking as if she hadn't paused, probably wanting to cover the awkward moment. "I haven't seen him since the service. He and his dad were close. I've always thought well of him."

I held up my hand to stop her. "Macon and I are estranged just now."

She tried not to ask, but the struggle was so evident on her face, her near-distress, that I relented, adding, "I hope he and I will work things out, but time will need to pass, Mom. Things were said between us."

Her face flushed. "Shame on him—"

I cut her off. "No, Mom. He was unfair, but he also had reasons to believe . . . Well, what he believed." I raised my hand again. "That's all I'm going to say about it. I don't want to discuss Macon."

She nodded. Her expression was perhaps a little sad, but maybe slightly relieved, too. Maybe telling what little I had, had been the right choice.

We ate, and when we were done, I started doing the dishes and Mom excused herself. She went upstairs and I let her go, glad to be alone. I turned away from those framed faces.

After a kiss and a hug, my mother left.

The quiet felt odd. It should've been nice, but

this big house was too empty. I stepped out onto the porch. The day's warming trend had held, and a couple walking along the shore were carrying their jackets instead of wearing them and their jeans were rolled up as they walked barefoot just above the fringe of the water.

But the sky was blue, the breeze was sweet, and it was too early to call it a day.

Mom had been clear about there being no reason not to stay for a while.

The framed photos on the counter caught my attention. Mom had meant well. But seeing them made me feel like some very important faces were missing.

I'd stuffed various last-minute items in some of my boxes and bags. Most were still out in my car, but in one of the bags I'd brought in were two more framed photos. I hadn't planned to display them, but . . .

Gregory. I held the five-by-seven portrait taken at the beginning of our marriage. I brushed my fingertip along his cheek, his smile. His eyes . . . I recognized those eyes. In them, I could see and remember the person I'd loved.

And then there was Macon. He had his

mother's coloring—sandy-haired and blue-eyed—but in personality, he was so much like his father. They'd been close. Gregory's illness had been very, very hard on his son.

I set the photographs on the counter next to the other photos, but I turned the frames slightly away. They'd be easily visible with deliberate effort but not so that I'd be surprised or startled if I happened to catch a glimpse at a vulnerable moment.

Someday, I told myself, it would be better.

Later, when I carried more items up to my room, I discovered Mom had made up my bed with the bedspread I'd brought, that my pillows were now neatly tucked into place, and a lovely pink and purple afghan was folded and spread neatly across the foot. I remembered that blanket from my childhood.

Walking into that beachy bedroom and seeing a few of my own things arranged there—cozy items that set it apart from the overall generic feel—gave me a warm moment and something gently squeezed in my chest.

I appreciated my mom . . . even if we drove each other crazy. I promised myself that I would do better as a daughter and a friend.

Chapter Five

The months spent preparing to sell our family home in Raleigh, and the anxiety of getting rid of things I associated with years of happy memories had been grueling. The tasks were greatly complicated by Macon's resentment and anger. And all that emotion was piled on top of my own grief. But last night—my first night at Beach Heart—had been different. I'd slept well. One good night's sleep couldn't cure the past, I knew that, but it meant that I wasn't as exhausted tonight, even after Mom's visit and the work of emptying the car.

Tonight, my second night at Beach Heart, I was restless.

I took another look around, this time without Mom pushing me. I checked every cabinet and closet on all levels of the house. I was already familiar with the kitchen because Mom hadn't left a single shelf unexamined. The fresh laundry supplies in the laundry recess had surprised me, but the assortment of cleaning tools and supplies in a small closet off the living room looked like they'd been around a while. Most of the closets were empty, as expected. A large built-in bookcase next to the fireplace was well stocked with books and puzzles for various tastes and ages. The shelves also held an assortment of entertainment options like DVDs and games. Thoughtful, and probably a standard offering for guests.

The difference was in the large master bath upstairs. As I'd discovered yesterday evening, that bathroom was stocked with plush new towels and washcloths. Those, plus the scented luxury soaps in that bathroom, had given me pause. Those soaps reminded me of Aunt Eva. They'd felt personal. Particularly welcoming. Those special items, and the homey touches Mom had added, helped me feel . . . not quite at home, but more *at home* than I could've imagined.

Were fancy soaps etc. standard? I didn't think so. There were no such special touches like detergent pods and fancy soaps in the east unit. Did that mean prior tenants had left those items behind on my side? That might apply to the laundry detergent. But the plush towels and soaps? Not likely. More questions . . .

When my evening tour was done, I was still

restless. I was not in the mood to read. The TV was working, but I'd watched too much of that during the long hours of night when I'd been on duty watching over Gregory. Aunt Eva's boxes awaited me, but I was avoiding those. Not sure why I was, but I admitted the truth of it.

The moon and stars called to me as they had last night. After a moment of hesitation, I asked myself, *Why not?* I grabbed the throw from the sofa in case it was chilly and went out to the crossover and the benches.

With the blanket around me, I settled on the bench and stretched my legs out along the length of the seat. The wood at my back was hard. Next time, I'd bring a sofa pillow to lean against.

Next time. Those words warmed me more than the blanket could've.

I rested my head back against the wood and stared amazed at the ocean and the night. The stars were scattered across the dark sky . . . But no, that word implied randomness. As I picked out a constellation or sought the brightest stars, I thought I must be experiencing the same sense of awe and mystery as ancient astronomers. Sailors had braved the vast unknown depths of the oceans, leaning solely on the stars as their map of the universe.

The moon and stars above were reflected in the moving surface of the ocean, creating patterns of light on the water as if no divide existed between the two bodies. Inside my head I felt the vastness, an echo, or maybe a call back to the expansiveness—an opportunity for emptying all the nasty stuff and allowing the free, restoring flow of fresh oxygen in. Watching the artificial lights on the horizon, I wondered where they were going. What were they doing? Oil tankers with a small crew of hardworking men? Maybe a cruise ship over there filled with families vacationing and playing. Those small lights might belong to a yacht.

And all so far away.

When I was a child, Mom told me my father was in the navy, that he'd left us when he found out I was on the way. He'd never been in my life, and generally speaking, I had so much love from Mom and Aunt Eva that I didn't miss him much, but sometimes I wondered. I never told either of them, but there were nights when I'd sit out here with my aunt and see the ship lights . . . and think that that it could be my father's ship, that he might come to see how his daughter had turned out. I'd hoped that he'd be proud and perhaps regretful over leaving. But he never did show up, and life went on.

Tonight, I wasn't subject to any such childish fantasies, but I did feel alone.

Lonely? Maybe, but in a good way, as if with distractions removed and with chaos blown somewhere out to sea, I could breathe.

Into my peace intruded a reality. Macon. I couldn't believe he was any happier with this ugly rift than I was. And if he *was* okay with all that had happened, then I'd never known him. Had never seen who he truly was.

If so, that would be on him, not me. When he showed up, I had to believe that it would be because he was ready to listen. To actually *hear* me instead of listening to his *own* pain and shutting out my voice. Hopefully, when he did arrive, I'd be able to hear him too, despite *my* pain.

When he came.

If he came.

I'd left a forwarding address at the post office, but it was to Mom's house. Macon knew nothing about me being here. He'd never been here. By the time his father and I had married, Aunt Eva had already moved inland. But Macon knew my mom. They'd gotten along well. So when he was ready, he'd know how to find me. I hoped that day would come.

For the time being, I would wait.

And that was okay because, for now, I was resting.

ଔ

The next morning, early on Friday, the boy was back at work. I saw him as I was returning from my morning jog. As I came near, I slowed, and then paused altogether for a better look at the tower and wall he was building. He was a busy boy. I hadn't seen a castle or even a washed-out pit when I'd been out for my early morning air. Joggers and turtles appreciated that.

Aunt Eva had always said that turtle season went from May to October, but ankles could turn year-round. Picking up after yourself—even on the beach—showed respect for yourself and others, including for wildlife. Another Aunt Eva rule.

The boy was upholding that rule.

I was tempted to speak to him. Maybe wish him a simple good morning? If he'd glanced up or had shown even a tiny interest, I would've. To do so without even that weak invitation seemed unwelcome.

I couldn't help a quick scan of the houses lining the beach, but I spotted no watcher, yet he seemed fine, so I decided not to disturb his peace.

Peace was too hard to find to disturb it so lightly. I knew that for sure.

Whispering a quick, "See you later," just loud enough to be heard, but not to be startling, I left him there and headed for the stairs to my crossover.

Peace. A beach view helped a lot and the sweet breezes and sunshine made it even better, but I needed more. A distraction or hobby—like Dylan and his sandcastles? Maybe a therapist?

I'd let the boy be my example. Busy without overdoing. Focusing on rest. But I needed to feel as if I'd accomplished something. And I thought of Aunt Eva's boxes, still waiting for me.

ૡ

I'd left those boxes with Mom since she'd received them from the attorney years before. It hadn't been an intentional decision, and I couldn't explain why I'd never remembered to claim them from her during our visits. But now Aunt Eva's boxes were stacked in the back bedroom, just as we'd left them the day before.

Mom had been offended that those boxes of mementos were all I'd received when Eva had passed. Mom had called them cast-offs that no one else wanted. But I knew Aunt Eva herself had packed these boxes because I recognized her writing—*For Emma*—and the perfect upright slanting and the decorative whorls. When I lifted one of the box flaps, I saw a scarf. I remembered the pattern. The colors. I'd given her this scarf for her birthday. Mom had taken me to purchase it, and I'd chosen wrapping paper, and I'd drawn and colored a card. That was the day I'd discovered the frustration of folding silk scarves.

Holding the scarf in my hands, I pressed the folds to my face. Ten years in storage. I supposed I could smell that mustiness. But was it purely my imagination that I could detect her scent in the fabric, too? I liked to think I could.

Gregory hadn't been drawn to the ocean or long walks along the shore, and Aunt Eva, while polite, had had no fondness for Gregory. I'd loved them both. I set the scarf on the bed. I hadn't made a deliberate choice of Gregory over my aunt but the laws of time travel and not being able to be in more than one place at the same time had made it impossible to give them both the attention they deserved.

I found a cigar box along with the scarf. I knew what that was about. We'd kept a stash of photographs in there. Many of them had been stained by my grubby kid fingers. My aunt and I had enjoyed them together and we'd spent endless hours chatting about the memories and the people.

Other than a quick flip of the lid to see if the photos were still there, I didn't look further. Too much emotion for me just now. I set the cigar box on the guest room bed beside the larger box it had come from, and quickly turned my attention back to the stacked boxes. But that was it for now. I left those flaps closed for now. Later, I told myself.

I made it as far as the door where I stopped and leaned against the door frame.

My emotions and my brain felt scattered.

Guilt was part of it, I supposed. I hadn't been there for Aunt Eva. I could feel my absence keenly in each object she'd packed and could only imagine what she'd felt.

I'd done better for Gregory, hadn't I? When I'd realized he wasn't cheating—that something was physically wrong with him—I'd stayed. Despite being on the brink of divorce, having spoken to an attorney, and already packing my bags—I'd stayed. Even though, in absolute honesty, I'd already felt emotionally separated from him, I stayed through the worsening years and then for the truly bad part. And it broke me in a lot of ways. And loaded me down with guilt. Perhaps enough to bury me.

Maybe that was the real reason for not wanting to open the other boxes. I had enough guilt. Did I want to invite more? Because when I opened these boxes all that crap was bound to come flying out and wrap itself around me.

I pressed my hand to my face, covering my eyes.

It was a sad, pathetic state to be in when the threat of finding forgotten treasures from the past could so terribly overwhelm the recipient, me, with grief and regret.

Was it about avoidance? Self-protection?

Shame on me, I thought. I pushed myself away from the doorframe and returned to the boxes, placing my hands flat against the cardboard. This box was marked in big letters: *DISHES*. Sounded innocent enough. I took a chance.

Aunt Eva's dishes were old-fashioned, everyday china with painted shells around the flat rim. I remembered them well. I ran my fingers around the rim of the platter. Yes, there was the chipped spot. I even knew how that had happened, and I smiled. Without hesitation, I carried the box into the kitchen and unpacked it, stacking the dishes on the counter.

I'd been afraid of these? I shook my head.

I'd use them. Why not? I'd wash up the plates and bowls and the rest and use them instead of the anonymous dishes that were in the rental's cabinets. I had pleasant memories attached to these dishes.

This time, I returned more easily, more comfortably, to the other boxes. I lifted the lid of another. This one had letters banded with ribbons and rubber bands.

The contents of this box looked more personal. Was that my handwriting on the envelopes? A long-ago child stepping out of time itself, to show up here? Below the letters was a small three-prong hinged cookbook. A leather-bound book that might be an address book or a small journal was next to it. My aunt had written her name on the cover. I felt strangely moved at the sight of her handwriting, so I didn't touch either of those. I needed to be in the right frame of mind.

I moved that box out of the way.

The third box—I lifted the lid and found a piece of artwork. It was mixed media collage combining color, fabric, pen, and paint arranged in delicate brushstrokes that shaped small flower petals and tiny green leaves with small buttons sewn here and there like berries. The framed picture was about sixteen inches square. The frame was a shadow-box type, but shallow and antique looking. It complemented the eclectic appearance of the artwork.

I remembered it well.

Aunt Eva had hung this on the wall of my bedroom—rather the room I'd stayed in when I was visiting. There'd been a desk in the room, and this had hung over it and was directly in view when I was lying in bed. It was the last thing I saw before the lights went out at night and the first when I opened my eyes in the morning light. It wasn't "dear" in terms of costliness, but it was dear in how it took me up, almost on a magic carpet, and returned me back to that time when my aunt had welcomed me at the beginning of each visit, had tucked me in at night, had scolded me when I left a damp towel on the floor—and so on. All the little memories that outlasted the temporary splash of bigger occasions.

I clutched the frame to my chest and stepped back intending to skirt around the boxes and leave the room, and I stumbled. The frame slipped from my hands and fell to the floor, the corner hitting hard, and I heard the glass break as I saw the frame split.

Uttering an instinctive cry that was short but harsh, I blamed myself for my carelessness. An accident, of course. Inadvertent but still my fault. *So typical of me. Why do I ruin everything I touch?*

I knelt there on the floor, suddenly still, listening to the silence filled only with the echo of my condemning words.

Had that thought really come from my brain?

That I ruined all that I touched? Hurt all that I valued?

Yes. Because despite all the years hanging on the wall, or in storage, the work of art had done well enough until one thoughtless moment in my care.

A poor wife, a poor stepmother, and a poor daughter. That is the proof of my life.

Where was this ugliness coming from? I pressed my hands over my ears, willing my mind to be empty, to stop. When the negative thoughts slowed, I knelt, moving carefully and deliberately, and focused on picking up the broken glass.

By the time I stood again, I was able to firmly reject the awful thoughts I'd had. I wasn't that person. Things went wrong, but not by my hand. I'd done my best to fix what was wrecked, and to soften the despair for others when it couldn't be fixed. That's who I was. And I needed to find a way to remember that.

I dropped the glass in the kitchen trash can and then assessed the damage to the artwork.

The glass was gone, yes, and the frame was

splintered, but it was still mostly attached due to the brown paper covering the back. It had a couple of small tears, as if fingers had pressed too firmly once or twice. An old label was affixed to the back of the frame. The gold-tone label and the black printing on it was faded. I carried it over to the door to the porch where the daylight was strong and examined it. The name of a business, Front Street Gallery, Beaufort, North Carolina was embossed on it.

The sun touching me through the window lured me out to the rocker. I carried the artwork in what was left of its frame to the porch and sat with it in my lap.

Could it be fixed? Was it worth the effort?

I liked this collage. The important thing was that it had been Aunt Eva's. It had mattered to her—enough for her to pack it with other things in those boxes. It meant something to me, too.

At the least, I could find a new frame and glass insert for it. That shouldn't be too difficult. But there were small areas of damage in the fabric. A few loose stitches. Nothing than could've been caused by today's fall.

Wear and tear over time perhaps aggravated

by a fall. Sounded like a commentary on life. And for some weird reason, that thought gave my spirits a lift, easing the annoyance and frustration over that moment of carelessness because, with rare exception, what was broken could also be mended. And if the result wasn't perfect, still it would be good enough.

From the end of the crossover, a male voice called out, "Ahoy, the ship! Request permission to come aboard?" The hearty shout was punctuated by a dog's bark.

Jake and Starfish. I sighed. But my spirits lifted a bit more. The sandcastle boy wasn't building today, but the sun was shining, and the day was warm and more people were out than there'd been before.

A little company might be nice, but I refused to respond in kind. I waved and called out, "Sure."

They ascended the stairs and walked the crossover to reach the porch. Before he unhooked the gate to my side of the porch, he said, "Am I interrupting? I don't want to intrude."

Star whined.

"It's all good."

They came through the gate. Starfish did a

quick sniffing tour of the porch, spent a great deal of time investigating the edges of the closed door, and then settled on the cool wood planks in the shade of the house, flopping to her side and exposing her neck. Cooling off, I supposed.

I offered, “How about a bowl of water?”

Jake said, “Star will appreciate it.”

“What about you?”

He shrugged. “Not for me, thanks.”

“I’d be willing to give you a glass.”

His expression went blank for a moment. After a slight pause which amused me, he laughed. “Very funny.”

“How about iced tea?”

“Thanks, but—” He stopped, suddenly focused on the splintered frame and artwork I was holding. “What do you have there? It looks broken.”

“It is. I dropped it.”

Somehow the frame made a quick passage from my hands to his, even before I knew I was releasing it.

“Nice. I like this. Too bad about the frame, but no damage to the artwork that I can see.”

“There’s a small tear.”

He examined it more closely. “Oh, I see. Yes.” He looked up at me. “Can probably be fixed.” He noticed the label on the back. “Oh, hey. It says Front Street Gallery.”

“You’ve heard of it?”

“Sure. They’re still in business over in Beaufort.” He grinned. “You should take it to them. They can probably fix it up and reframe it.”

I frowned. “Seems like a lot of effort to go to. It has sentimental value. It belonged to my aunt. But to go to Beaufort, to a gallery . . .”

“Doesn’t hurt to ask if they can and what it would cost, right? If you’d like me to, I’d be happy to ask them. I knew the folks who used to run the gallery. They probably still do, for that matter. I wouldn’t mind saying hello to them again.”

I reclaimed my picture. “No, but thanks, I’ll take care of it myself.”

He nodded. “It’s easy to find. Right on the main drag in Beaufort. Front Street. Lots of restaurants and shops there. I go over that way regularly. Should make for a fun afternoon if you have some free time.”

“Thanks, again. I’ll be right back with Star’s water.”

By the time I returned, I had my words picked and ready. I set the bowl down beside the half-sleeping dog and said, "I know I said this before, but forgive me for repeating it. I'm not dating right now."

His expression never altered.

"I appreciate you and Star being neighborly, but—"

"No worries. I'm pretty tied up these days myself. That said, if you're ever in the mood to get out and have a meal somewhere, just give me a call."

"Oh." I rubbed my hands together, feeling awkward. "I guess I assumed you were hinting we should go to Beaufort together. I shouldn't have."

He laughed. "Oh, you assumed correctly, but in actual fact, I am pretty tied up this week, so it's just as well that you turned me down before I asked."

What? That struck me as odd and it took me a moment to untangle his meaning which delayed my reaction, which was probably a good thing. I gave up the effort and asked, "What do you do, by the way? Here at the beach for employment, I mean. You said you'll be busy this week?"

He shrugged. “Jobs here and there. I work on commission, sort of.”

I frowned, waiting.

He looked at Star. She’d emptied the bowl with great messy laps.

“Let’s go, girl.” He turned back to me. “We’ll get out of your way.”

“What sort of jobs?”

He paused at the gate. “Let me know if you need help with that picture. As for jobs—I take those as they come. Maybe we can discuss it over dinner sometime.”

I crossed my arms. “Really? I was interested, but mostly out of courtesy. Should I care all that much?”

“That’s up to you.” Halfway along the crossover, he gave me one more wave.

An annoying man. From his poor timing to his poorly trained dog and his knack for saying the wrong things . . . Or was that deliberate?

As if I care enough to wonder even for a second about what he does to earn a living or to fill his days.

And as my mom might’ve said, he was probably halfway to crazy. There were days when she could say the same about me.

But Front Street Gallery . . . Why not take a drive to Beaufort tomorrow? Even nuts could have good ideas on occasion.

Chapter Six

On Saturday morning, I wrapped the framed artwork in a towel and placed it securely on the floorboard of my car. One quick look at the map of Beaufort showed how simple the drive was. Unless I missed the second bridge . . . in which case, oh well. I knew how to turn around and try again. I was a pro at that.

The sun was bright and the day was warm but not humid. It was the perfect day for a drive along Bogue Banks. When I reached Atlantic Beach I made the turn to cross the bridge to Morehead City and then turned right to follow the next bridge over to Beaufort.

I felt . . . almost good. Less drawn.

The streets of Beaufort, many old and narrow, were a little trickier than I expected. I missed the turn that would take me to Front Street and had to find a place to turn around and go back, but the view as I drove along Front Street with the quaint shops and a plaza with benches, glimpses of a boardwalk and the sound beyond, was worth doing twice. I pulled into the parking area right across the street, practically in front of Front Street Gallery.

The brick building was set back from the street. It looked like it had been a home long ago. Front Street, the park adjacent to other businesses, then the boardwalk and the harbor. A few boats rocked gently at anchor. The sign with the gallery name was out front and clear. From the sidewalk, I could see the sign in the door was turned to Open. I retrieved the towel-wrapped frame from my SUV and as I lifted it out, as a sudden wave of doubt hit me. It was all good and fine to be sentimental, but maybe my better choice would be to save myself the expense. Some things weren't meant to be kept forever.

I was here now. I could at least hear what they have to say.

Locking the car, I crossed the main sidewalk to the one that led up to the gallery and I ascended the stairs.

No one was in sight when I opened the door, but a bell—like a large cowbell— jangled overhead. I looked up and confirmed it was, indeed, a cowbell with a small sprig of blue flowers tied to it with a bow.

I scanned the store, taking in the display tables, artwork hanging on the walls and some small sculptures tucked here and there. Quite a variety of items.

The door closed softly behind me, but still I saw no one.

Before me was a large room with shelves and displays of ceramics and paintings on the walls, some freestanding driftwood sculptures including a set of herons, with round display tables in the middle of the room showing off touristy items like shell creatures and shell frames and shell sailboats, and so on. Once upon a time, art had been my thing. I'd majored in Art History in college, but never took it beyond that, not professionally. But Gregory and I had shared that interest in art, though our tastes were different.

A glass-topped sales counter was near the back of the room and next to that was an open door to what looked like it might be a breakroom. Perhaps the salesperson had just ducked into the restroom thinking they had a quiet moment?

Another door was adjacent to the breakroom door, but it was closed. I had a brief glimpse of a staircase and maybe a small hallway over by the far wall, but then suddenly the closed door opened a foot or so and a petite, dark-haired woman looked out, smiling at me. She had a phone to her ear. She gestured toward it then held up one finger—a request to wait. But then her expression changed to something that spoke of disappointment. The woman put her hand over the phone and asked softly, "I'll be right with you?"

I nodded and got a thumbs-up from the woman who disappeared back into what must be an office, but she left the door open this time. I walked over to the glass counter and set the frame down, then began a more casual tour of the items arrayed on the shelves and of the paintings and other artwork above. My attention got stuck on the carved heron sculptures. Two were full-sized—like adults—and the third was small. Presumably the baby. I touched the one nearest me. The gray wood was smooth, almost silky to the touch. The artist had used some sort of whitewash in streaks along the neck and on the back. There must have a lot of hand-rubbing to make those whitish areas look as natural as—

"Hi. Sorry for the delay."

The woman had approached so quietly that I

jumped in surprise. She said, "Sorry to startle you."

"No problem. I was enjoying looking around."

"Those herons are a beautiful set."

I gave them a quick smile. "They are, indeed." I saw she was about to make the sales pitch. "Oh, but I'm not in the market. Sorry."

"No worries. What can I do for you? And if you're just looking—and out enjoying an exquisite day—then that's fine too."

"I'm sorry for the interruption." I nodded toward the office door.

The salesclerk looked surprised. "Not at all. I appreciate you waiting." She gave a small laugh. "I admit, though, that I was a little disappointed."

My mind went blank. I didn't know how to respond to that.

The woman laughed again and said, "I noticed a package on the counter. Is that yours?"

Feeling on safer ground now, I said, "Yes. It needs repair and I thought you—the gallery, that is—might be able to help." But by now I'd seen that it didn't look like an actual framing shop, so I added, "If you do that kind of work here."

Sounding positively cheerful, the woman said,

"Well, then, let's go take a look."

As I followed her, she said, "I was disappointed because I was expecting a new part-timer. When I heard the bell, I thought you must be her. And I was so very glad because we are terribly shorthanded these days, and with the weather warming up, that will become more of a problem." There was a pleasant, almost bubbly quality to the woman's manner. As they reached the counter, she added, "Of course, I quickly realized you weren't a temp or a part-timer." She sighed. "My bet is the new gal isn't going to show." By now, the woman had taken her position on the other side of the counter opposite me. But she wasn't done yet. As she reached toward the towel, she changed course and instead looked directly at me and said, "Welcome, by the way, to Front Street Gallery. I'm the manager. Call me Maia. Thanks for dropping in and I hope we can help you."

"We?"

"The royal *we*, I suppose. Honestly, the young man who used to work here went off to college last year and only comes home for holidays now. And then the retired teacher who's been so dependable for so many years, has moved away permanently. But that's not your problem. It's just my way of apologizing for being so scattered."

I unfolded the towel. "You can see the problem."

"Oh, how sweet. Oh my." She gave it a sober look. She pointed at one spot and another as she said, "I can see the wear in some places. Nothing too bad. Mostly, it's just the frame?"

"It belonged to my great-aunt. She hung it on the wall of my room when I was a child. The room I always stayed in while visiting her. I came across it the other day and was surprised by the memories it carries with it. I know it's not valuable—"

"Oh, shush now. There are different types of value . . . and they are all valuable." She stopped and seemed to be chewing on her lip, but delicately—an indication of deep thought. She squinched up her face a little and said, "Hmm." She offered a quick smile then pointed at a spot where the ribbon and netting and needlework formed some sort of junction. "Do you see that there?"

"What?"

"Right in there."

"Some stitches . . ."

"Hold on." She pulled a magnifying glass from under the counter and handed it to me. "Point it right there."

"Oh. Initials?" But they weren't E.D. Not my aunt's initials. And I'd never known her to do this kind of craftwork anyway. "Is that a date?"

"Looks like a three and a four to me. Likely for 1934."

"I presumed she bought it here, but perhaps not." I lifted the framed work and tilted it upright so she could see the Front Street Gallery sticker on the back attached to the brown paper backing.

"Well, look at that. We do put a sticker on the back of work we frame, but that's old, too. Older than any I've seen around here. But that's neither here nor there. Are you looking at getting the frame replaced or the artwork retouched? If you are thinking of getting it touched up, then you'll want to do that before framing."

"I don't know. I was focused more on fixing the frame. I need a new one, I guess."

"Up to you, of course. But it's lovely work. Like a sampler but of keepsakes." She pointed at specific details. "For instance, that looks like a baby's ribbon, and this looks like a bit of tatting . . . Do you know tatting? Not too many people do that anymore. And these tiny bells and buttons must've meant something to someone." She rested her hands on the glass on either side of the artwork. "We don't do fabric or textile restoration here, but I know someone who can. Would you like me to contact her? Have her take a look and give you an estimate? Then you'll have the information you need to decide."

"Yes. Sure. That would be great."

"I promise we'll take good care of it. I know it's important to you."

"You are very kind."

Maia laughed. "Not at all. It's not only my job, but it's my pleasure to serve you—even if you *aren't* here applying for a job." She chuckled softly as she pulled out a pad of paper receipts. "What's your name and contact information?"

"Emma Dance." I recited my phone number and mentioned I was staying in Emerald Isle but wasn't sure how long I'd be there. "It's my great-aunt's house . . . or was."

"I'm sorry for your loss."

"She's been gone a few years. I do miss her.

But it's—rather *was*—her house that I'm staying at." Impulsively, I added, "My house now." I felt bold just stating it like that, but the woman, Maia, showed no reaction.

She nodded, saying, "I'll contact Mary right away. Unless she's out of town, I'll probably have an estimate on cost and timing within a few days." She wrote a short description of the artwork and a brief explanation of the tasks on the slip and then detached a copy. She stapled a business card to it and handed it to me. "And in the meantime, if you have any concerns, or a change in plans, just give me a call."

"I will." I looked at the neat handwriting and the staple. How long since I'd held a handwritten receipt? It brought to mind the trips with Gregory to fancier galleries in years past. I folded it carefully to slip in the zipped pocket of my purse.

In a different tone, one that said business had been attended to, Maia asked, "So you're just in the area for a visit or more permanently?"

I shrugged. "Not sure. Maybe for a while."

"Well, Emma Dance, welcome to our town and to our gallery. I hope you won't be a stranger." She was interrupted as her cell phone began ringing again, the sound coming from the office. "Oops, guess I left it in there."

"Thanks again. I'll see myself out."

"Thank you. I'll be in touch!" Maia said as she hurried to the office.

Well, that was done, I supposed. We'd never actually discussed options for reframing the piece, but that could wait, right? Until after the textile part, as Maia had referred to it, had been assessed to.

In fact, I was impressed that she'd given the piece such attention and consideration. It was sweet and it was quaint—and it meant something to me because it had meant something to Aunt Eva. But preserving the past wasn't always the right choice. Sometimes the choice to let the past go—to let it *be* the past—was the more reasonable, practical option. Sometimes the healthiest one.

Or did that only apply to memories and mistakes?

As I neared the door, I noticed the herons again. A little family. Cast-off wood. Cast off, in fact, by the ocean. Shaped and cherished into something else entirely. The ultimate recycling transformation by skillful hands.

There was hope, wasn't there? I touched my eye and found moisture on my lashes. Stupid. I hadn't cried through this whole awful years-long nightmare. I'd lost my temper. I'd been depressed. Angry. Guilty. Every negative emotion a person could pile into the baggage they carried around, unseen but keenly felt. But I hadn't cried. And I wouldn't now. The worst was over. I was in the healing phase.

I forced a smile, turned to the door, and opened it gently. The bell sang its goodbye overhead with a gentle clang.

ଔଷ

My hands felt empty. I felt empty. Deflated. I'd promised myself lunch. The streets were quiet, but several restaurants appeared to be open. I crossed Front Street to the row of businesses that fronted on the boardwalk with its pretty baskets of hanging flowers and view of the boats at anchor in the sound. It would be nice to maybe find one that offered seating with a view of the sound. And I'd take a closer look soon, but for now there was a bench calling my name. It had a nice shady spot in the bricked patio area. It was actually a relief to drop my purse on the bench and then sit down beside it. And just breathe and feel that soft breeze and the aromas from nearby kitchens. I closed my eyes.

It could only have been a couple of minutes—not much more than that—when I sensed someone nearby.

"Did I startle you again? I'm sorry. I often come out here to eat my lunch."

"Maia? Who's minding the shop? Did your help show up after all?"

"No such luck. But that's okay. It's early in the season and quiet today. I did flip the sign to Closed, but if I see anyone go up to the door, I'll trot back over there. Won't hurt me to miss a few bites of my sandwich." She patted her hip.

"Nonsense."

"So says the slender woman," she said, with a gentle teasing note in her voice.

I smiled. "No credit to me."

"Hmm. Genetics? I always say that if I'd been taller and liked chocolate less I'd be skinny, too. Mind if I join you?"

"Not at all." That's when I noticed she had two

bottles of water tucked under her arm.

She grinned. "Saw you out here on my bench. I'm territorial, I guess, but not nervy enough to invite myself to join you without bringing a gift." She handed me the bottle. I accepted it, and she settled herself in place, putting her lunch bag, shaped like an old-fashioned lunch pail but with zippers and compartments, in the space between us.

She pulled out an apple and offered it to me. "Like an apple?"

"No, thanks. I'm going into one of these restaurants as soon as I can decide which. Any recommendations?"

"They're all good. But." She pulled a sandwich from her lunch bag. It was secured in plastic wrap. She waved it like a prize. "You're not allergic to chicken salad, are you? I should ask, right?"

I laughed. "No, I'm not allergic."

"I promise I keep a clean kitchen. No pets or kids, so no surprises." She opened one end of the plastic and held it toward me. "Take half."

This woman, a stranger, a shopkeeper, had followed me out to *her* bench and was offering me half of her sandwich.

"Seriously. This is chicken salad. Super fantastic chicken salad."

Her enthusiasm persuaded me. I did as instructed, carefully extracting one half of her sandwich.

"Excellent," she said, and pulled the plastic wrap back from her half.

Carefully, tentatively, I took a bite. And another. She tore her napkin in half and handed it to me. I accepted.

"Oh my goodness, this is so amazing. Did you make this yourself?"

"I did. I don't cook a lot, but when I do, it's fabulous, and I don't mind saying so. My mother and her sisters taught me well. I like to bring my lunch and eat it out here, but usually it's peanut butter and jelly. I put a little more effort into it today, and I'm glad."

"I can't believe you're sharing your lunch with me."

"Why?"

"Well, because."

"I know. I'm teasing. But I've been alone all morning and it's looking like I'll be on my own this afternoon, too, so I've pushed myself onto you. I admit to being selfish."

"Oh, not at all."

"Well, I did barge into your thoughts. But I brought gifts, so . . ."

She finished the last bite about the same time I did. She reached back into her magic lunch bucket but bypassed the apple and came out with a package of cookies. Again, in plastic wrap.

"I can't claim to have baked these myself. But they are good."

"Oatmeal raisin?"

"You betcha." She opened the bag and offered me one. Which I accepted.

She said, "The collage you brought in for repair is very sweet. And unusual. I think someone treasured it."

"It was in my Aunt Eva's house when I was a child. I saw it there for . . . forever. Before she died about ten years ago, she packed away a few of her belongings for me to have and included the collage. I only found it again yesterday."

Maia finished repacking her lunch bag, now with the trash neatly folded. "Sure you don't want that apple?"

"I'm sure. Save it for your snack this afternoon."

She nodded. "Well, I think it's a good thing to try to fix it up. After Mary gives the estimate, I'll be in touch. So, either way, we'll talk again soon." She glanced across the street. "Got a customer!" She was up, with her lunch bag and water bottle tucked under her arm, waving as she crossed the street and called out, "I'm on my way!"

Wow. Like a hurricane. Come and gone. But a nice hurricane. Perhaps more like a gentle, but sudden spring shower? felt . . . *How did I feel?* Like a person. Just a person.

Which was nice.

I walked over to the boardwalk and leaned against the railing. The water was only a few feet below, lapping at the pilings holding up the boardwalk, and at the sides of the nearby boats.

How *did* I feel? Not quite so lank.

I leaned backward, my hands still gripping the railing and with my eyes closed, my face lifted to the sun.

Maybe hope was catching up. Maybe.

The benefit of this trip to Beaufort had already been reaped—broken frame or not. I turned and looked back across Front Street. Instead of hanging around, it seemed a good time to leave. I'd already had a bite of lunch, after all, and I wanted to carry this feeling of well-being home with me. Home?

To Beach Heart. Home for now.

I headed toward my car but didn't stop, instead I continued around it and walked back up the steps and into the gallery. When I opened the door, the bell rang again, though this time I hardly noticed. Maia was at the counter. She looked up. Her greeting showed both surprise and a welcome.

"Emma?"

"Before I go, I was wondering . . . How much are the herons?"

Maia grinned. "They are so beautiful, aren't they? And truly, not as much as you may think. Let me tell you about the artist . . ."

Chapter Seven

I couldn't afford them, but I bought them anyway.

The heron family looked a lot bigger carefully wrapped in paper and bubble wrap and lying on my car's back seat. Maia had seemed so pleased, and I'd been pleased too, even as my less enthusiastic, more budget-conscious self was alarmed by me nodding and saying I'd take them with me.

Funny way to declare I was home. To make my mark. I'd spent money I couldn't afford to fight the beachy décor. Which, of course, was a ridiculous concept. How much beachier could one get than life-size herons? But I hoped they'd look more like artwork, and less like my present décor which was chosen for cuteness and durability, and intended to survive all manner of tourists.

Somewhere in her sales pitch, Maia had mentioned that a friend of hers had purchased an egret, similar to the herons and crafted by the hands of the same artist, the first time the friend had come into the gallery. Now I was purchasing a small flock. A family. I had to laugh. And laughter was beginning to feel like a habit—if not a new habit, then at least one fondly remembered, and hopefully back to stay.

ଔ

As I drove home, from time to time I glanced into the back seat and caught a glimpse of the wrapped herons and felt a small thrill mixed with a little guilt. When I pulled into the parking area below the beach duplex, I opened the car door to remove the herons and felt a silliness rise in me. Like a warm hug. It was the most positive feeling I could remember experiencing in a long time. I was glad there was no one here to distract me, to interrupt the mood.

In fact, after I moved my purchases inside, I removed the wrappings and stood them next to the striped chair. After giving each a gentle pat on the head, I changed into shorts and a T-shirt and went out to the beach. Not specifically for a jog or a walk, or even to occupy my restless mind with whatever and whomever I found—whether with a boy building sandcastles or a chance meeting with *other* acquaintances—but just to enjoy the sunny afternoon and to *be*. To simply be. And this time, I took a bag with me in case I found a few somethings worth hanging on to.

☙

The next morning, Sunday, I slept in. Even as I woke, I kept the soft sheets pulled up around my face, enjoying the feel of the fabric against my cheek, in no hurry to emerge from that sweet space. Instead, I stayed curled under the blankets and remembered the Sunday mornings spent with Aunt Eva and going to church and Sunday School. I remembered the years of Vacation Bible School in the summers, and orange popsicles and sharing crayons with the other children when we colored pictures. I remembered the one kid who liked to eat paste. I remembered all of us seated in the grass, in the shade of a big tree, singing songs. A stream of memories like that flitted through my mind at will as I watched.

It was midmorning by the time I'd forced myself from bed. I showered and dressed for the day. It felt—*I* felt—relaxed and wonderful. But as soon as I stepped out onto the deck, I saw Starfish.

She was running back and forth along the beach, frolicking and splashing in the fringes of the wavelets, attacking them as if they were challenging her and must be driven back. Every so often, she'd return at a gallop to the sand to plop beside the boy, the sandcastle architect. Each day, even though he started afresh, his castles reached new heights, as if he was building faster to get higher before the tide came to plow it under and fill the holes, or the sun set and he ran out of time.

Star was free of the leash. From the crossover, I scanned the beach and then studied the porches that were within view from this angle. Where was Jake?

I had my laptop with me, intending to make a list of things to do, and things to consider while I was deciding how to move forward. As I walked along the crossover, I looked east and west, and back again, and I saw no sign of my red-headed neighbor. But down on the beach, Star saw *me* as I neared the benches. She gave a short bark and abruptly stood still. She braced her front legs a split second before she dug in and surged forward, flat-out running.

Toward the crossover stairs. Toward me.

Instinctively, I hugged my closed laptop to my chest and steadied myself against the railing to receive her greeting.

She took the stairs in two leaping strides, reached the top and turned the corner. I didn't try to avoid the inevitable, but merely hoped to lessen the risk. Starfish found me irresistible in some way I didn't understand. It would pass. All things passed . . . eventually.

But Star didn't touch me. She stopped two inches short of my knees, panting, wet brown eyes begging—hoping and pleading for an invitation.

Slowly, I eased a step over and then down to sit on the edge of the bench. Equally slowly, I held up my hand. "Sit, Star." Was my tone firm enough? Was I clear in my command?

She didn't sit. Or she did, kind of. Her back end lowered but hovered over the deck planking with her tail wagging furiously. She was panting so vigorously that droplets of dog spit were landing on my knees.

Hand still up, I said, "Sit. Stay."

I'd never owned a dog. Never had a pet of any kind. I had no clue whether I was doing this right, but so far, so good. Slowly, I lowered my hand to pat the top of her head. Her head remained absolutely still, but when I touched her, I felt the quiver vibrating throughout her body.

"Shh. Calm down, girl. Where's Jake?"

Mistake. Saying his name. I noted the error as she responded by putting her muzzle on my knee and resting a paw on my other leg.

"Stay, Starfish."

She heard her full name and did stop short of climbing into my lap.

I patted her soft, silky fur again. "You know what, Star? I think you're just spoiled. Spoiled rotten."

She continued gazing at me with those brown eyes and amping up the charm big time and she was wearing me down, but climbing up onto my lap wasn't negotiable. Nope. That tongue hanging out as she panted made her look thirsty. Should I give her a bowl of fresh water?

"You two are good friends now." Jake laughed.

He was standing below our perch. Barefoot in the sand. The leash dangled from his hand. He was wearing shorts, a sleeveless T-shirt and a smirk.

"Where were you?" I stopped stroking Star's.

I swear the dog looked disappointed, but as I stood to address Jake directly, she got the message and flopped onto her side, seriously panting now. "You abandoned your dog."

He looked surprised. "Me? No way."

"Look at her. She's practically sick from dehydration."

"Water, water everywhere, but not a drop to drink?"

"A rhyme? Who said that?"

"Not a clue." He came up the stairs to join us. He stopped at the spigot and turned the wheel ever so slightly, so the drips became a slight stream. Star jumped up and dashed over. Jake said, "I was visiting Mrs. Donley."

I must've looked blank. I felt blank.

"Dylan's grandmother," he prompted. "I took her a book. She was complaining that she hadn't had a good book to enjoy in a long time. I took her one."

My brain was trying to catch up—to make the move from abandoned pooch to Jake, the one-man lending library, with personal book curation and delivery, no less.

"Who is Dylan?"

He grinned. "The architect."

"Seriously? How did you—? Well, I presume you asked him his name. He didn't seem open to speaking with me."

"Mrs. Donley saw me talking to the boy one too many times, I guess, and came out to introduce herself. And to question me."

"Good for her." I patted the closed lid of my laptop. "As for Star, she was unleashed and unattended."

He shrugged. "She was with Dylan. And in sight of me over at the house with Mrs. Donley."

"I was about to get her some water."

He frowned. "Mrs. Donley? I think she's good. She seemed fine. Has access to plumbing and all that."

I bit my lip. Just enough to keep the hot words inside.

Jake grinned. "Sorry. I couldn't help teasing. The image of you and Star finally bonding made my day. I hope—sincerely—that she'll calm down and stop . . . greeting you so enthusiastically now." After a pause, he asked, "Mind if I join you?"

"I . . ."

"I won't stay if you're busy."

I nodded toward the laptop. "Hadn't really gotten started yet."

"Remote working?"

"Just checking email and such. Maybe make some to-do lists."

"I'll introduce you to Mrs. Donley, if you like."

"Another day."

"She says Dylan has problems. I asked because he doesn't talk, as you noted. Seems like he's hardly aware of anyone around him—unless you get close to his castle, that is."

"True." I'd noticed but I was surprised *he* had. And he'd asked the boy's grandmother about it. How nervy was that? Or caring? Even so . . .

I said, "So what'd she say?"

"He's not deaf. That's what I was guessing. She said that he doesn't talk much. He's . . . remote. He's always been that way but not this bad. After his dad passed, it got worse."

"How sad. But what about his mom? I assume she's getting help or therapy for him?"

"She does. She has to work, so Grandma stepped in. But the kid gets restless, agitated, indoors. Even outdoors if he's not allowed to wander. It's different at the beach, she said. Something about the ocean soaking up all the external somethings. Luckily, his mom's friend has this house and lets Mrs. Donley hang out there while Dylan's at the beach."

"But all by himself out here?"

"She keeps an eye on him. She said he won't go in the water above his big toe so no risk there. And he's peaceful. Rather, more at peace. Sleeps better. All that."

"But it's a rental, right? What happens when the season kicks in? I can't believe the friend can afford to forgo rental customers so his grandmother can hang out in the house while Dylan plays on the beach."

"True enough, I'm sure. They'll figure it out."

"Well. Interesting. Sad, too. At least he has his mom and grandmother to care for him."

Jake took the few steps over to the faucet and turned it off. "Come, Star. It's time to move along."

I almost quipped that it was too bad he couldn't stay longer, but managed to hold it in. He had more than enough ego to think I was serious.

Weird, though, how the verbal part of my

brain seemed to be working semi-independently of my judgment functions. Set free, maybe? Well, I'd better reign it back in because impulsive remarks never led to anything good.

After they left, I settled on the bench and opened my laptop. Lists? No, no interests in lists. Instead, as I watched Dylan moving around his latest castle, tweaking this and adding that, I thought of Macon again.

Instead of a list, I began a letter. It started, "Macon, I hope this finds you well. We've had our troubles—" I stopped, highlighted the words, hit delete, and tried again. "Macon, I hope that someday we can find each other again. Things can never be the same without your father, but . . ." And I continued typing until my stomach reminded me to eat.

I closed the laptop, knowing I'd never send this letter to Macon. Maybe it was simply a message communicated to the universe that might circle around until it found him. No, not that either. But one day, he'd show up, and it didn't hurt to practice what I'd say to him when he did.

Late Monday afternoon, Maia called with an estimate for the artwork repair and reframing.

"That was quick," I said, hardly believing it.

"Mary is getting ready to go out of town in a few days and said that if you want her to proceed, she'll get it done before she leaves. When she's done, I'll handle the framing here at the gallery. I can't replace it with the exact frame, but what I have available is a very close match. What do you think?"

The price seemed reasonable. Though, I reminded myself, for someone low on cash and with no job in sight—who'd just wasted a sum of it on a heron family—it was probably still more than I could afford.

I told her, "Yes, please go ahead."

"Will do. I'll be back in touch when it's done. Barring any unexpected holdups, should be a quick job. Quiet time of year, you know."

We disconnected.

A quiet time of year . . . I *did* know and was grateful for it. I'd been here at Beach Heart almost a week. Each night, just before I went to sleep, I stepped out on the balcony and thanked God for this gift. For however long it lasted, I prayed to enjoy it—to be a grateful person, instead of living under an anxious and fearful cloud. And I was feeling the shift. So each morning, I stepped out to the balcony again, to prove to myself that this gift was true. I was here, with the sky wide and enduring above the horizon, and the ocean, seemingly ever-changing but constant in its many faces, While I was standing on that balcony, I also sent Gregory one more mental apology, wishing I'd been able to express my caring in a way he could've understood before he died.

Doing this didn't erase the past, but it helped assuage the worst of my guilt over being here and alive and doing better now without him. By the time I'd taken a morning jog and had showered and dressed for the day, I was looking forward again—to the rest of today and to the good that tomorrow might bring. And I was okay for now.

On the downside, as I'd settled in and the newness was passing, I had time on my hands. Too much. I'd never had hobbies. Was now the time to learn some?

What I truly wanted was to redecorate Beach Heart West, but it would be costly. And when the day came that I had to move on?

I shook my head.

No, for now, the decor must stay as it was.

ઉ୪ ƒ

Per the calendar the management company maintained, renters for Beach Heart *East* were due in on Thursday. Most arrived on Sunday afternoons, but these had rented for not only next week, but also a few days in advance of that. So, Thursday. These were the first guests at Beach Heart since I'd arrived and, frankly, I was curious about how it would be.

The back deck had a privacy partition that shielded the one side from the other, but was really only a pretense of privacy, and the crossover—along with the benches and my imaginary figurehead prow of a balcony—would be theirs to use too. I would have to share.

I'd come here to hide. Had asked my mother not to tell anyone I was here. I'd avoided making relationships . . . not terribly successfully. And a few days from now, guests would be right next door.

It'll be okay, Emma. I smiled, pleased. Yes, it

would. It would absolutely be okay.

ଔଓ

I sat out again that evening in the twilight. It wasn't as solitary tonight. The beach walkers were up in number. All along the strand more beach towels were hanging from the porch railings. A child's squeal could be heard more often, or a parent shouting to a kid to come inside before it got dark. As the beach emptied of people it seemed to cue the stars to begin popping out. And it was peaceful. In me and around me.

ଔଓ

A couple of days went by. I did my own house cleaning since I wasn't paying the management company to provide that service for my side of the duplex. Pinching pennies where I could? Hah. And spending those pennies, plus a few more, to do things like restore an old picture with sentimental value and buy a family of herons.

My heron family was currently sitting over between the chair and the dining table, where I'd placed them when I'd brought them home. It was a temporary spot until I thought of a better arrangement.

No regret about those herons—I refused to allow it. But as I already knew, there was no money for new furnishings. Even so, I had Aunt Eva's dishes on my table, and a few knickknacks from our past situated here and there, including the framed photos Mom had brought and the ones I'd added—and the oceanfront, alive and constantly in motion but looking the same as it ever had. If there was a theme to the *new* "decorations" it would be *memories without the baggage*.

These were present thoughts about the future. As if I'd be here.

Could this truly be my place to build anew?

My heart beat a little harder and faster. I took a deep breath and let it out slowly. I felt . . . audacious. The possibilities scared me a little. But also energized me. I went through the main floor and opened all the blinds. The beach light streamed in, picking up the splash of colors in the room and glinting in the glass of the picture frames and reflecting across the ceiling. It was glorious. Fresh.

Like a fresh start.

Like a bubble of warmth and lightness inside me.

When Maia called on Wednesday and said she was finishing the new frame today and it would be ready for me to pick up tomorrow, or whenever it was convenient for me, I was super impressed.

"Already?"

"Yes, ma'am. Miss Mary was eager to get it done before leaving on her trip, and as for me, I don't do much actual framing anymore, but I've done a lot over the years and it's kind of fun to do something different but familiar. So, assuming no big interruptions happen, it should be ready."

"I'll come by tomorrow morning maybe?"

"See you then."

And she was gone. I set my phone back on the counter and stared at it. The interruption—this interruption—may have been providential. An opportunity to continue the upbeat feeling.

ଔ

The next day, Thursday, I arrived at the Front Street Gallery shortly before lunchtime. Maia was standing in front of some paintings and speaking with a man who appeared to be a customer. Maia was dressed as before in a dress and flats. Nothing over the top, but still dressier than most of the coastal shopkeepers I'd seen. The man wore khakis and sandals and seemed a serious shopper, but as they turned away from the painting, I could tell by the tone of their voices and their body language that the interaction was ending.

I'd stood quietly to the side hoping to communicate that I was in no hurry. As I waited, the sunrise–sunset series of small paintings they'd been discussing caught my eye, too. No, I could *not* afford them, but I stared at them wondering how difficult the scenes would be to paint. The splashes of color seemed so simple, so casually done, that I suspected it required a very skilled, talented artist to render it just so. Gregory had collected art. He saw art as objects of beauty or prestige that could be both enjoyed privately and shown off to guests. I enjoyed beautiful things, too, but for me art was a little different. My tastes were more eclectic. Perhaps pedestrian in comparison. But I never wanted to dim Gregory's enjoyment, so I tended to go along with what pleased him.

He'd purchased a beautiful still life while we were traveling in Italy. It had been given a prime spot in our home—hanging over the fireplace. One day, it had vanished, leaving a shockingly empty place on the wall. My first thought had been that Gregory had decided to hang it in a different spot—perhaps in his home office. He'd been spending a lot of time in there recently and seemed to be constantly shifting and rearranging his files and his desk setup. It was unlike him, but I thought he'd just grown dissatisfied with how it looked or functioned for him. But the painting wasn't in his office.

When I asked him where it was, he suggested we must've been robbed. He became agitated and the suggestion quickly escalated to insistence. Before I knew it, he was calling the police.

I remembered that day with confusion and distress. It was like being caught—trapped—in someone else's crazy dreamscape. It didn't make sense but I couldn't quite grasp why. And then, while we were speaking with the officers, one of them who'd been taking a look around, spoke from the kitchen doorway, saying, "Ma'am? Ms.

Dance? Is this the missing painting?"

The painting had somehow found its way into that space between the refrigerator and the cabinets. Gregory looked at me as if I'd played a trick on him, perhaps had sabotaged him.

"You're in deep thought again."

I jumped. Literally.

Maia touched my arm. "Where were you? I noticed you staring at Anna's paintings, but I think you'd gone elsewhere—somewhere much farther away?"

I rubbed my face. That time-travel yank feeling. "I'm fine. Just a memory."

"Sorry."

"No, I'm glad. Feels rather like I was rescued."

She smiled. "Come with me."

I followed. She led me to the breakroom.

"Have a seat."

"Oh. That's okay. I—"

She paused and looked back at me with her hand on the fridge. "Are you in a hurry?"

"No, but I don't want to interfere at your place of business. I truly am okay."

"Oh, I believe you. No, this is about me. Folks

have been coming in steadily this morning—no moment to grab a drink or a bite. That's good, right? But this present lull won't last. I can make coffee or hot cocoa or . . ." She reached in and came out with a pitcher of iced tea. "Will you drink iced tea?"

"Sure, but . . ." I gave up. I recognized how she'd asked the question. *Not would you like a drink or can I pour you some*, but in such a way that I'd seem foolish to persist in refusing. Plus, I was thirsty. "Thanks."

Maia nodded and set the glasses of ice and tea in front of us at the table. She placed her glass at the seat at the end where she would have a view of the door. "I'll be able to cover the door from here." She nodded. "I'll be right back."

She dashed into the small office adjacent to the breakroom and truly was back in a flash carrying a package that I knew must be my artwork.

"Good time to take a look." She set it in front of me and then sat in her seat with a sigh. "My feet will be delighted to take a break." She took a long sip and set the glass back down. "It's *sweet* tea. Hope that's okay."

"It's delicious."

She opened the brown paper wrapping. "What do you think?"

It was beautiful. Not classically beautiful, perhaps, but the stitching that had worked loose was now tight and neat, without even a sign of a repair. The colors had been touched up on the piece. If I hadn't known about the fading, I would never have picked up on the retouching.

"Nice. Very nice."

"Yes, she's a wonder."

"How much do I owe?"

"Actually, it came in under the quote. We'll settle up when you're ready to leave. I'm just delighted to see a friendly face that isn't . . . Well, that said, I guess you *are* a customer." She shrugged and chuckled softly. "You mentioned visiting you great-aunt as a child and now being back at her house at the beach. I imagine it's wonderful being back where you spent part of your childhood?"

"Beach Heart. That's the name of the house. I'm glad to be back . . . if a person can ever truly *go* back. That said, there are lots of good memories." I ran my fingers around the frame of the collage. "I've been thinking that good memories can sometimes hold you back, but they might also tempt you onto a new path, a better path, forward."

"Like starting over in hope of making more good memories?"

"I suppose. I wish that, if I'm starting over, I could've gotten started sooner. I feel old."

Why on earth was I saying all this to a near-stranger?

But her eyes were kind, and her appearance and manner were welcoming and showed a gentle amusement.

"You aren't old. If you are, then I am too." She shrugged. "Besides, it's all relative, right? It all depends on which side of the number you're looking from. And does it even matter? There's no better place to erase a little age and fatigue than the beach. The ocean. The water. All that good stuff is like a tonic."

"What about you?" I asked. "You're the only one I've seen working here. Don't you get overwhelmed?"

"Ah. Well. I am here an awful lot. Which is hard because I've only been married a year. My husband travels a lot, so it's challenging. I have several part-time people who fill in, but my core support has . . . Well, life happens. Between illness and folks moving away and such, I'm left in a lurch. It's been off-season, so until recently it's been quiet generally, but business is picking up early this year."

The kindness was still apparent in her eyes, but the amusement had vanished from her face. Marriage was never easy, but at least the first years should be good. And here was Maia finding it difficult to simply get out of the office. Not a good start to a union that was supposed to last a lifetime. And yet a good, solid start guaranteed nothing, as I knew.

Maia said, "Oh dear. I've done it again. You have that look again." She touched my hand. "I didn't keep you here to make you sad. I should be getting back to work anyway."

I picked up my picture and followed her out of the breakroom and to the counter. I had a home. I was thrilled to have it. I loved standing on the balcony and sitting on the bench and watching the ocean and all that. But inside . . . I sighed. For a person who claimed she wanted to be left alone . . .

well, I was lonely.

That was life, right? The balance was always off.

Maia accepted payment and rewrapped the brown paper around the frame. "Would you like a box to carry it in?"

"No, it's small and light. Thank you so much, and thank you for your kindness."

"Not at all. Thank *you* for hanging out with me for a few minutes."

"You've helped me. I appreciate it." As I stepped away and started walking toward the door, I turned back and added, "If there's ever anything I can do to help you, just let me know."

Maia laughed, her eyes twinkling, and just as casually she said, "Anytime you need a job, you let me know."

I heard in my head, *Turn around and get out the door*, but instead, I felt my shoulders moving upward in a slight shrug and heard myself saying aloud, "Unfortunately, I don't know anything about running a gallery I haven't held a paying job in . . . well, thirteen years." And then I added a careless laugh to show my words held no particular meaning and no underlying message.

And I saw Maia's expression change from already disengaging, to surprise and then to speculation. She said, "If you are interested . . . Honestly, I love it here—I always have—but I don't know if it would be something you'd enjoy. It's quiet now but will get very busy in season. Lots of lookers or folks wanting souvenirs to take back to the pet sitter and such, as well as those shopping for artwork for display. Quite a mix." Maia leaned on the counter and gave me a long look. "If you *do* decide to stay around for a while, let me know."

I was all set to agree with her and hurry to the door when she said, "That said, if you think you might be interested but want to chat or get a feel for the work, give me a quick call or show up for lunch and we'll talk about the gallery and what's involved."

Managing a quick smile and a short word—*thanks*—I was out of there.

And I didn't stop until I'd passed my car, crossed the street and the park, and made it to the boardwalk. There, I grasped the railing and stood gathering my wits. I'd been so rattled. Had hardly seemed able to even control my words or behavior.

Did I want a job? I needed one. But did I want to jump into a job—a commitment—right away, the first job that came along? Plus, from Beach Heart, Beaufort wasn't just around the corner. It was a bit of a drive. Not impossible, but for a part-time retail position . . .

And then it hit me—she hadn't been serious. Or I'd read more into her words than she'd intended. Who would hire someone like me practically right off the street? The gallery had valuable items and handled money. They'd have concern over their reputation, too. I'd already told her I had no recent work experience. Maia was just being kind, or perhaps teasing.

With that thought, I found my calm and returned to my car. I drove back to Emerald Isle to keep my appointment with the management company.

And the reality of that—of *me* meeting with the management company about a valuable rental property—was almost mind blowing as the unexpected job offering.

Not a job offer, I reminded myself.

The meeting went well. We kept the west side rental paused for now. I made it clear that I was unsettled about future plans, but should soon know how I wanted to proceed, but we'd keep the current terms active for the east unit.

They were pleasant and professional and seemed to understand. I was reassured. But I needed to talk to someone and when I began to prattle on, I realized it couldn't be these people. They were polite, but they had work to do.

After I left their office, I went home and walked out to the porch and called Mom. I should bring her up to date anyway and since I was in a chewing-the-details-over kind of mood, the timing seemed good. But she didn't answer so I left a voice mail, just saying I was good, and had called to say hello.

I stretched my legs out on the crossover bench and opened my laptop, making notes about the conversation with the management company and such things, along with the questions I never thought to ask in the moment. It was quickly done, but I continued sitting there, and heard noises back in the direction of the house.

Yes, it was Thursday. The renters.

I knew they were there. I'd seen the car parked below. There were shoes scattered on their side of the deck by the door. But they were very quiet. As I sat, I heard them coming, walking softly and speaking low to each other. As they reached me, the woman offered a soft, "Good morning," and I responded. Reserved, unobtrusive people. As they continued past, I wondered if this would be the usual? I suspected not.

The couple went down the steps and crossed the dry sand to the wet and set off walking along the water.

Aunt Eva had trained me early *not* to say, "My aunt owns this place" to the renters. She'd said it was an omission, yes, and perhaps a redirection, but not an actual lie. That it was better for all concerned because it was important that the guests deal with the management company. If we tried to do the job of the management company, it would be a poor experience for all concerned.

I remembered listening carefully and saying, "But if they ask . . ."

"Who? Ask what?"

"The kids. They ask me where I'm from, which is okay, but then they ask when I got here and when I'm going home and all that."

"Just tell them we have a long-term rental

arrangement. Which we do. We just happen to have it with ourselves. No middlemen."

"Middlemen?"

"The folks in the middle. Like the management company."

Now, as I sat on the crossover watching my current guests grow small in the distance, I understood. Who could tell what would happen as renters came and went, but for now, I'd watch and learn, and find out for myself. As Aunt Eva had said—we wanted this to be a positive experience for all concerned.

Staring into the distance, I saw a man and his dog walking this way. The sun glinted red on both his hair and the dog's.

And I stayed where I was, except that I closed my computer and shifted my legs, putting my feet down onto the floor planks. As if . . . *Okay, just say it, Emma.* As if to clear the bench for someone else to sit, who might care to join me here, despite the perfectly good, wide-open, mirror bench. And chew over some thoughts with me.

In fact, they might not even stop…even if they spied me here watching them.

I waited to find out.

Chapter Eight

As Jake and Star waved and walked down the stairs to the beach, I thought of something Aunt Eva had said about a quarter of century ago—that there was joy to be found in ordinary tasks and simple moments. It seemed to me that it was the same with laughter. Simple laughter. Honest laughter. Shared laughter. And thinking of laughter reminded me of friends, and specifically of Jake and Star. It was a great gift to laugh. To be able to laugh. To spend time with someone who clearly enjoyed hearing you laugh and was willing to go out of his way to make it happen, even if it made him look a little foolish.

Like Jake. I suspected some of his remarks were deliberately intended to be amusing, or amusingly irritating.

He was charming in a disarming way. And Starfish, with her easy, sometimes overly adoring manner, helped me to be comfortable around him. He was also, to my detriment, perhaps, a little too convenient. I needed someone to talk to, but I also needed to be fair to him. Respectful. Thus, when

Jake reached the bench where I was sitting and joined me there, I said, "I need to be totally honest with you."

He looked around as if I might be talking to someone else.

"I'm serious, Jake."

He nodded. "Is this about not wanting to be friends? Have I already worn out my welcome?"

There was still a hint of teasing in his voice. But I wondered if it might be a defense to protect himself from rejection. I didn't want to hurt him.

"No," I said. "You haven't and I appreciate your advice about the picture with the broken frame, and also the help you gave with getting the boxes, and even the chair, into the house. *But.*"

"What?"

"I need to be clear. I'm single now, yes, but I haven't been single for long. I wasn't being coy or leading you on when I said I wasn't open to relationships now."

"What happened?"

A quick gasp escaped me. I would have to talk about this sooner or later. Wasn't the passing of time supposed to make it easier? How much time was enough?

I said, "My husband died. Recently."

"I'm sorry."

The apology was there in his eyes. He hadn't even needed to utter the words for me to understand that he cared. I felt a bit like an overripe apple about to drop off the tree and in need of a soft landing—which was all the more reason to be honest, even if it ran him off. Especially if it ran him off. That might be best for all concerned.

"He died recently, but he was ill for a long time." I couldn't say to him that I'd talked to an attorney about a divorce because I'd thought my husband was cheating on me. I'd done that instead of realizing sooner that he was that . . . his brain was failing him.

"We didn't know what the problem was for a while. His age, his health, were all good. By the time I understood something was physically wrong, and more time passed after that before I could convince him to see a doctor. He resisted." The words got away from me. "I tried to get his son, my stepson, to help, but he refused to see the problem." I stopped and regained my control. "It was hard for everyone."

"I'm so sorry. Words like *sorry* don't seem to

really cover it, but that's the best I can come up with."

Meanwhile, Star had laid her muzzle across my thigh, clearly sensing my sadness and offering kindness. My eyes stung but I was pretty sure I wasn't going to full-out cry. Not with Star's warm brown eyes meeting mine, and when I looked at Jake, I saw kindness in his, too.

I cleared my throat as I tried to remember that I didn't have to lay my heart bare for anyone, however pleasant or kind they seemed. "Everyone has tragedy in their lives. I wish it had been different. But I can't go back and redo it. I have to move forward." I stopped to breathe and covered my shaky composure with a shrug before speaking again. "But relationships . . . This isn't personal. I don't think I'm fit for . . . not even for friendship yet. One minute I'm up and optimistic and the next I'm . . . down and not very nice. I just need to decompress, to rest for a while. I'm not someone that anyone can count on just yet."

Surprise showed on his face. But I let my words stand as said.

Jake said, "Fair enough. We're neighbors. We'll wave when we pass. A little chitchat here and there. And if my dog comes to visit and gets thirsty, you'll give her water?"

"Of course."

"How does neighbor-friendly sound?"

"Neighbor-friendly?" Surprising myself, I smiled. "Okay by me."

We sat silently for a few minutes enjoying the spring breeze and companionship.

Out of that still moment a thought came to me, and I spoke it aloud. "I do have news. Well, it's not actual news, but something that came up because of the advice you offered."

"My advice?" He sat back again.

"About the broken collage? I took it to the gallery in Beaufort."

"I hope it was a good thing that came out of it."

I laughed softly, feeling suddenly awkward. "Maia runs the gallery. She suggested I might come to work for her." I let it hang there, suddenly out of steam. Embarrassed.

"That *is* interesting. Are you considering it?"

"Full disclosure—I'm not sure she meant it. She probably regretted the suggestion as soon as the words were said. But maybe not." I shrugged.

"Regardless, it got me thinking and that's a good thing. I don't have any real work experience, so taking a job would be good from that perspective. For the résumé, right? On the other hand, I don't know if I'll stay here or for how long. I wouldn't want her to regret investing the time in me."

"Well, but no one ever knows how long they'll be anywhere, do they?" He shrugged. "Even when they think they do. The best we can do is live our days. We can plan and try to be flexible. But we don't control our fate."

"True enough. But to be counted on? When I don't know myself what my future looks like?" I pushed a windblown lock of hair out of my face. "For instance, just over a week ago, I never expected to be here. Not even close."

"Yet here you are."

I shrugged. "Exactly."

"And it's good so far?"

His question surprised me. I nodded. "Yes. In fact I'm happy to say that it is exactly what I need."

"Well, then."

"Well what?"

"Unexpected. Unplanned. But beneficial. Taking things one day at a time isn't always the answer. But you've been through a lot. Maybe you've earned this."

"No, I haven't earned this or anything."

"You're hard on yourself."

"Maybe."

"So back to the job question. If you think you might enjoy the work in the gallery, like talking to customers and such, then why not give it a try?" Leaning forward, slightly toward me, he shook his head. "Sorry. Here I go giving advice again."

"I think I wanted an opinion. Maybe a sounding board."

He nodded. "Happy to be of service, then." He shrugged. "You know, though, personal life and work are different. Drop the personal, practical concerns for now. You can never tell what the future will bring. You might enjoy working in Beaufort, at the gallery."

Star must've sensed Jake was about to leave because she sat back and glanced up at him. Jake smiled softly and scratched her head.

"It's time," he said. He rose, adding, "Must be close to the supper hour. Her inner clock—or should I say *dinner* clock—is impeccably accurate."

I stood too. "Thanks for dropping by."

He met my eyes. "I'll be seeing you around, neighbor?"

"I'll be here." I smiled. "For a while, anyway."

He said solemnly, but kindly, "Don't leave without saying goodbye, please. It wouldn't be neighborly."

For a moment, neither of us moved, but it didn't feel awkward, and in that space, I said, "In actual fact, I have no idea which door to knock on should the need arise to say goodbye."

He pointed to the east. "Down the street that way. The yellow house."

ଔଔ

When I woke the next morning, I washed up and took a slow, easy jog on the beach, accompanied by the most glorious natural artwork than I could ever have expected to witness in the form of dark and light, from low mist rising to towering clouds defining the cloudless area of sky, with those clouds changed in succeeding shades of deep blue to lilac to lofty white and tinged with gold.

I stopped to watch morning unveil itself

around me. To see the sea birds skimming the waves. To wonder how those birds speeding above might appear to the fish below. Like dark clouds passing overhead? Or shadows? But these shadows sometimes dipped low and snatched up the unlucky fish that happened to be swimming right next to you. I'd felt a lot like those fish—going along, oblivious, until without warning one's world devolved.

Made it hard to trust, as Mom said.

And yet, here I was, still standing, specifically with my feet cooling in the damp sand and with the morning chill wrapping itself around me as I absorbed the beauty of creation. I got moving again, and by the time I'd finished my morning run in the most amazing gallery imaginable, I still wanted to talk to Maia about the possibility of a job, so I showered, dressed a little more professionally, and hopped in the car.

This opportunity—if Maia was sincere about it—was probably the gentlest, most appealing way for me to enter the workforce again after so many years.

With retail and customer experience, I could gain confidence, and have current information to put on my résumé. And in an art gallery? That sounded cool, especially combined with my degree. Felt like something I might be able to build on.

Doubts hit when I pulled up and parked in front of the gallery. I sat in my car, thinking. If I walked up those steps and went in through those doors, it would be a huge step, almost an act of declaring that *maybe*, just maybe, I *might* believe in a better future. The downside was that a job like this wouldn't pay enough to be my sole support.

But did I need that? Presumably the rental income from the other unit would help. But what about unexpected emergencies or repairs? And taxes? I had an appointment to chat with the accountant recommended by the rental management company. We'd discuss all that. But what this job could be? A jumping-off place, a place where I ditched the old, failed life and moved forward into creating a new one.

Maia was standing at the display window, facing the street.

It was time. I opened the car door and stepped out.

She moved to the gallery door and pushed it

wide to greet me, smiling and saying, "I'm glad to see you!"

So she *had* meant what she'd said about a job. I was immediately caught in the push-pull of conflicting waves of gratitude and doubt.

She stepped aside to allow me in. "Can you give me a hand?" She pointed to a painting that was hanging askew on the wall. "I was trying to figure out what to do when you stepped right out of your car. Thank goodness you're taller than me."

A stepladder was positioned below the painting, but the shelves below it prevented the ladder from being close enough for an easy reach. The painting's position looked perilous. Not just for the painting, but also for the items in the area below it.

Maia said, "This hanger came loose somehow." She showed the crooked hanger on her palm. "I wanted to take the painting down for a customer, but then I couldn't dislodge it from the other hanger or get this one back in. I was wishing for a couple more inches of arm length when the light glinted off your car and caught my attention." She smiled. "I thought I might have to go out to the street begging for help—and then there you were. Do you mind?"

"Happy to help." I set my sweater and purse on a nearby table and climbed up. I was able to lift and unhook the painting without difficulty and lowered it down for Maia to take from me before I descended the ladder.

"It's a beautiful work," I said. "Some combination of wood and paint?"

"Yes, indeed. It's a local husband and wife team. They craft the wood in tones and textures and layers, then come in with the staining and painting. Their beach scenes are the most popular here, but they also do other images."

"Nice."

Maia had carried the picture over to the counter and was wrapping it up. "The buyer is coming by later to pick it up." She taped the corners of the paper, then cut a length of cord to wrap around it and slipped an artificial flower in the bow she tied. She looked up at me. "Are you here for business or a visit? Or to have our job chat?"

"Yes, the latter," I said.

"Let me set this in the office and we'll talk."

She carried the painting into the office, and I got a peek into the small room. Nothing remarkable, but it was neat and well-ordered. She went from there to the breakroom and I followed.

"Have a seat," she said, "I'll keep an eye on the door."

"Sure." I felt stiff suddenly. Awkward. As if I didn't know quite what to do.

"Emma, you look like you might run. I promise there's nothing scary going on here. How long has it been since you interviewed for a job?" She paused and waited.

"I worked right after college, but then I married and . . ." I rushed to add, "So at least thirteen years, except that I did work briefly a few years ago and so I interviewed for that, but . . ."

She held up her hand to stop me. "Don't be nervous. This isn't a regular job interview anyway. I don't want to hire someone who gives me all the right answers. I want honesty because I want this to be a good decision for both of us."

She motioned to me to sit. Somehow, I did.

"I'm sorry. I don't know why I'm so nervous. Maybe I'm worried about promising more than I can give. I don't want to let anyone down."

Again, she waved at me to stop. “Deep breath,” she said.

“I’m sorry, Maia. I thought I could do this.”

“You’ve been through a lot.” She must’ve seen my shocked expression because she hastened to add, “I can recognize it in you. You hide it well, but hiding it isn’t good. It can’t last. It only damages.”

A kettle whistled. Maia stood. “Hot chocolate,” she said. She returned with two mugs. “I assumed mini marshmallows.”

I smiled a little. “Sounds perfect.”

We sat across the table from each other with the aroma of chocolate and marshmallows scenting the air like potpourri. Some of my tension eased.

Maia asked, “So you thought that what we talked about was worth a drive up this morning to continue the discussion. What about working here appeals to you? No schmoozing, please.”

“Fair enough.” I took a deep breath, feeling the chocolate infuse me. “I haven’t worked a paying job in forever. I need to find a job but have no idea what. I have nothing to put on my résumé. No employer is going to be interested in the trips I took with my husband or the upholstery fabric I chose for the living room sofa."

She didn't speak, so I paused for a sip of cocoa and to breathe again.

I continued, "I've always loved art. I majored in art history, but it seems like a lifetime ago. I worked for a small office. Just office work right out of college while I looked for something more in line with my degree, but then I got married and my husband liked to travel, so that's what we did. I did have a job briefly about three years ago, as I mentioned, but then…well, my husband got sick—a degenerative brain disease—and I quit that job to take care of him. He passed three months ago."

Trying to stick to the important points and not get lost in the swamp of details and regrets, plus wishing to get it all said fast, I continued, "I want to be fair to us both. I don't know if I can stick this out. I don't know where I'll be a month from now. Probably in Emerald Isle, but maybe not. I could be wasting your time."

She frowned slightly, then asked, "What about *your* time?"

"Mine?"

"Yes. What would you be doing if you weren't

working a day job?"

I grimaced. "Looking for a job."

"You said you are living in your aunt's property, right?"

"True. It's mine now. But it doesn't come without financial obligations."

"You wouldn't earn enough here to pay for a beachfront lifestyle."

"I don't need to, at least not yet. My expenses are low at this point. This is more supplemental. I'm meeting with an accountant in a few days. She'll help me sort out the reality pennies. Meanwhile, I need to figure the way forward. And I don't want my decisions to negatively impact you here at the gallery if it doesn't work out for me to stay."

"At this time, we're talking part time hours while you decide if you like the job, and while *I* decide if you can handle it. It's retail. Art history? Office work? Could make a difference. One can never be sure, but a certain bent of mind, combined with the practical experience of being here—it could work out. But this is not the kind of shop that most people think of when they hear the word *retail*. It's very specialized. You'd need to learn who the local and regional artists and artisans are. That's what most of our clients are looking for, and our clients are both local and otherwise. That's where our greater profit is. But right alongside those traditional works of art are the shell creatures and souvenir knickknacks." Maia added, "And they all matter."

Emma waited, sensing that Maia wasn't done.

"This is the end of the slow period. The season will soon be in full swing, and this is the time to finish getting the store, the stock, ready. It's a good time to try things out, and even better if it works well for both of us because, if so, I'd want you to stay for the busy season. That said, I understand things can change. What I *don't* need is someone who shows up for a week and then starts being late, or not showing up at all."

"I'm not that person."

"I'm sure of that." She went on to talk about the work, the hourly wage, and the number of hours I could expect at this time. She finished, "If you're interested, I can give you the paperwork to fill out, and you can take it home with you. It will feel more real. If you decide that you'd rather not take this step, then call me this weekend, or on

Monday morning, and no harm done."

I nodded.

"One more thing. I have a special project in mind for when I don't need you to cover the sales floor." She stood. "Come with me. This may not be something that will appeal to you, so you should know in advance. It'll be dusty, boring work. Come and see, and you can add that into your considerations."

We walked from the breakroom back through the sales floor and past the office to the stairs that led up to the second floor. A sign hung from a chain that blocked access to the stairs, stating that the area above was not open to the public.

"This chain and sign are intended to keep folks from wandering upstairs thinking it's part of the sales area. It was never a problem until it was—which is a commentary on life or human nature, I suppose. Since I'm here alone a lot over the winter months, it was best to put up the sign."

The stairway was narrow and poorly lit. I followed her up while holding tightly to the railing. At the top was a small landing with doors opening off it—one on each side. The air up here was thick, hot and stuffy.

"I used to leave the doors wide open for light and air circulation, but they stay locked now for the same reason I put that sign on the stairs below. We only use these rooms for storage." As she turned the key in the door to our left she added, "Many years of untended storage, unfortunately." She opened the door wide.

It was a relief to see the daylight. It brightened the place, though the stuffiness remained. Maia went over to a wide three-paned bow window and, with an effort, she pushed one of the side panes up a few inches. The air improved immediately.

She said, "I keep the windows closed because birds and insects can fly in and get shut up in here for days or months. Bad for them and bad for the building."

As she spoke, I was looking around. I saw attempts at orderliness in the stacks of old and new boxes. There were open areas of the floor and room to walk, so that was a plus.

An antique love seat or settee upholstered in a worn green-purple flowered brocaded fabric was pushed back against the window. Pillows with gold-colored tassels were arranged on it, and a small lap blanket was neatly folded on the seat. I wasn't sure what to call this particular piece of furniture, but given its placement conveniently next to the window with a view of Front Street, and the cozy throw on the seat, and the convenient side table with a small lamp next to it, clearly it was not as forgotten or neglected as everything else in this room seemed.

I may have made a noise, because Maia said, "Alternate workspace and occasional breakroom. Someone's old divan. It's been up here since before I arrived."

Divan. I noted the word, filing it away.

Maia added, "It can be a good spot to get away for a break." She glanced at me with a small grin. "The rest, however? It's badly in need of sorting and inventory."

I took a few steps farther in. "Do the other windows open?"

"Some, but I'm very cautious, as I said. Can't risk forgetting and leaving them open to weather or birds or insects. They'll get in here and create havoc, and the weather can change suddenly and do real damage."

"What about the other rooms?" I pointed toward a double door between this room and the next. They were pocket-style doors that slid back on each side into the wall.

"Yes. There's this room and one beyond the double doors. On the other side of the stairs are two much like these. In the back, connecting this side and that, is an ancient bathroom. Please don't use it. The water is turned off. If we decide to use this space again, we'll have to get the plumbing checked in there. For now, use the facilities downstairs. At any rate, the rooms on that side were kept mostly clear of storage. I drew the line at allowing any more space to be filled before this side is cleaned up."

"So you want the contents of these two rooms listed and…sorted out? Or just listed?"

"We'll start with listing it and marking the containers with an inventory sheet of some kind. I'll make whatever decisions are required regarding what to keep or not, and how best to rearrange the storage space."

I nodded. "I can do this, for sure."

Maia cast me a quick, assessing look. "Then why don't you start on Monday? We can ease you into the sales floor work. Frankly, this is without doubt, the best time of year to work up here. Come dressed for dusty work—should you decide to accept it."

After an assessing look of my own, I nodded, saying, "Let's go for it."

She added, "I park in the space behind the building and come in the back door. You'll do that, too. I'll be here at nine a.m., so any time after is fine. Shall we plan on three or four hours a day? Give it a week and if it's not for you, you can walk away with no worries."

"It's a plan."

"Excellent," Maia said. "I'll bring the supplies you'll need, and you can bring your patience and attention to detail?"

"Definitely."

Chapter Nine

Doubts set in before I'd reached the bridge to Morehead City. They were expected, but still uncomfortable to deal with. The positives and negatives began populating the imaginary tally sheet in my head as soon as I left the gallery and seemed to be arguing back and forth with me caught in between. By the time I'd crossed the second bridge over to Atlantic Beach, the positives were solidly trouncing the negatives. I wished for the confidence to simply grab the positives and run with them.

I needed, wanted, wished for someone to discuss this with. Gregory had been that person for me. He always said that doubts and what-ifs clouded the thought process, and he had a way of trimming away the distractions. It had become a joke between us. I would come up with the what-ifs and Gregory would slay them by putting them all into perspective and balance.

Just thinking about the good days before those days were lost . . . I was missing Gregory again—my Gregory at his best. I'd always remember him that way.

As for Aunt Eva? I smiled as I drove the miles along Bogue Banks to Emerald Isle. Aunt Eva's first rule wouldn't cover this. Her second rule about not bringing chaos into the beach-life bubble might apply better, but it didn't help me solve my lack of confidence or belief in my judgment. I could imagine she would tell me to either vacuum or take a walk on the beach…my choice. Because fretting over something never solved anything. Not one thing.

And she was right about that.

I remembered what she'd said about worrying. That it was best to just live your life and leave the worrying for when things actually went wrong. That doing so would make you better able to roll with the punches when they came.

And she was right about that too, because I had other things to consider and needed my brain cells for *those* issues.

For one, I had forms to fill out this weekend. Secondly, I had to figure out what to wear. Casual clothing, yes, since I'd be working in a dusty attic. But not *too* casual. I didn't want to give the impression that I didn't know *how* to dress for a job. What else? It all swirled through my head, but in a happy way.

When I reached home—*home . . . the word felt so natural and so pleasant*—I went inside, dropped my tote on the chair, said hello to the herons, grabbed a glass of iced tea and went out to enjoy the mild weather, the sunshine. Seeing no one around, I walked to the end of the crossover to stare at the ocean, listen to its music, and feel the fresh salt breeze. It was a slight breeze and the scents it bore lingered sweetly in the air around me. They may have brought memories with them because suddenly I was thinking of Aunt Eva and silently telling her about this relatively audacious thing I'd done today. I thought Gregory might be hearing it too and cheering for me.

A short bark caught my attention.

Jake said, "Don't move."

I frowned and of course I moved as I looked down at him.

He shook his head sadly. "You've broken the spell."

"Spell? What spell?" I scoffed.

"The one I was caught in." He shrugged. "Magical."

The sun glinted on his reddish curls. His eyes were focused on my face.

"You're teasing me."

He shrugged. "Maybe, maybe not. A penny for your thoughts? Though, if that expression is anything to judge by, I'd guess that whatever you were thinking was worth a great deal more than a thin bit of copper."

I groaned, showing my neighborly disdain for his approach. The way he spoke . . . he always sounded like he was making a pass.

Or was that me, and how I was hearing it?

Slightly embarrassed by my attitude, I put on a smile as I said, "It was something a little fun. Not a huge thing. Just . . ." I shrugged.

"Oh? What's that?"

I could've invited him to join me on the crossover. I didn't. Yet this current arrangement had the odd feeling of a balcony with shades of Romeo lingering below. I said, "Remember that visit to the gallery and the possible mention of a job?"

"I do."

"Well, it's official. Sort of a trial run to see if both of us—Maia and I—are happy with how it works out."

"Wow. Nice. You'll be selling art?"

"And souvenirs." I added, "But I'm starting with doing an inventory of the things stored up on the second floor."

"Wow, again. Sounds interesting to me. To you too?"

"For now, yes, it's good. I'm more comfortable doing that than going right onto the sales floor. I have a lot to learn about the business."

He nodded. "Very sensible."

"It will be good to get out. To have a purpose." Actually, I surprised myself by saying that. Suddenly, I *wanted* company. "Would you and Star care to join me for a bowl of water? A glass for yourself, of course." I grinned.

He grimaced. "Sorry. I'd love to but can't. Star and I are heading home from our walk. We took it early today because I have an appointment to keep this afternoon."

"Ah. I understand."

He nodded again, but in a way that struck me as tinged with sadness. I didn't know what to say, and then I was glad I didn't say anything because his expression cleared.

"We'll see you later."

"Later." I lifted my hand in a wave, and they turned and left. I stared, watching them as they went.

Just as well, I thought, because I had an appointment to keep, too.

ঔৣ

Gregory and I had had an accountant who tallied up our taxes each year and gave advice on how to lessen the tax burden, and he'd filed paperwork, including taxes, for us. Gregory had handled our finances otherwise. If things had been managed differently, I might have become aware of irregularities sooner. When our world began crashing, I looked to our CPA and expected him to understand what was amiss, at least from the financial perspective, or explain to me what I must surely be misunderstanding—to no avail.

He said that, looking back, he'd noticed changes in Gregory, but nothing obvious. By the time the next tax season was approaching Gregory had done so much—withdrawals, transfers, and things he called investments but couldn't explain who, what, or why—that I ran to him for answers. The accountant tried to help me sort it out, but his help was minimal, and it cost money, too, and soon I realized I couldn't even afford that.

Even now, it caused my heart to race and my head to spin to think of it. Still too fresh. I'd cleaned the mess up as best I could while also overseeing my husband's care, and the accountant had done what he could with the taxes and such, and I'd appreciated his help, but I had no wish to reengage with him in my new situation.

When I'd spoken with the property management company and explained that I'd never handled this type of property before, the agent had given me the name of an accountant in Morehead City who worked with a lot of their clients.

Honestly, I didn't see how I could afford an accountant, but for some things you just had to find a way. I'd have to afford at least a conversation with her because I needed her expertise.

ᴓ

The meeting went well. I was already thinking of

questions I wished I'd asked. When I had a real list, I'd give her a call, but for now I was digesting what I'd learned, and understanding that the limitations I'd assumed, were in actual fact, true. And that was especially true of discretionary spending. Like redecorating.

Based upon my meeting with the accountant, the gift of having expenses paid for the remainder of this year and the property conveyed to me without encumbrance was a blessing, but next year, when it came time to file, the value of the property would be taxed. I would need to be prepared to pay. But then again, the accountant pointed out that if I fell short in being able to pay the taxes out of what I saved from the monthly rentals, then I could easily borrow against the property to cover it.

There was also the matter of those debts left over from Gregory. A part of me resented that they'd followed me here to my new start, my fresh future, but resentment fixed nothing and so I'd told the accountant about them. She reminded me that once the deed, now in my name, showed up on my credit report, creditors could put liens against the property.

She added, “For this amount of debt . . . it’s just not that much, but the interest and late fees will keep building.” She shook her head. “Pay them off and be done with it.”

“I’m paying what I can, but . . . After I get a good job, I’ll be better able to manage them.”

“Ms. Dance, you are the owner of a valuable property. You can borrow against it and clear those outstanding debts.”

Borrow? That’s the last thing I wanted to do.

I’d heard the phrase—*turning over in one’s grave*—and I could almost feel Aunt Eva doing exactly that.

The accountant said, “I can see in your face how much you want to avoid that.”

I said, rather boldly, “I don’t want to sell it either. My aunt wouldn’t have wanted that.”

She shook her head. “No, I certainly do not advise selling. You’ve been the owner, and living there for not even two weeks? The value of this property is such that you’ll want to avoid incurring the capital gains taxes.” She went on to speak more about that and I listened, but the idea of it—that while I might not be able to financially afford to keep Beach Heart, selling it and paying taxes and real estate agent fees would be costly. Selling would fritter away the monetary value of this amazing gift for little purpose.

I felt rather trapped with no obvious exit.

"Talk to the creditors and set up a payment plan. My best suggestion is to investigate getting a loan against the equity in the property." She named a local bank and recommended them. "But remember, you don't have to do any of it today. You have some time to see how it all shakes out. You might find your budget stretches farther than you thought it could. And in a couple of years, if you want to sell it, it might be more advantageous."

"Thank you. I appreciate your help." And I did appreciate her giving me that last bit of advice about not rushing into big decisions.

After I was alone again the options weighed on me. The remaining debt was small but when you're broke, you're broke. The accountant had made it sound simple. Borrow against the equity to pay off the rest of Gregory's debts. And borrow against the property to pay the taxes in the new year. What if my car needed repairs? Or an appliance failed? Would I just keep borrowing?

She'd talked like it was all logical. Just business. That I could count on revenue to eventually cover what was owed.

I'd never managed the money matters. Gregory had. By the time I was trying to engage with it, it was more a matter of unraveling puzzles and putting out fires. I couldn't risk more of that. I couldn't live through that again.

Childhood memories and being able to return to the place where I'd been happiest, was a blessing, but I couldn't pay the bills with that. It was hard to trust in the present or the future. There didn't seem any safe choices . . . no clear decisions . . . except one. Whether it was because I didn't want to let my aunt down again, or I didn't want to give Beach Heart up, or even if it just came down to taxes and losses—selling Beach Heart was not an option.

ᘓᘐ

When I returned home, I was discouraged. I stood in the living room and looked around seeing the beach art décor. During the week and a half that I'd been here, the furnishings had bothered me, especially the grinning dolphin. Not much. Just an irritation. Like that speck of grit that gets into your shoe and finally, you reach a point when it doesn't matter where you are or what you're doing, you simply must stop, take off that shoe and shake it out.

I wasn't at the shaking-out point, but the need was growing. I suspected that my dissatisfaction came from visiting the gallery with the artwork—hence I now owned the herons—but it was also the realization that I was likely staying for a while.

But there was more to Beach Heart than the décor. There were the wide windows fronting on the ocean view. The porch and rockers. The crossover with its benches, and the railing at the end where there was nothing but that bit of wood and a stretch of sand below between me and the infinite horizon.

Standing in the living room, I closed my eyes and listened. The ocean moved with a distant low, shifting roar. I went out and stood briefly on the porch and then walked along the crossover and down the stairs until I was barefoot in the sand and feeling the warm, dry sand shifting beneath my feet as I walked toward the water. I stopped short of the wet sand and sat, my gaze focused beyond myself on the horizon. Then I pivoted, still sitting cross-legged, and stared back toward the houses. They lined the strand—colorful and large and welcoming. And one was mine.

I had this chance. This gift.

Maybe the loan, then. And I could take on second and third jobs . . . I gathered handfuls of sand and let it sift between my spread fingers. The sand felt clean and light. I was reminded of fine grains funneling through an hourglass. It spoke of time.

Time could be cruel. Time could be a blessing. It depended upon what one was doing while those seconds of life passed.

And I had time to consider what was best to do.

Did it make sense for me to go elsewhere? I'd have to pay rent, and eventually a mortgage if I was able to find employment that would support more than a basic apartment.

The most comforting thought I'd taken from the meeting with the accountant was that if I found a job, lived economically, and saved as much as possible toward that eventual tax bill—and had regular renters in the other unit—I didn't need to go anywhere else for the time being unless I wanted to. At least until the taxes caught up with me.

And while I might be finding the décor somewhat tedious, I could live with it.

That evening, I carried the repaired collage up to my bedroom. An orange plaster seahorse was hanging between the dresser and the door. I took it down from the wall and settled the repaired picture on the hook. It didn't take up much real-world space, but in effect, it spanned how many years between past and present? A bunch. I stepped back to admire my work and was pleased.

☙❧

It started raining on Saturday afternoon and continued through Sunday. The rain arrived with a cold front and temps dropped. Beach walks held no temptation—not for me or anyone else. I might have been alone on earth, especially after the renters packed up and left midmorning. I put some soup on to simmer and went to the storage bedroom. I went through a couple more of Aunt

Eva's boxes, but each item held memories or a question—why'd she pass this or that *whatever-it-was* on to me? Both the memories and questions made me feel alone and lonely.

I wrapped up in a blanket but stayed on the porch and sipped a cup of hot tea. Even in this stormy mood, the ocean was beautiful. Exquisite in its moods, even the ominous ones like today. But it was also cold. There was no warmth in its touch.

The wind in the eaves whistled and sang as the storm moved in and whipped around the house. I listened to it like an old friend. When I was a child, it had sounded like whispers, like conversations overheard but too distant to discern the words. Tonight, I heard those wind voices again, and I remembered when Aunt Eva had tucked me in to sleep and I'd asked her what the wind was saying. She hadn't known, nor had I, but tonight, I was pretty sure it was wishing me well on the new job and new adventures.

ଓଃ

Monday morning arrived and I awoke thinking

that almost two weeks had passed since I'd met with Mr. Smithson, had accepted the keys and moved into Beach Heart. It had been a tentative move-in at first. Now? It no longer felt tentative, but not quite permanent either. For the time being, it was okay. That in-between status felt comfortable and appropriate. I was moving forward, and, to that end, I about to begin my first paying job in years.

I wore jeans and a button-down cotton shirt, but also brought a change of clothing—a pair of dress slacks and a nicer blouse—which I left hanging in the car. Shortly before nine a.m., I sat in my car in the small parking area in the alley waiting for Maia.

She arrived soon after, seeming almost surprised, but distracted. She greeted me briefly when I met her at the back door where she disabled the alarm and we walked in together.

I set the folder containing the completed forms on the breakroom table. "I'll wait here until you're ready to review the forms and talk?"

She nodded. "Grab a coffee or whatever and I'll be back shortly." But no sooner than she returned, a customer entered. Maia said, "Take the clipboard upstairs and take a look around. Get a feel for the upstairs and start a list." She passed me a small key ring. "These will open all the doors up there. I'll give you a yell to come down when we can talk."

As instructed, I went up the stairs, unlocked the door on the left and went inside. The wide doors between the front room and the back, had been left open. So, first, I simply stood there, wondering where to start.

One box at a time, right? Okay.

Checking one box and shifting another out of the way, looking through, behind and so on, I tried to figure out whether any logic had entered into how these items were stored and soon knew the answer was no. It was mostly chronological. Wherever there was space when things were brought up here, that's where they'd been deposited. Some shifting of boxes and bags had occurred over that time, too, so in the end, it truly was a random assemblage of many years.

As I generally became familiar with the items stored and/or abandoned up here, I began working out a process and started a list.

Midmorning, I stepped downstairs to check on

Maia, wondering if she'd forgotten me, but no, she was assisting a couple who were interested in a painting. I didn't interrupt but went quietly back up the stairs.

Customers kept coming in. A busy Monday was good for the gallery, but it was impossible for us to sit down and have that official chat in the breakroom. I worked upstairs, sorting through the stored items, until Maia dashed partway up the stairs to tell me I should call it a day when I was ready. That we'd have our talk tomorrow.

Noon already. Hard to believe.

I left that day, satisfied. Working on the inventory list gave me a sense of having accomplished something tangible and useful, important or not.

Oddly, though, I wondered if I should stay to help. I almost offered, but really, without knowing my way around the sales floor processes, I'd be more of a hindrance than a help.

The day was warm and sunny. At home, I changed to capris and a short-sleeved top and pulled my hair back. Taking a sandwich and a glass of tea out to the porch, I noticed that Dylan was back. He was building down by the water, as usual, so I took my lunch to the end of the crossover, set my drink on the railing and leaned there to watch him while eating my sandwich.

Dylan wasn't alone. A teenage girl was with him today. Their backs were to me, and I watched their interplay—his awareness of her and small interactions with her, and how she acted alongside him, but separately. She hummed a tune, just seconds here and there, and when she did, he stopped. Listening, I was sure. I heard no words exchanged but they were companionable. Star joined them, both children making over the dog while attempting to protect the sandcastle from a canine disaster.

It was an undeniably pleasant, peaceful interlude, and Star's presence meant Jake must be nearby. I scanned the beach strand and saw him walking my way.

"Hello. Join me?"

He was up the steps in no time.

"How'd it go?" he asked, as we walked the short distance up the crossover to the benches and sat.

"Good. I enjoyed it. I was doing inventory and I'm not sure I'd want to do that kind of work long term. But for now? For today? It was perfect."

He smiled. "Glad to hear it."

"I spoke to an accountant, too." I hadn't meant to say that. I shook my head. "Not today. A few days ago."

"Oh?"

I shrugged. "I was worried about making ends meet with taxes and other expenses and such." I waved my hand at Beach Heart, as tall and imposing as ever behind us.

"Always good to be informed."

"It's vital to be informed. Not simply to trust . . . never mind."

"You aren't sure you can trust the accountant?"

"No, not what I meant. It was so crazy with my husband. He . . . not meaning to, I'm sure . . . but he did a lot of financial damage that was awful to clean up. Expensive, too. I assumed he and the accountant we'd dealt with for years knew what they were doing. Truth is, my husband handled most of it, and I didn't know how badly he'd mismanaged things until it was almost impossible to sort it out. Plus, by then, he, himself, needed very costly care." I pointed at the house again. "So, this amazing gift . . . I want to be sure I do everything I can to avoid losing it." I was sorry I'd started this line of talk and dearly wanted to change the subject.

"Emma, I think you should have lunch or dinner with me sometime."

"Jake," I said with a cautioning look.

"Remember, we already agreed. We are neighbor-friendly, and neighbors do share meals on occasion, as do friends."

I nodded. "They do. That's true."

"You need to get out and have fun. Have you gone anywhere other than the house, to work, and the grocery store?"

"True enough, though I've hardly started the job. Haven't been here all that long anyway."

"Just short of two weeks," he said. "And you already have a job."

I grimaced, slightly embarrassed. "If I like it and if I can keep it. Tomorrow is only my second day."

Jake returned my grimace with a grin. "I go up to Beaufort about once a week. If I were to turn up there one afternoon as you were getting off work and invite you to lunch, would you feel stalked?"

"Stalked? Maybe."

"But not terribly annoyed?"

"Maybe not terribly." I couldn't decide whether I *should* be annoyed. "Jake . . . I appreciate you as a neighbor."

"It's a deal, then. I'll apologize in advance that I don't always know when I'll be coming up that way, and I know you don't want me to make a special trip. It's not like it's a date or anything, right?" He tried to look serious, but the grin kept trying to break out. "So there won't be much notice. If it isn't convenient when I *do* show up, we'll try again another time."

"A bit over the top, but fair enough." Thinking of our neighbor-friendly conversation, I offered him *my* hand this time, saying, "It's a deal."

He looked surprised, but accepted my hand and held it for a moment before gently releasing it. "It's a deal, Emma."

Chapter Ten

As I was leaving the house on Tuesday morning for my second day of work, the reality of it gave me both a thrill and a shudder.

Was it the work or the commitment that worried me? Not the work. With time, I could learn that. Was it the commitment…the fear of falling short of expectations…of failing again?

As before, I was a few minutes early. When Maia arrived soon after, she smiled when she saw me. “You came back.”

I responded, “Yes.”

“Come have a cup of coffee or cocoa. Your preference.”

I followed her in, feeling awkward. I noticed she was pale. Maybe she was a little off kilter this morning?

She dropped her purse off in the office and came back to the breakroom where I was waiting.

“I was supposed to come today, right? You seemed surprised.”

“Oh, yes. My goodness, yes I’m glad to see you. I was afraid the dust and tedium of inventory might've run you off."

My tension eased. "I didn't mind at all. Some of the items up there are interesting, and it's a simple job. A good way for me to start."

We each took our mugs of hot caffeine, and she gave me a longer look as we sipped. I was relieved to see her color was returning to normal.

She asked, "You slept well? You look it. I think the beach agrees with you."

"That much difference between yesterday and today?"

"Between that first day you walked in here and today. Given how exhausted you looked the day we met, I wondered if you'd be able to hold up to the physical labor and, admit it, the tedium of inventory." She tapped the side of her mug with her index finger. "I guess that's why I was a bit surprised you didn't call out this morning and instead showed up, actually beating me here again." She nodded. "I was pleased to see you." She set the mug down. "Mind unlocking the front door and flipping the sign? I'll check the phone messages."

"Happy to." I gave my mug a quick rinse, set it in the sink, and then went to the sales floor.

The main salesroom was lit only by the morning light filtering in through the large front window and the plate glass door. The room and its contents had a suspended air, still and undisturbed, as if not yet awakened by the new day. Through the window, the buildings on the far side of Front Street looked almost as still and quiet as the gallery. I moved closer. The park, the bricked surface I'd walked on, the trees and benches, and beyond it the boardwalk and the dappled waters of the sound. I was part of this brand-new morning. Brand-new day. A fresh start. And the bell hadn't even rung yet. But it would. I flipped the sign and unlocked the door, and then I reached up and with a slight hop, I was able to touch the bell and ring it. Two bell notes followed by a slight echo. I might have even laughed as I did it. When I turned back toward the room, I saw Maia standing in the office doorway watching me.

Thrown off, and feeling rather silly, I shrugged and said, "Bell works."

Maia raised an eyebrow in question, but only said, "Good to know."

ଔଡ

Upstairs, as I was working through the items for inventory, I found a photo album near the divan. It seemed to be a history of Front Street Gallery and I took a break from shifting boxes and classifying the various 'inventory' I'd found. I sat on Maia's divan and thumbed through the pages of the album. Men in tall hats with canes. Women in heavy dresses and broad-brimmed, netted hats. This was a history of the building, of the people who'd lived in it, and its changing face over time as it became the gallery it was today.

The breeze came through the open window behind me with scents of water and streets and restaurants and so on. I enjoyed the photos that showed Front Street over the past century and a half. Much was the same. Much was not. The photos of flooding from past hurricanes were sobering. It drove home to me that beauty didn't come without potential cost. How would I handle a hurricane coming ashore with Beach Heart in its path?

I closed the book. Time to get back to work. Likely Maia could hear the floorboards squeaking over her head when I was moving around, and she might worry if she stopped hearing those noises.

Most of the boxes seemed to have been stored here in good faith—as if someone had truly intended to return to deal with them in the near future. Others had been carried up and left in what was clearly an intent to simply get them out of the way—a dumping ground of sorts.

There were file cabinets in the adjoining room, but access to the drawers was blocked by boxes stacked in front of them. Most of those boxes were also full of documents and assorted paperwork. It seemed to me that the original intent had been to store the shop records here, but over time the system had broken down. When I found something unexpected, or that seemed out of the ordinary, I set it aside in the back corner by the locked door that Maia had indicated was a bathroom.

A broken toy. An old frame. A few dusty books. Maia could check them out later. None of the items seemed to have monetary value though some were obviously antiques, or maybe just old. In a box of torn and faded Christmas decorations, white feathers caught my eye, fragile looking and delicate, peeking up from a jumble of old red garland. Carefully, I moved the garland aside and pulled out the treetop angel.

I held her, amazed. Those fine delicate feathers weren't feathers, but rather carved and painted with such finesse that I had to touch them and run my fingers along the seams and edges to convince myself that she was, indeed, made of some very light wood. Balsa, maybe? The angel's hair was dark but with shots of gold and red and a delicate halo—like a crown—graced her bowed head.

How could I leave her in the back corner on the floor with the broken and dusty objects? She was only a piece of carved, painted wood and rather nicked and worn—but she seemed precious. Not deserving of being forgotten. Lost.

I carried her to Maia's divan and settled her in the soft, secure area where the pillow met the sofa back.

Shortly before noon, I heard light footsteps ascending the stairs. I greeted Maia at the landing.

She said, "You've been working up here for almost three hours straight. I didn't want to interrupt, so I stayed away, but I'm curious. How's it going?"

I gestured toward the door to the front room.

"Take a look."

She did. She walked through the front room and into the back room, taking a cursory look around before returning to me. "I like the progress. Is there anything else you need? Labels? Other pens? What can I do to make this easier for you?"

"So far, so good. I'm numbering and labeling the boxes as I go and noting the contents on the inventory list. I've sorted the boxes into groups to some extent. After I've gone through a few more boxes we should talk about how best to proceed with the different groups. If we can review this tomorrow or the next day to ensure I'm on the right track, I think that will be good."

"So you'll come back again?"

"Yes? You want me to, right?"

"Definitely."

I smiled, "Then yes, I'll be back tomorrow."

Maia said, "Oh, who's that?"

She was looking past me, and I turned to see. It was the angel on the divan.

I smiled as Maia walked over and picked her up.

"She was in a box with old Christmas decorations most of which are probably too torn and dirty to be of use, but she seemed . . . special. Rather than put her back into the box or in the corner with the other items that I didn't know what to do with, I set her over there."

"She's lovely." Maia checked the base and around the wings and skirt. "No markings to identify the maker or owner."

"Assorted odds and ends are in the corner of the back room for you to look at in case you want to hang onto them. I don't know that you will. Some broken toys and odd bits. Didn't want them to get lost amid all the boxes and stacks."

"Thanks. I'll check them out later. For now, could you stay a little longer? Maybe thirty minutes? I was tied up with a customer downstairs and I'd love to go the restaurant across the street and grab some sweet tea and a sandwich. If it's a problem, feel free to say so."

Suddenly, painfully aware of the sweat stains on my shirt, not to mention the dust I'd picked up going through years of undisturbed storage, I touched my hair and tugged at my shirt.

"Maia, I can stay, no problem, but if you're asking me to mind the sales floor, I don't think I'm fit for that. I'm a mess."

"You'll be fine. Walk around with the duster and anyone who comes in will get the picture."

"I have a clean blouse and a pair of slacks hanging in my car. If you can give me a minute, I'll do a quick change. Can't do much about the rest of me, but it's better than the way I am at this moment."

"You brought a change of clothing? You are a prepared kind of gal, I see. I like that. And yes, please change if you'll feel better about it."

I set the inventory list atop the nearest box. "I'll be super-quick."

I might've heard her speaking as I hurried down the stairs to the main floor, then dashed through the sales area to the breakroom, but I didn't listen because I was in motion. I kept going, focused on fetching the clothing from my car, and as the exterior door shut behind me, I realized I didn't have my car keys. They were inside with my tote bag. Nor did I have the code to get back inside the building.

Would Maia realize? Would I have to walk down the short alley and back around to the front of the building? I felt so stupid. So eager to please, I'd made myself look foolish. Unprofessional.

The door opened. Maia said, “You’ll need the code.”

“Yes,” I said. “And my keys.”

She stood aside and I went in. I’d left my tote bag in the cleaning closet in the breakroom.

Maia smiled. “You’re welcome to keep your bag in the office. Just set it in the corner where I won’t trip.” She paused, then added, “I’d like some company for lunch, if you can stay for a little while after I get back.”

“Sure.”

“Then think about what you’d like me to fetch for you while you change. I usually have the salad, but their burgers and chicken fingers are good, too. Today, I have a yen for a chicken salad sandwich.”

“I’ll be right back.” My face was flushed. I tried to reclaim my cool along with grabbing my fresh clothing. She was waiting, holding the door open for me. I brushed past her and headed to the restroom to change.

In the mirror, it was clear that I’d been doing dusty work—it showed in my face. But I was struck that there was also color in my cheeks and my eyes were brighter than they’d been in ages. Maybe even a warmer brown. Funny. The activity? Maybe that was part of it, but I'd been busy with Gregory and then moving out of the house, too. No, this was a different kind of busy. And it felt good.

I folded my dirty shirt and jeans and rejoined Maia in the breakroom.

She handed me a slip of paper with the door code and a phone number.

"You won't have a problem, but if you do, just give me a quick call. I'll only be two minutes away, if I run." She flashed me a smile. "I don't run often, but I can. Shall I get you a sweet tea? What else?"

"Sweet tea is good. A small salad maybe?"

"If there's anything you actually hate salad-wise, tell me now."

"No anchovies, please?"

She laughed. "Got it. I'll be right back."

"Let me grab my wallet."

"Nope. This one is on me." As she grabbed her purse from the office and set off across the sales floor, she said, "I usually bring my lunch, but today we'll have a treat."

The cowbell clanged, and she was off and moving in the bright sunshine. From the window,

I watched someone wave from the other side of the street. Maia waved back. A car slowed as it passed her and I saw a hand shoot out through an open window, also waving.

Early in our marriage, Gregory and I had traveled so much that it was hard to feel a sense of community. When things went wrong, I didn't have friends I could trust to share my worries and fears with. By the time, I was in survival mode—trying to care for Gregory and hang on to what was left of the life we'd lived together—I was isolated. Hardly knew my neighbors at all and I'd lost touch with college friends. There was mom. I'd wanted to tell her, but I hadn't. She and I had totally different styles when it came to managing troubles. Words were her thing. For me, endlessly talking about problems never seemed to solve them, but only added torture to the mix.

Watching Maia being recognized and greeted even as she quick-walked down the sidewalk. It didn't make me jealous, but for a moment I felt . . . illumined. I heard the echo of long-ago words in my head—what Aunt Eva had said about appreciating ordinary things. She'd been telling me to appreciate the joy to be found in ordinary tasks and ways, not just things.

My aunt's words were in my head—but this time with a new understanding that came from my recent hard times. She wasn't speaking about *having* things, but rather of the blessing of a place to call home, the joy of having the health and funds to take care of it, and the stability of circumstances that allowed you to enjoy your life without constantly having to anticipate the next blow. It was that practical and emotional stability that allowed a person to trust and to enjoy today.

I'd taken that for granted until I no longer had it. And I wasn't back to that stability yet, but I was feeling the potential for good in my life again. Plus, I was still holding the card Maia had given me with the key code and her phone number written on it.

I laid the card on the counter, slightly out of the way but handy in case I needed it, and I put my keys in my tote bag. I set my tote in the office this time instead of in the cleaning closet.

Every time something moved out on the street, I suffered a small shock of alarm. Was someone coming? That person on the street . . . were they about to climb the steps up to the front door?

No and no. No one entered at all. It was uneventful. By the time Maia returned, I'd given up *alarm* as an automatic response. It was pointless anyway. I'd dealt with so many unhappy things in the last few years and fright or worry had never prevented any of them. I would greet whoever walked through that door and take it step by step. But when it opened again, it was Maia, juggling tall cups of iced tea and bags that must surely contain food.

We settled at the breakroom table, as we'd done before.

As we dug into the food, Maia asked, "So what do you think?"

"About doing inventory? It's interesting."

"And what about being left here all by yourself? I wouldn't be surprised if it freaked you out a little. It did me, way back when. I never let it show, but I felt it and over time, it faded. Funny, though, that after all these years, I sometimes experience that feeling again when a customer walks in. That sort of *What if*? And the *what-if's* are limitless, let me tell you, but time and experience helps. Now I just cover it with a smile and greet the customer. I've never yet run into a problem here that I couldn't resolve." She shrugged. "Or apologize for when I couldn't."

I smiled, if a little sheepishly. "I had a moment of panic, but knowing you were close by, I was sure I could stall anyone long enough for you to get back here to rescue me. But . . ."

"But what?"

"Maybe it would be good if you showed me around the counter and register and all that? In case a situation arises when you aren't nearby. I'm sure you have a list of emergency contacts and other things that would never occur to me to ask about."

"Good thinking."

And we did. After we ate, we took a quick run through the forms I'd filled out, and then Maia explained her processes and how to manage the payment devices, and we laughed a lot. We also went from wall displays to table displays and Maia talked about her suppliers—the artists, including the creators of the souvenir items—and talked about them as if they were friends—a community. What she showed me was pretty simple and altogether felt more like planning a vacation than learning a new job. When a customer did come in, she indicated I should stand at the counter and observe the interaction.

I did and I felt content. I watched her easy, conversational exchange with the woman who was admiring a trio of dunes paintings, and it struck me that I'd been lonelier for simple companionship than I'd dreamed.

Beach Heart had been an unexpected gift, and it had already changed my life for the better, but somehow, the gift had been twofold. I was being offered friendship. Both here and back at Beach Heart itself. Jake and Maia were each bringing human warmth into my life. And there was Starfish, too. I'd never been around animals much, but I could see the value there. All I had to do was allow it in and take a chance on it being real.

If I could combine the ocean vista with the companionship, the sense of community that I saw in Beaufort at the gallery and along Front Street . . .

Now that would be truly lovely.

Chapter Eleven

Instead of working only three hours on Wednesday, I stayed at the gallery until mid-afternoon, and enjoyed myself. It was only my third day working at the gallery, and I knew if I took this job long term there would be times when it didn't feel so new and fun, but today was good. For now, that was enough.

When I left work, I walked across Front Street to the shady park area with the benches and then continued to the boardwalk where I stood at the railing gazing out at the water and enjoyed the breeze. Over lunch, Maia mentioned she kept a small apartment in town. She'd lived there before her marriage. She and her husband had a place outside of Beaufort, but it was a bit of a drive. She often stayed in town at her apartment because it was handy and when he wasn't traveling, he stayed there with her.

How long could they do that? I didn't ask her, but I'd seen that question in her face when she was telling me.

The scenery was beautiful here, no question.

Would this work for me? It could, I supposed, but I missed the ocean. The sound. The drama. The almost otherworldliness of it—of nature that sang siren songs and drew us into the beauty while the impartial, inevitable nature of nature itself promised nothing beyond a beautiful moment—moments that said enjoy now because, insofar as nature was concerned, there were no guarantees.

I went to my car and drove home with my window partway down soaking in the scents as I traveled the miles toward Beach Heart. When I got home, I went straight out through the French doors. This day was very different from my first return to Beach Heart. No gale was blowing. There was no need to cling to the doorframe to stay upright, nor was I getting pounded by an unexpected rain squall and going all frantic over a child who was doing fine.

Not everything was terrible. Not every ending was a curse.

And I felt so much stronger. No lankness. My hair, my complexion, mirrored my feeling of wellbeing. And when I smiled, I was feeling it inside again.

I felt . . . if not quite whole, that I was getting

closer every day.

As I strolled along the crossover, I noted shells lined up on the railing near the water hose. Trails of sand ended at the hose, though a pair of sneakers and some sandals had been left behind at the base of the steps.

I stood at the end of the crossover on what I now thought of as my crossover balcony and picked out my current renters from among the people on the beach. They seemed happy. One of them, a small boy, was working hard with Dylan and both seemed content. I felt much like a queen surveying my lands and loyal subjects. Actually, all things considered, me standing on this balcony at the end of the crossover, might more appropriately classify me as a figurehead like those carved wooden figures that perch on the prow of sailing ships—and yet, I'd never felt less wooden. Still vulnerable, still worried, but alive. Still apart, but also feeling a sense of community.

And hopeful. Yes, I felt hopeful.

There was a difference between the serene, scenic boardwalk view in Beaufort and here—this place of ocean and sky. The Beaufort boardwalk view was beautiful but standing here before the ocean, my skin tingled, and the rhythm of the waves echoed in my heart.

I belonged here.

And I was hungry. I went into the house to have an early supper.

ശ്ശ

After I'd cleaned up the kitchen, I noticed Aunt Eva's cigar box on the table and thought of the photo book I'd found upstairs in the gallery while doing inventory and then the general good will I felt around me there, which edged open the emotional door—the one that had closed more and more firmly over the last few years. Perhaps those photos recalled to my mind the cigar box because after supper, I settled on the turquoise seashell-print sofa with the TV playing nothing in particular in the background, but with Aunt Eva's cigar box on my lap. I opened the lid.

A few of the photos were black and white. One of those showed a much younger Aunt Eva in short shorts and a halter top with the ocean behind her, so I knew it was taken at the beach, probably here at Beach Heart. On the back, in her own hand, was written Eva and Warren Douglas. The man with one arm around her and holding a fishing net in his other hand must be my deceased uncle. There were also several faded Instamatic photos. I recognized myself as a young child in a couple of them. I was out on the beach and usually in constant motion, so I tended to be a blur in photos from my childhood. In one, though, I was kneeling in the sand and building a castle in the same area that Dylan preferred.

A wider group photo showed Eva and a tall man with a bunch of kids in a grab bag assortment of summer shorts and T-shirts lined up in front. I picked myself out from among them.

I studied my great-aunt Eva's face, at least the teeny tiny image that showed in the photograph. Her body. Her posture. I remembered her as very old. Or was that the perception of a very young me? This woman didn't look old. Late forties or early fifties, maybe. It was hard to tell given the fading of the photograph.

Dropping the photo into the box, I put my head back and closed my eyes.

Theses photographs recalled the past—my past. They had nothing to do with Macon, or even with Dylan, but somehow they pulled it all together in my head and brought back to me most keenly the time when Macon had been the child—about Dylan's age—and I'd been the adult, yet so very young myself when his father had introduced us. Macon had seen me as grown up—an adult like his dad. I recalled his quiet, almost sullen standoffishness on the day we met, which passed soon enough as we built a relationship.

I'd been proud of that. Not quite his mother, but someone he came to trust and love like an older sister—as I'd told Aunt Eva I was hoping for.

But time passed, he grew up, and when things went wrong, I was handy to blame. Gregory broke my heart, but it was that wound from Macon that persisted in causing me pain. Because Gregory, as it turned out, couldn't help what he'd done. But Macon knew better. And he was still alive and could still be reached.

But not by me. Not yet. Maybe someday I'd try.

I put the cigar box aside, stretched out on the sofa, and reached up to pull the blanket down and over me. I'd channel surf until I found something mindless that would bore me into not caring.

But the cigar box was still in my view. And that silly time-travel sense washed over me again. Of memories. Of hugs. Of scents and sounds, including laughter, as Aunt Eva laughed at some foolish joke I told, or laughed in delight when I'd performed the perfect pirouette in the middle of this very living room floor.

Of Macon when he won first place in the science fair. Of Macon when he was sad about his friends or a girl, and talking to me made him feel better.

My eyes stung. Abruptly, I sat up. That stupid dolphin was grinning at me from the wall. I stood, went straight to it, fidgeted it off the hooks, and carried it to the back bedroom. I left it there and shut the door.

The herons seemed almost to smile at the dolphin's departure. Which possibly showed I had totally lost my sanity.

The moon was bright. The air was mild. I hesitated because I'd already changed into my nightgown. I laughed. It didn't matter. It would look like a simple white dress in the dark. If anyone saw. If anyone cared.

I grabbed the sofa blanket again, and a pillow,

too, as I passed by on my way to the door.

ଔଷ

I hugged the blanket close about me. With the slight breeze, the night was chillier than I'd expected. Up next to the house, it was warmer, but I wanted to stroll out to my balcony—the one at the end of the crossover that stretched toward the ocean and ended somewhere beyond the horizon yet stayed above the crowd, above the reach of most dangers. I hugged the blanket around my arms and shoulders and lifted my face to the night sky, my eyes closing as I let it in. *It*. What was *it*? Whatever, so long as it was good and uplifting. I craved all the *feels of it*. To remember and recapture it.

But when I opened my eyes and beheld the stars, the moon, the shades and textures of the night sky, I felt it—*joy*—all the stronger. Yes, *it* was joy and the beauty of it almost took my breath, but the aloneness of it, despite its glory, added a sharp edge that frightened me.

You could not lose what you did not have. But having it didn't mean you could keep it.

My hand to my throat, I sighed. Even fright was welcome, so long as there was plenty of room left for hope too. For a future.

"Emma? Is everything okay?"

Yes, it was Jake. Starfish was at his side. Both were staring up at me.

Startled, I asked, "How did you know I was out here?"

By the moonlight, I could see the ghost of his smile, a hesitation, and then he said, "I'm tempted to tell you that the stars called to me, and that the moon invited me to walk this way. But I have to admit that Star and I take this walk almost every morning, as you know, and again every evening. Star expects it. We're a little behind schedule tonight." He shrugged. "But that other stuff? Stars calling me and such? It sounds much better, don't you think?"

I smiled despite myself. His words were mocking, and I should probably be annoyed. But his tone offered something else. I chose to go with the tone.

"Indeed," I said. "Almost poetic."

"What brings you out into the night, Emma?"

I shook my head, shrugging at the same time.

"Actually, I think the night, the moon, or maybe the stars *did* call to *me*."

There was a moment of silence between us before he answered, "We only walk a little farther than this. Star expects it—which means more than you might understand. She appreciates routine and isn't really open to negotiation, so here we are. Won't you join us?"

I brushed at the blanket I was using like a shawl over my nightgown. A simple cotton affair, but it covered more than most warm-weather attire. Even, it was a nightgown.

"Not dressed for it?" he asked. "Who's to see? I promise not to tell. Maybe, in fact, the night was calling you out for a moonlit walk on a peaceful beach with a neighbor-friend and a dog who adores you."

Funny thing about the word *and* being a conjunction. Its placement in this sentence, and me not knowing where the comma fell, if a comma was even required here, made me uneasy. Instead of a comma, perhaps it needed only a pause about the length of a heartbeat to tell the intent of the speaker. But the key was the verb, *to adore*. I was almost certain I'd heard Jake say *adores,* the singular form. That would refer back to only one noun, Star. So it was still all good, and I could breathe again. Neighbor-friends—that was us.

"Not far," I said.

"Not far," he echoed.

As I held my blanket shawl in place with one hand, I navigated the steps with the other hand on the railing. When I reached the sand, I lifted the hem of my nightgown to keep it safe from the sand and the water. When I reached Jack and Star, she apparently took that as an invitation to sniff my feet. I reached down and scratched the top of her head, speaking softly to her. Satisfied, she was on the move again, resuming her walk. Jake and I moved quickly to catch up.

"Shouldn't you have her on a leash?"

"Probably. But really, she never takes off without permission, except when she sees you."

"That's odd, isn't it?"

He shrugged. "Not odd. But it *is* interesting. I've asked Star what's so special about you—you know, special from her particular viewpoint—but so far she hasn't shared."

I shook my head. "You can be rather silly. I expect you've heard that before."

"Sigh," he said, and then he did exactly that, sigh, before saying, "I'm serious often enough. Sometimes the other side of me breaks free." He paused. "So how is the job going?"

"Actually . . ." I drew the syllables out long. "Surprisingly well. Early days, right? Might not stay quite so shiny in my mind, but for now, I'll stick with it."

"Your boss seems happy too?"

"Yes. Again, early days. Plenty of time yet for me to mess up."

"Or to be brilliant."

I laughed, but quietly. "That too."

The sand felt smooth beneath my feet and the moon gave enough light that I could walk barefoot without too much worry over broken shells. Funny how the thin film of water left on the sand after the wave rushed out seemed warm. Like it was insulated. Science could probably explain that, but I didn't need the explanation. My brain had already played with sentence structure and conjunctions and comma placement tonight. At the moment, I had the smooth, silky sand beneath the soles of my feet, the moon and stars above, and companionship—pleasant companionship. That was enough.

"I worked five days this week. Morning hours. And she asked me to stay a little later today, so she must be satisfied with how it's going thus far."

"I never doubted she would be."

"Hah."

"I just didn't know how it would be for you. If you'd want to continue with it."

"Reasonable concern. For several years, my life has been a long road with a lot of changes when I least expected them. When I came here, all I wished for was the opportunity to hide and rest and figure out who I am now, after…everything." I waved my free arm. "I got this. A job and—" I broke off before saying *friends*. That felt too intimate out here under the moonlight.

"Time to rest . . . that's what you found here, right? Mostly, anyway."

We'd stopped and were standing at the edge of the water, my toes at the lacy tips of the waves just before they outreached themselves and then ran back to the ocean. Star was nosing at a shell half-buried by the outgoing tide.

Jake said, "You went through a lot with losing your husband."

I bit my lip, then pressed them together, not wanting to speak about it.

He repeated, "For the most part, with coming here, you got what you wanted, right?" He paused, but I still didn't reply—silent now because I couldn't believe what he'd just said.

It had never occurred to me to want Beach Heart. I hadn't even known it was possible.

Had I gotten what I'd wanted? A deceased husband? A lost stepson?

Had Jake lost his mind? I felt like I was losing mine.

He added, "I think this is what you needed."

Did he expect a response? He'd thrown a lot of words at me and some of them sounded critical. Others sounded . . . I didn't know . . . almost as if he was seeking reassurance for himself about *my* life. While I struggled, he added, "As for a place to hide? Well, that could work anywhere. Certainly at the beach, but," he shook his head sadly, "I'm sorry to say that I don't think you are very good at hiding."

I went from confusion to bemusement to laughing out loud. Mom had said the same thing to me about hiding, hadn't she? I said, "Oh, shut up," but good naturedly.

I hadn't seen his tension until it was now easing. He said, "I apologize for presuming I know how you're feeling."

Shaking my head, I said, "Don't. Everyone has something they're dealing with. As for Beach Heart and the beach itself? It's a blessing I could never have anticipated. The good memories. It's healing, you know? As for the gallery, so far, so good. I think the job, or the people there . . . there's healing in that, too. And the best thing is that I don't have to make any hard decisions. No one is battering me with demands or complaints. I can relax and think or not think. As I choose."

"That sounds good."

"It does."

"Ready to head back? I think Star is going without us. She's serious about her routine. I believe I mentioned that."

"Yes, thank you."

"Thanks? For what?" he asked.

"I won't tell you. It will go to your head. You're already outrageous enough. But consider yourself thanked."

As we neared the crossover that would take

me back to Beach Heart, I found my steps slowing. Jake matched his pace to mine, and Starfish paused and turn back to look at us, a question obvious in her pose.

"Emma—"

"Good night, Jake. I enjoyed the walk. Thank you again."

He nodded. "Good night." Then he walked on, caught up with Starfish, and the two of them disappeared from the moonlight as they passed into the darker shadows of night.

My own journey took me back along the crossover and into the house—into Beach Heart and to my bed for what turned out to be the best night of rest I'd had in I didn't know how long. Maybe years and years. Before I fell asleep, I thought of Aunt Eva, of Jake and Starfish, and even of my mother. And I promised myself that I'd reach out to her and be kinder to her. More welcoming. Because she did love me, I knew that. And I loved her. And I was feeling stronger now.

Baby steps, maybe. But getting there . . .

ঞ৪৯

When I woke the next morning, stretching and remembering those pre-sleep thoughts and how it felt like my life was finally coming together, I felt great—until I saw the clock and realized I hadn't set the alarm and that I was going to be quite late to my fourth day on the job.

Tangled in my sheets, I rolled out of bed, literally, and hit the floor clumsily before scrambling to my feet.

In one big whirl of movement, I raced through washing up, brushing my hair, and all the other stuff that I'd normally take my time with, and I stayed so focused that negative thoughts couldn't get a foothold in my brain. I settled into the car knowing that I couldn't try to make up time on the commute. The drive was the drive and getting stopped by an officer would *not* help me to get there sooner. That exercise in patience—sticking to the speed limit on ten miles of nearly empty road—was excruciating. I considered calling Maia again but didn't. Somewhere in the maelstrom of getting myself together this morning, I'd called her—words and apologies and excuses at the ready—but had gotten her voice mail. I'd left a message but she hadn't responded. I could only assume she was busy—which meant my absence was all the more egregious.

You aren't that important. Not to the success of the gallery. And somewhere in that repeating thought was Aunt Eva's voice saying, *"Do your best. That's all you can ever do. Just be yourself."* But by the time I arrived in Beaufort and drove up the small alley to the parking area behind the gallery, my insides were a mess.

And I didn't see Maia's car. Any car.

I pulled in, grabbed my tote bag and punched the code into the door lock. I dropped my tote bag into the seat of one of the plastic chairs, took a deep breath, and stepped out to the sales floor expecting to see Maia despite the lack of her car, but I didn't.

Instead, the only person in sight was a guy. Someone I'd never met.

Chapter Twelve

The young man was slim, dark-haired and wearing a clean dress shirt that needed ironing. He was holding one of the souvenir shell creatures and he looked up at me as I hurried though the breakroom and out to the sales floor.

He was alone.

Did he work here? Was he a customer? I glanced at the front door. The sign was turned to Open and the bolt was flipped back. Had Maia not locked it yesterday when she left? Could he have wandered in?

"Hi," he said, his expression hovering somewhere between surprise and welcome.

I glanced toward the small office. The door was open. No sign of Maia being in there. Now what?

"Is Maia here?"

"Not yet. I'm Brendan."

Something nibbled at the back of my brain. Something Maia had said. I stepped forward.

"I'm Emma Dance."

He smiled. Relieved. "Good. I thought you

must be. Nice to meet you."

"Maia?"

"Not in. Maybe later. I'm home from school for a few days and she called me this morning and asked me to open for her. She said you'd probably show up."

"I'm late. Overslept. I left Maia a voice mail, but she didn't respond." Almost reflexively, I checked my phone. She'd called him but hadn't called me or responded to my message? "My ringer is off. How did my ringer get turned off?"

Brendan laughed. "My psychology professor might call that the realization of a subconscious wish."

I hardly acknowledged his words because I was flipping the ringer switch back on and checking my messages. If I hadn't been so frantic earlier, I would've seen the notifications popping up on my phone. I listened to Maia's voicemail thanking me for the head's up that I'd be late but was on my way. She added, *"Brendan is home for spring break. He'll open the shop and work with you today. I'll be in later, if I can. Call if you have any questions. You should be fine. Brendan is comfortable with the gallery processes."*

Now I gave Brendan a longer look. He looked pleasant. Maia trusted him.

"Is she sick?"

He shrugged. "She didn't say."

"So I guess I'll get back to working on the inventory? Unless there's something else I should do? Do you need my help down here?"

"Sure, and no," he said, but as I turned to go back to the breakroom for my tote, he added, "You know, I was thinking I might rearrange a few things."

Had he asked Maia's permission? "Like what?"

Still holding the shell creature in one hand, he used his free hand to point at a few paintings, and then at a standing sculpture—a large carved driftwood piece of a seabird perched on top of a piling. The base looked like a puddle of netting had fallen around it—also carved.

"I'm thinking these should be grouped together." He pointed at the corner near the display window. "Maybe grouped with the coffee table books in the display window." He waved the shell creature in the air. "Maybe pepper it with a few of these. A broad appeal, you know?" He grinned and added, "I'm also studying marketing."

I tried to see his vision but couldn't quite get there. Grouping expensive items together with the souvenirs? The actual art with the shell creatures and glossy books? Gregory would've scoffed. I simply didn't know.

"Have you discussed it with Maia?"

"No, but I think she'd like it."

"Clearly, she trusts you." I shrugged. "I think I'd discuss it with her first. But if you just want to go ahead, maybe start with what's easy to move? Not the paintings on the wall, but the standing sculptures and adding the shell creatures into the window?" I nodded. "Meanwhile, I'll be upstairs. Give me a yell if you need me."

"Will do."

My gut instinct was that if Maia wanted things changed, she would tell us. On the other hand, I didn't want to shut down interest and creativity in the people who worked at the gallery. It would be interesting to see how flexible Maia was in working with her employees. Gregory wasn't. He had strong ideas about art and traditional approaches.

I got a cup of coffee from the breakroom and

climbed the stairs up to the second floor. I set my cup on the side table next to the divan, and then opened the window a few inches. The breeze was blowing in across the water, and it must've started back over the Atlantic Ocean because it still carried a distinct chill, but the freshness was welcome.

I sat on the divan and gathered my wits. The morning had scattered them badly. And how unexpected it had been to find Brendan here instead of Maia.

I hoped she was okay.

At least I knew where to focus my efforts today. Right here. I sipped my coffee wishing I'd had something quick to grab on my way out of the house to take with me to eat. I'd noticed crackers in a cabinet down in the breakroom. If I couldn't slip out to grab a bite, perhaps I could help myself to a package of peanut butter crackers. I was hungry.

I smiled. It felt good to be hungry. To have an appetite. To be alive.

To walk on the beach in sunlight or by moonlight. Alone or with a friend. And his dog.

Or to be here, doing a job that wasn't

prestigious or glamorous, but filled some need in me that I didn't entirely understand.

Brendan reminded me of Macon, back when Macon was in college. So busy. So full of life and of learning things, both in college and for his personal growth. But seeing that age and the feeling of invulnerability that usually came with it, that of expecting to live forever and to be forever young—all that reminded me of Macon, yes, but also of the self I'd been a few years ago.

Partway through the morning, I took a break to check on Brendan and to visit the restroom and grab a bottle of water from the breakroom fridge. I'd made good progress upstairs, but really wanted to go over it with Maia.

"Have you heard from her, Brendan?"

"A text. She'll be here around lunchtime. She said to wait here and not go out for lunch."

I nodded. "Okay, then. Thanks."

Back upstairs, I tried to get back into the work, but instead, I looked at the keys Maia had given me. Maybe I'd earned the opportunity to check out the rest of the second floor? Maia had asked me not to use the bathroom up here, which kind of indicated that she didn't mind me checking things out. Right?

First, I unlocked the bathroom door. . . and yes, it was a bathroom. Little black-and-white tile squares covered the floor, and subway-style white tile was on the wall up to about chest high. The fixtures were old, but apparently had been cleaned well, the water turned off, and then the room had been left to time. I ran my fingers along the curve of the clawfoot tub and then over the fancy spigot and handles. The tub was lovely. And permanent, no doubt. I couldn't imagine carrying it down those stairs.

There was a window with frosted glass on the back wall. Another locked door was on the other side the room.

I left the bathroom, going back the way I'd entered, locking the door behind me.

Next, I went to the stair landing and opened that door to access the far side. As Mom might say, the alternate universe. But no, there was no mirror image here beyond the physical layout. This room faced Front Street and also had a lovely view. I stood there at the window watching the people coming and going down on the street. A woman was walking a dog along the boardwalk and I caught glimpses of her and the water between tree boughs in the park.

The differences between this side and the other was that, most noticeably, this room was empty, but also the room behind this one wasn't just another room. It had been someone's kitchen. Not fancy and the stove was ancient in modern terms. There was no fridge and probably had never had a dishwasher. The locked door to the left would lead to the bathroom. There was also a closet door in the corner next to the where a fridge would've been, if there'd been one.

The closet door was double-bolted and wouldn't budge. Because I couldn't help myself, I tried the keys, and also did some energetic yanking, but no good. Maybe it wasn't a closet? Someone had worked hard to make sure it wouldn't open. Make me wonder if this wasn't a closet, but rather stairs to a back entrance? Maybe.

I stood between the two empty rooms, looking back toward the front window and then at the kitchen again.

Dust was everywhere. Litter, the kind that seemed to accumulate from nothing given enough time, was scattered in the corners. The wood floors were marked and scarred but nothing terrible.

In the photo album by the divan, there'd been pictures of a family standing on the front porch. Of a woman gazing out of an upstairs window. Probably from the turn of the prior century. People must've lived up here over the shop for a long time after the first floor was turned into a store.

It seemed a waste as it was now. Then again, storage space was valuable, too. This was a small living area compared to modern day expectations, at least outside of big cities, but the street and water views here were amazing.

It made me think again of how it might be to live in town.

To be here. Not *here*, but living in a flat like this.

But I'd miss the ocean.

I would. That was true. If I could help it, I wouldn't give up Beach Heart for any reason, much less for the convenience of living closer to work. Nor for the community feel of being in town.

A person had to be happy within, or they wouldn't be happy anywhere. That might not be one of Aunt Eva's rules, but it should've been. I was making it one of mine.

ଓଃଌ

I'd returned to inventorying the last boxes in the back room. The idea of tackling the filing cabinets was rather daunting, and I would not dig into a century or more of paper records without Maia's specific guidance. The lunch hour was near when I heard Brendan calling up the stairs.

He was probably hungry. I remembered Macon at that age. Always hungry. As for me, those crackers I'd eaten hadn't lasted long, and I was hungry, too.

Maybe Brendan had heard from Maia again. I trotted down the steps and didn't see him, but I heard voices coming from the breakroom and found him and Maia there.

As soon as I saw her, I blurted out, "Sorry I was late. I overslept."

Maia looked startled.

Holding up the carryout box, Brendan said, "She brought pizza for lunch." He placed it on the table and handed me a paper plate and a napkin. "Let's eat before another customer walks in."

Maia said, "If one does, I'll take care of them."

I surprised everyone, including myself, by

saying, "I'll go out and greet them while you finish eating. If it's something more involved, you can rescue me."

Maia smiled, "Like Brendan rescued us this morning?"

Brendan bowed, slice of pizza still in hand.

All this good will was almost too much for me. I turned my back to them and took my time getting a glass of water. I blinked and breathed and then turned back toward them.

"Thank you both—for the rescues and for the pizza."

Maia said, "When the bell rings, we'll all run out together and scare the heck out of whoever walks in." She shrugged. "Or we'll invite them to join our pizza party."

We laughed. And we ate. And we talked.

In some ways, it made me sad for what I'd lost with my stepson. But it also gave me hope. And meanwhile, my life was growing in better ways, and I had no idea that a whole new shake-up was coming.

Later that afternoon when I returned home, I called Mr. Smithson. I'd been here more over two weeks now. Really, closing in on three weeks. Surely, it wasn't too soon to ask again about the man who'd given me Beach Heart.

There was no answer, so I left a voice mail. "I'm enjoying being at Beach Heart. Thank you for your part in making that happen. I would very much like to meet with Mr. Grimes and thank him. You mentioned his ill health, but I am hoping he's doing better now and open to speaking with me. Please let me know. Thanks." I added, "If I don't hear from you, I'll call you again. Soon."

I heard nothing back from him that afternoon, but I didn't know how to judge what it meant, or whether it meant anything at all. In fairness, it was a beautiful time of year, at the end of the work week, and I wasn't his client. His client was the man I was curious about. What was Alan Smithson's incentive to call me when he surely knew exactly what I was after and wasn't open to making that happen?

When I went to bed, I set my alarm. I wouldn't be late for work again—not if I could help it. Tomorrow would be my fifth day on the job. I was getting the hang of this and I liked it.

ଔଓ

Mr. Smithson did not return my call. Despite the message I'd left the day before saying I'd call him again, I decided that if I didn't hear from him by the time I left work today, I would drive directly to his office in Morehead City. Maybe I could catch him before he took off for the weekend.

This morning, only Maia and I were at the gallery. I arrived slightly before her and let myself in, and at opening time, I flipped the sign and unbolted the door. It wasn't likely that an actual paying customer would walk in before she got here. If someone came who was just window shopping? I knew enough about art and beachy stuff to keep them engaged until Maia got here. She hadn't called or texted, so I knew she was on her way.

When Maia arrived, she thanked me for opening the store.

"I haven't touched the register, though," I said. "I was hoping you'd be here before I risked resetting the wrong things and causing a headache."

"Well, then," she said. "We'll go over that this morning—after I've had a cup of coffee and a moment to orient myself."

"I'd like one, too. What do you take in yours?"

"Bless your heart and thank you," she said, and went on to tell me her preferred blend. As I went to the breakroom, she headed to the office and called after me, "Brendan is working this afternoon and this weekend. I'll be in and out to help him."

I joined her in the office.

"Maia, excuse me for saying this, but you are always here. How can you keep up this kind of schedule?"

She didn't answer right away. "It's the time of year. I'm used to it. It gets very slow during the off season. You won't believe the difference when late April hits. And by May, whatever isn't ready for the summer season—well, forget it. There's no time after that. Or so we hope. After all, without the customers, there's no gallery, right?"

"Of course."

"And yet, because it's so much slower during the winter months, I can't afford to keep the same year-round help. Unnecessary both in amount of work and in terms of payroll. So we reduce hours and I cover those myself with the help of a part-time person as best I can. Summer, though, that's when we shine. I'm hoping you'll work out and want to stay. That you'll be good with the customers and business and that you'll be content with what I can offer you."

Pressure. Yep, I was feeling it.

I said, "So far, so good, right? I'm not tested though. Hard to promise how well I'll do when the crunch is on."

Maia fixed her gaze on me. "I have instincts. Good ones. It's all up to you, but don't give up too quickly." She paused, then asked, "Have you considered whether you'll stay or move on? How's it going for you at the beach house?"

"Getting settled in. Nowhere else I'd rather be right now."

"Good. Glad to hear it." Maia smiled. "Then let's keep moving forward, shall we?"

We went through the register opening procedure again and this time I made notes. It wasn't hard, but only a lack of familiarity with this type of equipment.

Maia said, "Instead of working upstairs this morning, why not stay down here. You can help me dust and arrange and such. I'll show you how I maintain things, like making sure the paintings aren't about to fall off the walls, and that the shell creatures haven't lost a limb or an eye."

"Sounds like fun."

"We can also chat about Brendan's idea to move some of the items into a new display. It has merit, but . . ." And she continued speaking as we went about the morning routine. Routine for her. New to me, but easy. As easy as breathing.

This was vastly different from sitting in college lecture halls about art history and I'd never had any experience with retail except from the customer side of the counter . . .and yet, I suspected I could become quite good at this.

ঔ

The afternoon had turned warm as the day went on, and the late day air still held that warmth. After I left work, I did as planned and drove straight to Mr. Smithson's office in Morehead City. The small parking area in front of the building was empty of cars. The building itself looked empty, but I got out of the car and walked up to the main entrance anyway. The hours on the door included Friday hours, but a sign was posted saying the office was closed until Monday.

Mr. Smithson. Where are you?

Was he elusive? Or simply on a trip? Maybe he'd had a family emergency. What about his receptionist or assistant? Who was Ms. Carroll anyway? She might be his mom for all I knew.

But did his absence—or even his failure to return my call—indicate some sort of fraud or shenanigans was going on?

Not necessarily.

I leaned back against my car, thinking. There was an actual part of me that was okay with the lack of contact, with the office being closed. After all, if Mr. Grimes didn't want to be contacted, then I should honor that, right? There was some piece of me that felt it was important to thank him face-to-face. There was another part of me that said I should just roll with it. To be grateful and not push myself on a man who'd tried to do a nice thing.

Don't look a gift horse in the mouth. That was one of mom's favorite phrases when I complained about something not being quite what I wanted. It was Aunt Eva who'd explained it to me, saying, *If someone gives you a gift, you say thank you. Don't parse out the flaws.* I'd been a smart aleck, saying, "And what if I don't want whatever the gift is?" She'd answered, "Be careful how you handle that because you may not get a second chance at what's being offered."

So I was grateful yes, but I was also uncomfortable. Was I grateful enough to ignore my discomfort over not knowing every detail about why and who?

I wanted to know. That felt reasonable. But if the giver wanted to keep it otherwise . . .

Maybe it was good Mr. Smithson wasn't here.

The answer seemed obvious. Even if all of this—including Beach Heart being mine—crumbled around me, I could still enjoy today and tomorrow and the day after. For now, instead of angsting myself to death, I could drive home, kick off my shoes and sit on the porch or take a walk along the beach.

I could give Mr. Smithson a few more days.

In the end, no one knew how long the good would last, anyway.

ଓଃ୫ଠ

I stopped at the grocery store on my way home and as I carried the bags up to the front door, I saw a folded slip of paper taped to it. Pulling it free, I took the paper in with me.

It was a note from Jake inviting me to join him on the crossover bench at six o'clock for cake.

Cake?

Hmm. Wasn't sure what to make of that. What? Didn't know what to make of cake? Of cake with Jake, no less. *Hah*. I was a poet.

And I was intrigued.

A taste of cake with Jake.

I laughed, amused at my wit, and amused by my amusement.

Was I ten again? I didn't care. It felt so good to laugh over cake that I laughed some more.

In anticipation of the expected cake, I ate a salad for supper and at six p.m. I exited the sliding doors to the porch carrying two glasses of iced tea.

ଓଃ୫ଠ

He was waiting at the benches, sitting facing the

house. As I walked along the crossover, I noticed the end of a piece of fabric, like a table runner, laid across the bench seat and rippling slightly in the breeze. On top of the runner was a square plastic container holding four cupcakes fresh from the grocery store.

Cupcakes? Yes, with napkins alongside.

Jake rose as I approached.

"Hello, there," I said, offering him a glass of tea.

Star was napping on the crossover in the shade cast by the railing. She gave me a sleepy look, lifting one eyelid to greet and assess me.

Jake spoke softly. "She's annoyed about the c-a-k-e. It's not good for her."

I smiled. "And it's good for us?"

"It's cake," he said. "Of course it is."

Star grunted and gave us a super sad, defeated, but pleading look.

"No, Star," he said.

I settled at my end of the bench. The runner and cake were between us. It felt nice in a cozy way.

"To what do I owe this honor?"

"A party. Congratulatory."

"For what?"

"Your success on the job." He gestured at the cupcakes. "There's an assortment. You get first choice."

I chose chocolate. Because. And it was good.

"I believe we already established that my new job is a one-day-at-a-time kind of thing. I was late yesterday morning. Maia was good about it, but it's still a poor impression."

"Stuff happens."

"No truer words." I consumed the last bite, then said, "What about you? Can we celebrate *your* job, too? I'm still waiting to hear how you support yourself. Why the mystery?"

"No mystery."

"It's always just you and Starfish out here." Star made a noise at hearing her full name. "Sorry, Star. My bad." I turned back to Jake. "You said it's your sister's house? What about a wife and kids? I'm guessing you aren't married because a wife would surely object to you visiting me almost every day and bringing me cupcakes."

I said it lightly, thinking I was being witty and clever and full of my newfound optimism, but there was a part of me that needed to know. It was a heady feeling, but as soon as I uttered my little jest, I saw his expression and knew I'd gone astray.

"Sorry? I intended a joke."

He shook his head. "You couldn't know." He must've seen my expression because he added quickly, "We're divorced. I'm sorry it happened the way it did, that's all. It's in the past."

"Children?"

He shook his head again but didn't speak.

"I'm sorry," I said. "You brought me cupcakes to congratulate me on showing up for my job and I've ruined your efforts. Just know that I get it. I truly do. The choices we make . . .the consequences we live with . . .they can be a burden."

He nodded. "You mentioned about your husband dying. Are you doing better with that?"

I looked at my glass of iced tea on the railing. The sunlight was now filtering through the glass, lighting up the warm brown liquid and the facets within the ice cubes, and I wished I could capture that. But all things changed. Even beauty couldn't be held close if it depended upon the durability of an ice cube.

I wiped the condensation from the side of the

glass with my finger.

“A penny for your thoughts? Or another cupcake?”

“Upping your bid?” I smiled. “No, I’ll save the second cupcake for later, if that’s not too presumptuous.” I picked up my glass and drank a long sip, wanting that golden liquid in the sparkling ice while it was at its best.

“My thoughts? There was a young man at the gallery yesterday. He worked for Maia until he went off for college, and now he’s back on spring break so he’s picking up some hours. A nice young man. Reminded me of my stepson . . .as he was maybe eight years ago. When life was still fresh for him, too, and full of promise.” I smiled at Jake, but sadly. “Remember when you thought you’d live forever?”

He nodded. “I do.”

“And then the time comes in your life when you’d rather not.”

We both fell silent, and that silence stretched out between us.

I’d done this. My fault again. I’d cast a pall over our little party. I had to fix it. I struggled for a way to do that and managed to say, “Life is hard.

Living it can be overwhelming. It's a struggle to get through each day. And then the day comes when it gets better and you see the value of today—of living today instead of focusing your hopes on what's to come. When a good day lived in its proper moment becomes infinitely more valuable than promises of a distant future."

My hand was on the railing, as was his, and it seemed to me that his hand had edged forward. His fingertips were still several inches away from mine. But a slight lean forward, a small stretch from either of us, would cover that space.

I didn't know him. Not in a real way. In fact, the truth was that I didn't even know myself.

I leaned back, withdrawing my hand from the railing.

Meanwhile, we'd attracted an audience. Several seagulls were sitting nearby, waiting down on the sand, but keeping a sharp watch up our way. One bold bird had landed on the opposite railing and his eyes were focused, absolutely on the moment —this moment when Jake's partially eaten cupcake was sitting on a napkin between us. Star looked up and half-raised as if sensing her hopes of getting even a crumb might be forestalled by the intruder. She jumped up and barked. The gull lifted off but didn't go far before landing again, that beady eye trained on us—or the cupcake. Star whined.

I said, "I believe our party has been crashed."

"It seems so." Jake patted his thigh. "Here, Star."

She came toward him, but meekly, with the best manners on display.

He took that last bite of uneaten cupcake—vanilla with a nearly microscopic bit of vanilla icing still on it and offered it to Star.

That eagerness, that desire in her expression . . . I vaguely remember wanting something so very badly that I'd felt that too but despite the extreme temptation she stayed put, primly seated though still quivering. Jake set the paper on the planks. "Good girl, Star. Eat your cupcake."

And she did.

"Wow. Now that's either amazing training or amazing control or both."

"She's been going to obedience training which means I go too. They tell me what I should to do or not do. They are training me well."

I laughed again, and Starfish smiled with a tiny vanilla crumb moustache speckled on her muzzle. The seagull flew away. All was right with our little world again. At least, for the moment.

"Aunt Eva would approve."

"Aunt Eva?"

"The collage with the broken frame belonged to her." My hand was back up on the railing. "Funny, isn't it? I haven't laughed this much in years. And in fact, if not for Aunt Eva's collage—and me being clumsy and breaking the frame—I never would've visited Front Street Gallery and seen Beaufort, met Maia, and gotten a job. In fact, if you and Star hadn't come along as I was sitting here examining the damage, I might never have gone to the gallery to ask about getting it fixed. Life's so random, right? Or is it?"

An odd expression crossed his face. His hazel eyes looked troubled, and the color had darkened like the ocean when a storm was approaching.

He said, "We had a son. We lost him . . .long ago. Our marriage didn't survive it. I don't want to discuss it. I hope you understand."

I did. I understood so well that I didn't need to say it aloud. I merely nodded.

Jake went on to say, "Random or planned? We never really know, do we? We just do our best to dance to the tune that life plays for us."

As I watched him, I saw him mentally shake off the sadness that had settled around us.

The sunlight was slanting in as the sun moved lower toward the horizon, preparing to set over The Point. The Point was at the westernmost end of the island and out of our direct sight, but the light burnished the entire oceanfront with a golden cast for a short time, saturating the colors of the green growth and the wooden crossovers, and the world around us glowed. As the sun reached its lowest point, the color would drain, shades swiftly losing their color in favor of the oncoming night. But for now, in this hushed moment, I stared, mesmerized, as the late-afternoon light touched Jake's reddish curls, tipping them with a bit of gold. And Star, too, her coat catching fire in this golden hour, as she stood there watching us expectantly.

Jake sat straighter and I knew he was about to leave. So did Star. He said, "It's time Star and I headed out for our last walk of the day."

I stood, too, and boldly asked, "Mind if I join

you again?"

He smiled. "Happy to have you along. We'll wait here if you want to take the cupcakes inside and grab a sweater or something. Gets cooler down by the water."

As I walked away, I heard him say, "Your hair looks golden in this light."

He'd spoken so low, so softly, that by the time I understood he was speaking to me, I was almost at the door. If I paused, the action was infinitesimal before I decided to keep moving.

I'd heard him. He knew I'd heard him. For now, I'd let that be enough.

Chapter Thirteen

It might or might not have been cooler down by the water. I put a sweater around my shoulders and thought no more of it. Jake and I exchanged the occasional spoken remark—no long or deep conversations—only an appreciation of the sunset and companionship. Faint threads of color were starting to work their way around from the actual sunset happening to the west of us, toward the end of Emerald Isle, where the White Oak River flowed out to the ocean at The Point. I hadn't been down there since I was a kid. Aunt Eva and I had hitched a ride with a neighbor who had a truck, and he'd driven us down there to watch the moon rise as the sun set. I'd never forget that.

In the dimming light and growing shadows, Beach Heart became only one among all the other hulking dark shapes of the buildings lining the oceanfront. But there on the beach, walking down along the waters edge with Jake and Star, I'd never felt more comfortably at home in my life. After we'd reversed direction and walked back to the crossover, Jake and I touched hands, and then stepped back from each other. I couldn't read Jake's face, but suddenly I felt shy.

"Come, Star," he said. "Good night, Emma."

I smiled into the darkness, making out his features by only the ambient light, and responded, "Good night."

They continued onward, and I returned to the house.

The walk had been lovely but left me restless.

Ultimately, I might not be able to stay even if things went well, but my new motto was that this day was important too, and it meshed well with Aunt Eva's wisdom about the great pleasure to be found in the joy of ordinary days and ordinary tasks. I'd already taken that dolphin down because I couldn't look at the TV without it being right smack in my line of sight. But the heron family sat where I'd left them. Aunt Eva's boxes were still stacked in the street-side bedroom. I'd started on them, but still had a few to go through.

It all spoke to a lack of commitment. Of not making a stand.

There were things I could do, but hadn't. My instinct said to wait.

And yet, today mattered regardless of

yesterday or tomorrow. And I wouldn't have missed this day for anything. Today was a jewel of a day to be remembered and treasured.

But just as Brendan had wanted to regroup the displays in ways that were more pleasing to his eye, I could do the same. Small things. Slight shifts. That could grow? Of course. It didn't have to be a big commitment. More of an exploration of what my heart and my instincts were trying to tell me.

If I were going to commit to staying here, what would I do?

I thought of the paintings I'd seen at the gallery. There were a couple that, if I could afford them, I'd hang here. Some of those sunset paintings, and one that was of dunes and sea oats and such, but with actual material in the paint. The lure to touch and go *aw* was almost irresistible. I'd get a new couch, too. And if I were going to go that far, I'd have the picture hanging hardware pulled out, spackle and sand the walls, and then paint these rooms. I'd bring color to these walls instead of doing it via smiling dolphins.

Picking up the herons, one by one, feeling the smooth wood, so silky to the touch, I tried them in different locations, but none felt quite right. So today was not the day. But it was always good to have options and possibilities.

I'd know when it was time to make that stand, or to choose, or whatever.

It was for me to decide.

૪ઙ

It wasn't until later that night as I was getting ready for bed that I wondered what it would be like to walk with Jake, maybe holding hands, or with his arm casually around me.

I wondered how it would be to kiss him.

The initial thought shocked me and yet felt perfectly natural at the same time. The idea itself felt objective. Not as a plan or something to fear or even as a fantasy. No more than a simple wondering.

Because I was coming alive. I pressed my hand to my chest and felt my heart beating.

Alive again.

Jake and Gregory couldn't have been more different. First, there was the age difference. Jake was about my age. Gregory had also been more ambitious and self-directed, and I didn't get that feeling from Jake. He was more laid back. And while he seemed light-hearted and open on the surface, today had proved to me that he was harder to read than I'd guessed.

Only time together would help me understand who he was at heart.

Would we have that time together? I hoped so.

I left the curtains open that night, as usual, and pulled the covers up around my shoulders. I lay there on my side watching the lights in the sky above and the lights moving along the horizon, and I knew the wind had picked up as I listened to the music it played via the eaves. Sometimes musical, but at times it sounded like a whispered conversation, its words and meanings elusive. But as I slipped into sleep, I understood that the differences didn't matter. It was all beautiful.

☙❧

On Saturday morning, Maia called. She said she was nearby visiting a friend in Emerald Isle and was hoping it was convenient for me if she dropped by Beach Heart while she was in the area.

"I apologize for so little notice. Is it a good time?

Stunned, I said, "It's fine. Do you need directions?"

"No, I know the way."

I wanted to ask if there was bad news, if maybe she was coming here to fire me, but I didn't. I kept the "worry" words inside, bottled up, and hoping to find them an overreaction. The nervous stomach, the incipient panic—it was all there on the edges, but I was determined to trust to better things than assuming disaster. This was out of the ordinary, a surprise, yes, but that's all it was . . . hopefully. I did a quick tidying up of myself and the living room.

A surprise could be good, I reminded myself.

But this one wasn't. I felt it in my bones.

When the doorbell rang, I opened it wide, inviting Maia in. She was dressed as if on her way to work. But she'd come here first. Again, I felt that warning surge of panic.

"Come in. This is a surprise," I said as she stepped inside. "Can I offer you a glass of iced tea?"

She smiled. "Sweet tea?"

"Is there any other kind?"

Maia laughed. The sound was soft but didn't reflect in her eyes.

"Have a seat," I said. "I'll be right there."

As I was pouring tea over the ice in the glasses, she asked, "Mind if we sit outside?" She was standing at the glass doors looking out toward the ocean.

"Outside is fine," I said. "I'll join you there."

I grabbed a bag of cookies and tucked it under my arm and carried the glasses. The cookies would give my hands something to do when they wanted to twist my fingers or cover my face. I felt it all coming on. Bad news was screaming in my head like an outraged harpy who'd been ignored for too long. My hands were shaking as I approached the door to the porch. The ice clinked in the glasses almost like an agitated strap of jingle bells.

Maia was there, opening the door for me. I set the glasses on the table between the rockers, and we sat.

"Want a cookie?" I asked.

"Not yet," she said.

And at that moment I knew without doubt that this was most definitely *not good.*

She sipped her tea. The breeze was lovely and warm. The most recent east side occupants had left early this morning, and at some point today the cleaning crew would arrive and then tomorrow the next renters would show up and be hauling their weeks' worth of supplies up the stairs, but today it was private out here. I thought of all that because I saw her looking around curiously. Then she surprised me by saying, "Friends of mine own a duplex nearby. One or the other of them lived there in *their* west side on and off for years. I would often sit on the porch, rock in the rockers, and visit." She gave a short smile. "They're either gone now or have moved over to the sound side of the island."

"As a child, I sat here with my aunt when I visited her. Just sitting and chatting and rocking and sipping tea. It's a lovely memory."

"Mine too," she said. She set the glass on the table and looked down at her purse on her lap. "Speaking of porches and your aunt Eva, and good memories—I am here to apologize for an oversight. I don't know quite how to approach this, so please forgive me if I do it clumsily."

I was impatient. "Sometimes it's better just to

get it said. Are you firing me, Maia? Or letting me go from the gallery for some other reason? Please know that I appreciate the opportunity you gave me. I'll be disappointed, but I'll deal with it. I know how to receive bad news."

Maia looked aghast. "Fire you?"

"This past week was great, and per our conversations at the gallery, I thought it was going well for all concerned, but I understand things can change in a moment. When one least expects it." I forced myself to stop babbling and simply said, "I thought you came here to tell me now instead of waiting until Monday when I'd be seeing you back at the gallery anyway." Now a shock hit me. "Or is this about you? Oh, Maia, I hope you're okay. I've been . . ." I swallowed the words. They felt so intrusive. I softened them to, "If something has gone wrong, you know you can count on me."

Her jaw had dropped, her mouth was agape, and her eyes were wide.

"Maia? Are you okay?"

"Oh my," she said. But she said it over and over. "Oh my goodness." She reached out and touched my arm. "Breathe," she said. "Please, for both our sakes, sit back and breathe." And then she added, “I believe I’d like one of those cookies after all.”

As I unfastened the bag, glad to have something to do, to focus on, she said, “I knew you had some lingering trauma from all that you’ve gone through, but we are going to figure out how to help you get past that. I promise you.” She accepted the cookie from me but didn’t eat it right away. I did. I had to do something. A cookie was better than nothing. I broke it in half and nibbled on one end.

Maia said, “I did come to deliver something, some news, and it might not please you. Or it may be old news to you. But not knowing, it made sense to me to bring it here—away from a more public place like the gallery.”

I chewed the cookie just to keep the nerves down and stared at her. Waiting. For the next blow.

“That art collage with the broken frame? You brought it to the gallery to be fixed.”

“Sure. Of course. It’s hanging on my wall upstairs.”

“Well, Mary, the lady who did the repairs, had some health issues directly after. Apparently, the trip she was preparing for was to go to the hospital for surgery. Outpatient, I believe, and it went well, though she was kept abed for a couple of days at home. She's doing fine now, so she was sorting out her work area and discovered this."

Somehow Maia was now holding an envelope—a rectangular white business envelope—in her hands. "When she took the backing off the frame, she found a folded piece of paper. She put it aside and somehow something else got set on top of it, and she forgot. As she was putting her work area back into order, she found this and remembered immediately and brought it directly over to the gallery just before closing yesterday. She apologized profusely. To be honest, I don't think she even looked at it when she first found it, else she would never have forgotten about it, but when she found it the second time, she did. I know this is private, and she was embarrassed but I'm quite certain you can trust her discretion. She truly is a lovely woman."

Maia handed me the envelope. It was a crisp, pristine envelope, so she must've put the paper in it for the purpose of this delivery. She said, "It isn't all that remarkable anyway, except in how it was sealed inside the frame." She drew in a deep breath. "Would you like me to leave? Just say the word."

I shook my head. Words were beyond me. I was terrified. Of a neatly folded piece of paper.

It wasn't ancient. It was oldish. The paper was clean and in good shape, as if someone had treasured it—and then had hidden it away in the back of the framed collage.

A birth certificate. Eva Deveraux Douglas and Warren Douglas, parents, and the infant, Emma.

My first reaction was how sad that Aunt Eva had lost a child. She must've since I'd never met that Emma . . . her Emma . . . Emma Douglas.

With the same birth date as me.

And then the realization hit me that the Emma Douglas referred to on this certificate was . . .

Me.

Chapter Fourteen

My vision blurred. A buzzing noise filled my ears. I closed my eyes and shook my head to clear it so I could think. This made no sense.

Maia asked softly, "Did you know about this?"

"No. I mean, I have my birth certificate. And it isn't this one. This makes no sense."

In a steady, calming tone, she said, "You're in shock. Can I get you anything?"

"You don't understand. I *have* my birth certificate," I repeated. "I have multiple copies. I was born Emma Deveraux, to my mother, Maureen Devereaux. My father is listed on it, but they weren't married, or even together. He wasn't in our lives when I was growing up. I was raised by my mother." I opened the certificate to scan it again, saying, "There must be an obvious explanation I'm missing."

I reread it line by line, over and over, but nothing changed. I tore my eyes away and tried to focus on the horizon—that unbroken, unfaltering line—to find some logic in this puzzle.

Maia said, "One of them could be an amended birth certificate. Like they do in an adoption where they seal one and make a new one?"

Queasiness began to twist my stomach.

"Mom said my father was in the navy. He was local for a while, and they met and fell for each other. It was a whirlwind relationship. She got pregnant and he left, but she always said having me was the one thing that made it all worthwhile." I shook my head. "As for Aunt Eva, her husband, Warren, died when I was very young. Two years old, I think. I have no memory of him at all."

Maia urged softly, "Ask your mom, Emma. Ask her and give her a chance to help you make sense of this."

I picked up the envelope to return the certificate to it, but as I let it fold along the it's accustomed lines, the sunlight caught faded writing on the back of the certificate. It was written in pencil and almost unreadable except in this brightest light of a beachfront morning.

To my dearest baby Emma,
Perhaps this is cowardice or selfishness,
but I choose to believe it is love, and if fate

should ever bring you to find this, please know how much you were loved by us all. You are my heart wherever you are. Eva

You are my heart…

My heart could not survive this tearing and pulling. My brain could not survive this clash of what I knew as fact and what made no sense. Forgetting that Maia was there, I put my hands over my face.

Her voice came through to me as if from a distance, saying, "Call her, Emma. Call your mom." The porch planks squeaked as Maia rose from the rocker and came to stand beside me. "If you want to talk, to vent, to do whatever—you are always welcome to call me anytime."

I let her go. I sat there, my hands still over my face and the envelope on my lap. I felt trapped, unable to think or move forward. I'd been wrong when I'd made those early assumptions about Gregory and what his changed behavior had meant. But this? No matter how it was explained, there'd been lies told. Lies that many of the most important people in my life had been a party to.

Lies and secrets borne of lies. There was simply no way around that conclusion, or a way around the pain and confusion. But that was as far as my brain could take me. Now my hands were back on that envelope, and the only thing I could see before me was the meeting place of sea and sky.

I don't know how long I sat there—apparently captive to my brain trying to fit and refit the puzzle pieces together, to force them to mesh, to make sense, so I could figure out what to do in order to move forward. And it hurt. From my throat to my jaw to the crown of my head.

Could I trust anyone in my life? To claim everyone was against me seemed self-serving, even self-indulgent, but in all honesty, I was beginning to think it might be truer than I could ever have imagined. None of those who'd been closest to me for all my life could be trusted.

"Emma?"

Jake. Standing down along the crossover. "Mind if—" He was interrupted by Star galloping up the crossover to greet me.

Biting my lip, trying to keep the despair and distress discreetly hidden until later—later when I'd better know what to do with it—I greeted Star, scratched her head. By then, Jake had joined us.

"You looked so deep in thought, I was hesitant to disturb you." He gave me a long look. "Are you upset? Anything you'd like to talk about?"

"No one can be trusted." I blurted it out, angry.

Jake's face changed. He looked . . . I didn't know the words to describe it, but he looked as if he was seeing an Emma he'd never seen before—one he wasn't happy to meet. I didn't care.

Jake took a step back. He said carefully, ever so gently, "I'm very sorry, Emma. I'm sorry you were hurt. No one meant for that to happen."

"What are you talking about?" I blurted out. "Why are *you* sorry? It's not your fault. As for the intentions of others . . ."

He paused, a long, perhaps confused pause, then said, "I'm sorry because you're hurt. I'm sure whoever hurt you didn't do so intentionally." He was speaking carefully, choosing his words and tone precisely. He added, "I'm glad it's not because of what . . . because of something I did."

"My mother. My great-aunt." I made a rough noise and stood up. "I don't want to discuss it."

Again, ever so carefully, Jake said, "Okay. How about a walk, then? Shake off some of the excess negative energy?"

"What are you talking about?"

"You're angry, Emma. Clearly. I'm relieved I'm not the person you're angry with, but sometimes people do things—well meaning, with good intent, but that end up looking different afterward. Decisions or actions that are awkward to confess or explain."

"It's not about you, Jake."

"As you said, and I am sincerely very glad to hear that. But I can't leave you like this."

"Why not? I've already told you that it's not your problem."

"But it is, Emma. We're friends, aren't we?"

He'd made no move to sit in the rocker, but he was leaning back against the railing now, looking a little less fraught.

Jake was concerned about me. Even Starfish had stayed close. She was, in fact, sitting on my feet and half reclining against my shins, offering her own special comfort.

"It'll be okay," I said, sounding unconvinced, but it was a truth. I'd learned that if misfortune or pain didn't outright destroy you, eventually it worked out one way or the other. The trick was being alive and of sound mind when it finally did.

"I don't think it's a good day for a beach walk. Or even for companionship. I'm not fit for that just now."

"If you want to talk, Emma, or if you don't want to talk but just want distraction—I'm pretty good at that. Just call me."

I gave him a cold stare. "Ironically, Jake, I can't do that. I don't have your number."

A surprised look crossed his face, then he smiled. "I believe you are correct." He rummaged in his pockets. "I seem to have left my phone at home." He held up a pen. "I don't have paper." His eyes lit on the envelope I was holding, but I didn't offer it and he didn't ask. Instead, he said, "What's your number? I'll text you mine."

"Seriously? You can remember it until you get home?"

"Not a chance. *But*"—he held the pen poised over his forearm—"go for it."

I was surprised. I didn't think anyone had ever written my phone number on their arm or anywhere except the usual—on paper. To see if he'd really do it, I recited the numbers for him. And he did.

He'd done it. I could hardly believe it. In big, obvious numbers. A foolish, empty gesture. It annoyed me. This was not a day for lighthearted foolishness. To be annoying back, I said, "What if it rains before you get home?"

He turned to survey the sky. "Blue sky all the way today. Today is a day for bold, brave tasks, Emma. It's a seize-the-day kind of day. And if by some chance I fall into the ocean and these numbers vanish…you'll see me back here all the quicker to ask again, and again, as often as needed."

With a slight bow, Jake left. Starfish followed, but reluctantly, and only when Jake patted his thigh and called her to him.

If no other kindness could touch me that day, still the empathy of a dog hit the mark squarely. That, and of Jake wanting to ease my pain.

Seize the day?

A blue-sky day. Was this a day to tackle difficult or unpleasant things?

To give my mother the chance to explain exactly what she and Aunt Eva had done thirty-seven years ago and had kept secret from me?

I didn't feel bold or brave. Merely destructive.

But there were things that struck me—Jake writing my number on his arm. Starfish offering the best comfort she could. Maia coming all the way to Emerald Isle to share this with me in person. By now she was surely back at the gallery and working—always working. But she'd given up her morning to share this—this envelope—with me face to face.

I could've taken the time to pull out my birth certificate, but why bother? I'd seen it many times through the years. When I'd registered for school, when I got my driver's license, when I obtained my passport… All of that was done decades ago. Before I'd left home, Mom had given me the original embossed copy along with multiple other copies. They'd always been accepted. I'd never needed to ask for a new copy from the state's Office of Vital Records.

In recent years, we hadn't traveled. There'd never been a discrepancy noted in the past, but systems and databases got updated regularly now, even going back in time and updating retroactively. At some point, the copies I had might not pass unchallenged.

I stared at the horizon and wondered…if I

asked for a certified copy from the State now, which one would they send?

ଔଡ଼

"Mom…." I dropped the phone mid-thought. Clumsy. I grabbed it back and heard the voice mail instructing me to leave a message. "Mom," I said again, and then abruptly ran out words. I hit the disconnect button. I had to gather my thoughts before attempting this. Driving up to Greenville was out of the question. I was shaking, and every time it seemed to be lessening, it started up again. I drank a ton of water. I tried dialing again, but when the voice mail started talking at me this time, I hit the disconnect button so hard that the phone scooted across the countertop and hit the floor. I tripped over the edge of the carpet and hit the floor and found myself face-to-face with the heron family.

Enough. Maybe Jake was right. Maybe Maia was, too, about venting. I got back to my feet and left my phone where it landed and went outside to try to breathe.

ଔ

I made it to the water's edge, where I sat. The waves rolled up, barely touching my toes at first, but then coming closer and higher, touching the hem of my capris. Still I sat, watching the horizon, following the waves rolling in. Nothing brilliant occurred to me. I couldn't clear my thoughts enough to think. Perhaps I didn't want to think.

A red bucket bumped my foot, was then lifted by an encroaching wave, but before it could be swept out, a child was there, rushing into the water to grab it. Dylan. He didn't speak, but I felt his acknowledgment of me when he sat only inches away.

His thin, bare legs were wet and covered in sand except for where a few bruises showed and a scrape or two. I remembered the same with Macon. Dylan pulled his legs in to sit cross-legged and let the water bring sand into the bucket and he'd hoist the bucket and let the wet sand slide back out. He did this over and over. It looked like my brain felt.

A tear rolled down my cheek. I reached up to brush it away and Dylan scooted closer. Still not touching me, but I was almost afraid to move lest he move away. I kind of liked him sitting there, trusting me.

Macon had too. Once upon a time. It seemed so long ago.

I needed to reach out to him. Before too much time passed. Before anger and resentment became ingrained between us like a habit.

No one should live with that bitterness inside them. It was a killer. Of joy. Of all things good.

I pulled up my knees wanting to put my arms across them and hide my face, but as I did that, staring down between my arms at the sand and the water washing across the surface, a shell was revealed. Each fringe of wave rushed up and claimed a little more of the sand to reveal the shell movement by movement. A beige shell. With high well-defined narrow ridges that began at the narrow point and ran back—in perfection—to spread across the wide arc of the bottom.

With each wash of the incoming waves, I waited to see a crack or a chip, but none appeared. It was, indeed, perfect. When the next wave came, it lifted a little and shifted a fraction. The next wave claimed it, picking the shell up and dragging it a few inches down the sand. I grabbed it.

I caught it in my hand. That bit of perfection. Like a moment in time. And instead of letting the ocean take it home again, I held it on my open palm in front of Dylan…until I was sure he saw it, was aware of it. I felt the strength of his stare. And then his fingers moved deftly—not actually touching my hand—and accepted the gift.

From the corner of my eye, I watched him examine the shell now displayed on his own palm. After a minute that stretched out long, he stood and trotted the few steps over to his castle. I watched as he pressed the shell into the wall of the castle just over what I imagined to be the door, but he'd turned the shell such that the narrow point was at the bottom and the way it sat, pressed into the sand, looked for all the world like a heart. Turned up like a horseshoe might be…perhaps to keep the luck or love in.

A short distance up the beach, in the shade cast beneath the end of my crossover, sat Dylan's grandmother in a lawn chair with an umbrella—one intended for rain, not for sun, over her head and keeping watch. This was the closest I'd been to her. I lifted my hand in a wave, and she returned it. In the background, Beach Heart stood as ever, knitting past and present together in one magical swoop. And as I took in the aura of the house and all the memories that came along with it, my eyes caught movement on the porch. A woman—my mother—waited at the railing.

She wasn't waving. She was staring either toward that horizon that often mesmerized me, or at someone who might, or might not be, her daughter.

Chapter Fifteen

Even if Mom had left Greenville as soon as I'd called—or tried to call—even if she'd seen those calls cut short the moment they were made . . . How could she have accomplished the drive here so quickly?

Or . . . how long had I been sitting out here?

The sun was almost at its zenith and Dylan's grandmother's shade was only a narrow band of shadow right up against the wooden posts of the crossover.

I stood. My shorts were damp, and the sand was itchy. I walked past Dylan and his grandmother and trudged up the steps to make my way along the crossover to the porch where Mom was standing.

"I'm sorry," she said. "I came as fast as I could."

"I'm going to change. I'll be back shortly." I left here there and walked inside.

I changed to dry clothing. I didn't rush, but I didn't delay either. This had to be faced.

She'd stayed on the porch, was still standing

at the railing and staring out across the ocean.

I opened the door and asked, “In or out?”

She glanced at the privacy partition.

“No one’s over there today. The next guests arrive tomorrow.”

She nodded. “Then out here, maybe? Might I have something to drink?”

As with Maia, I brought two glasses of iced tea out to the porch, but unlike with Maia, this time I left the cookies in the cupboard.

We each took a rocker and I said, “Please explain to me who actually gave birth to me. Please explain what part of my history is the truth and what is a lie.”

The coldness in my voice both frightened and reassured me. I had to listen. I couldn’t do that if I was hot with anger or overwhelmed by emotion.

She reached down beside her rocker and retrieved a shoebox she must’ve brought with her. I hadn’t noticed it before this moment. She set the box on her lap and opened it carefully. Ever so gently, she reached in and took out a tiny yellow dress. She displayed it across her palms with her fingers spread wide. A dress. A very light yellow in a delicate cotton fabric with a gathered skirt and pleating on the tiny bodice.

"I brought you home in this. My daddy—your grandfather—bought it for you while I was still in the hospital. This dress and the shoes. He brought it to us while you were still in your bassinet in the maternity ward for you to wear home." She nodded toward the box. "Please take that."

I reached across and took the box from her lap. There was a tiny pair of white satin shoes with lace trim and teeny tiny embroidered yellow flowers.

"Hold them," she said. "He bought those, too, and brought the outfit to me when he and Momma came to meet you in the hospital."

"I just want the truth."

"Hold them, Emma. Those shoes were bought for you with love by your grandfather and grandmother. They were chosen by them and brought by them to the hospital—all out of love. To welcome you into our lives. That is the truth."

I gave in and took them in my hands. So tiny.

"At the time, we didn't know that M

Momma was already sick and would be gone in less than a year. We thought we had it all planned out. We three would raise you together. They would help me. I was supposed to be starting college soon. Despite the challenges we knew your arrival would bring, we never ever discussed not having you or me giving you up. We saw ourselves as a family and as a team."

"Where was my father? Did you tell the truth about him?"

"The choices I made with him were ill-advised. He left when I told him I was pregnant. You know all that. Except he wasn't in the Navy. He was a kid I went to high school with. He talked big, but as I later realized, he was immature and spineless. I've told you before that having you made all that heartache and disillusionment worth the pain. But I'll tell you bluntly that I consider myself fortunate that he ran away. He wasn't who I thought he was, and I believe his departure was a lucky escape for all of us." She breathed. "There, I've said it aloud."

"Yet another lie."

"Lies, yes. Or just people making good choices and poor choices, and doing the best they could at the time?" She gave the dress a last look and asked, "Can I have the box back please?"

I put the shoes back in the bottom and handed her the box. Carefully, she refolded the small yellow dress and laid it on top.

All I felt was resentment about the lies, and also about her obvious attempts at manipulating my emotions. I must've made a noise of disgust because she said, "We aren't done yet. Not if you want the *full* truth. To know everything."

Everything? How much more was there to know?

"About Aunt Eva, you mean?" And I cringed at my own tone—so dismissive and rude.

"We didn't know when you were born that Momma would be near death in six months. Dad was totally overwhelmed taking care of her, as I was. I dropped out of college that first semester and took care of you and the two of them. It was grim. I was so young and not prepared for that kind of responsibility." She added very softly, "It went badly."

After a pause, Mom continued, "Aunt Eva knew what we were all dealing with, of course. She visited to see you, to see her sister-in-law—my momma and your grandmother. She was terribly worried about her brother who was going downhill fast with all the worry and grief. One day she suggested she and Warren could take you for a while. That would give Dad and I a break to focus on my mother and, maybe, the chance for me to reenroll in school. We didn't discuss or even think of adoption at that time, but that changed." She shook her head. "From the first moment I knew I was pregnant, it never once occurred to me to give you up. Never. But now…we—Dad and I—were overwhelmed. I saw his stress and his decline, and I wasn't much better. Aunt Eva offered a rescue."

She brushed at her lashes. I tried not to see.

"It seemed to make sense at the time. Aunt Eva who was childless and clearly adored having you with her full-time. You would have the financial and emotional support of Uncle Warren. They could provide you with an amazing home and I would have unlimited, close access to you. For legal and practical purposes, it made sense to make it official. Hence, the adoption."

"Sounds like a lot of justifications to me. Lots of excuses. Why was I kept in the dark?"

"Eva and Warren were stepping in as parents. It made sense. We kept it simple. We were just broadening the circle of people around you who cared about you—who loved you." She shook her head. "That said, I know it sounds…less clear now all these years later. And remember, Aunt Eva was several years younger than your grandfather—in her early forties. No reason in the world she couldn't adopt and raise a child, especially one she was in love with from the moment she first laid eyes on you. I knew you'd be safe with her no matter what the future brought."

"What changed?"

"Warren died. When you were two, he simply didn't get up one morning. Aunt Eva had lost her sister-in-law, my mother, a year earlier. Now my father, her beloved brother, was failing. On that dreadful morning when her husband wouldn't wake, she tried over and over, until she was finally convinced he was gone. Gone. It destroyed her. I swear she aged ten years in that one day. Within weeks, she'd lost so much weight, she was gaunt, and her hair went gray. This time I saw the same truth she'd seen with me—that she wasn't fit to care for a toddler. I packed your belongings, carried you and your things out to the car, and she never interfered. From that day on, you lived with me and Dad, and when you were a little older you stayed with Eva for summers and holidays. It seemed a good solution for everyone.

"I always knew that one day we'd have to explain this to you. Each time we had to pass the birth certificate hurdle, I expected a problem and was prepared to tell you, but as time went on and nothing happened it was easier to let it be. To wait for the right time . . . and the time never came."

"Until it did."

"Until it did. And I have another confession."

I felt a little bludgeoned.

"When the attorney turned Aunt Eva's boxes over to me to hold for you, I went through them. I wondered if she might have kept something from that time. I hadn't found the revised birth certificate from the adoption among her papers when she passed, and I wondered . . . So when you called, I knew. That's the *only* way you would've known after all these years . . . from something you found in Eva's boxes. Am I right?"

"She'd sealed it in the back of collage frame. The one she'd hung on the wall of my room here where I'd see it every morning, and the last thing I'd see each night."

"Someday I'd like to know how you came to find it in there, but not today. Today I'm too full of the past. One wouldn't think it could hurt so much after all these years, but I keep the pain close, because I want the joyful memories to stay sharp, too." She shook her head again. "I don't know if you'll ever forgive me for keeping all this from you and for not being a better mother, but please know it was well-intended."

"The legal, official birth certificate is the one showing Aunt Eva as my mother?"

"Yes, I suppose so. When we were doing the adoption, I told them all that I'd lost my original certificate. Dad had gotten extra certified copies, too, because that's just how he was, and I remember being amazed he'd do that. But when it came time to…give you up legally, I couldn't bear to let those go along with you and your baby things. I kept them hidden with a few other items as keepsakes. When Eva allowed me to take you back, I asked her for the amended birth certificate, but she pretended *she'd* lost it." She shook her head. "I knew it wasn't true." She sighed. "Thankfully, those original certificates and the photocopies of those, gave us what we needed. That's how I got you registered for school. I held my breath wondering if someone would check against the state records, but they seemed satisfied and never asked questions, so it worked. It also worked for your driver's license," she shrugged, "I don't know whether there weren't databases to check against, or maybe it wasn't the procedure back then . . . or maybe it was a simple error. I don't know and I didn't ask. Didn't dare risk raising suspicion and, well, it worked out." She smiled sadly. "I made sure you had plenty of copies hoping that you'd never have to request a new certificate from the state."

She'd protected me. Bad her choices? Were they good? Maybe. Maybe not. But once I was an adult, she should've told me the truth. That said, I'd had my own distractions. I had not made myself available and had often made a point of avoiding her, so she wouldn't see the secrets I was hiding.

I put my hand over my face again.

"I'm so sorry, Emma. It's been a burden all these years. Every time I'd convinced myself that we'd made the best decision possible, something would happen and I'd see that gulf between us. In the end, when you were dealing with so much—marriage and then your husband's illness—I blamed myself for not finding a way to fix whatever was wrong between us."

We sat together in silence. I couldn't think of anything useful to say. Snarky remarks kept popping into my head, but they seemed purposeless. Unworthy. So I sat in much the same way as I'd sat alone in the home I'd shared with Gregory on that last day.

I said, "Aunt Eva loved this place. She said it was the place she felt most herself, especially when times were rough. That it was her anchor."

"She and Uncle Warren brought you here. This was your home with them. This is where he died. I suppose the best and worst of her memories resided here. She couldn't leave one without giving up the other."

"Memories don't reside in spaces and places. They are within us. They exist where we are."

Mom looked at me, her head back against the rocker, and smiled. "True. But the fact remains, that when the bad memories swamp the good ones, we are eager to move away from that place."

"Sometimes practical considerations outweigh any others. I had no choice but to sell our house."

"What happened, Emma? I'd like to know. I

wish I could've helped you."

"No one could help me. Or us. By the time I understood something was truly wrong with Gregory, it was too late." I felt my lips pressing together and my jaw tightened. "In fact, I'd gotten a job thinking he was cheating and that I'd be on my own soon. I'd seen an attorney and started divorce proceedings. Did you know that? Of course, you didn't because I didn't tell anyone. I didn't know how."

I sat in silence for a long moment before continuing, "When Gregory finally went to the doctor and we learned there was a physical explanation for the odd, secretive, illogical behavior, we also found out there was nothing to be done but to manage his care. That was what the doctors said. *Manage his care.*" I shook my head.

"But Gregory had done things. He'd sold valuable items for pennies, had moved funds around. With the help of the accountant, I untangled things as best I could because the care and medical bills cost money—money that had disappeared." My last words were ragged. I breathed in deeply and held the breath inside me.

"I'm so sorry you had to go through that, and

go through it alone."

"Macon thought I'd been diverting the money for my own purposes, especially after he discovered the divorce papers. Snooping. I don't really blame him. He was as confused and worried as I was. But he didn't give me the benefit of the doubt. He didn't trust me." I looked at mom. "That's how it feels now. You didn't trust me to understand about what happened when I was a baby. I get it that you didn't tell me when I was a child. But as an adult . . . even then you didn't give me the benefit of the doubt."

Very, very softly, she responded, "I think that goes both ways, Emma." When I didn't answer, she added, "I think it goes back to the chaos of the beginning and the back and forth in the years that followed. I understood that you bonded with Aunt Eva. In some ways, I was glad because I knew that if anything happened to me that she'd protect you, take care of it. I knew all that and allowed it to happen, and the fault for that lies squarely with me."

She stood. I looked at her, surprised.

"If there's anything else you'd like to ask, you're welcome to do that now, or later. Anytime, of course. I'll do my best to explain, but I think we've pretty much covered it. Now it's up to you to decide whether to forgive me." Again, there was a pause. A waiting moment that stayed silent. She continued, "For now, Ross is parked below. He doesn't mind. He's probably napping."

"He drove you?"

"Yes. I was trying to get out of the house, all frantic, after I heard your message . . . or rather the lack of message. When I tried to back out of the driveway, I hit the mailbox, and at that point, Ross insisted on bringing me. I think that was probably a good thing. I was upset. Also, he has a heavier foot on the accelerator than I do. He got me here faster than I could've managed."

I stood, too. "Thank him for me. As for forgiveness, the anger is mostly gone. Now I'm just confused. I can't figure out who to blame. I accept that you all did the best you could do. Meant well, and all that."

"You were loved. Well loved."

My eyes stung. I ignored them. "I accept that. But you should've told me."

"You are right. If I could go back and redo any of it, I would've done exactly that." She kind of smiled. "I almost did, in fact. Remember that day when you came home from college and told me there was a young man you were interested in? Before Gregory. I almost told you then. But I didn't. Again, I say, I'm sorry, Emma." She added, "Mind if I use your bathroom before I leave? All this iced tea . . ."

I opened the door and stood aside to allow her in.

I set the drinking glasses on the counter and saw the cigar box of photos waiting there. I flipped the lid open and looked at the messy assortment of photos—black and white, faded color, even more faded Instamatic. Some faces I could attach a name to and some I couldn't. For instance, in the group photo of Aunt Eva with a tall man and a group of kids in front, one of which was me. I was young…maybe four or five?

Mom joined me at the counter. "What's this? She asked. "Oh, the photos. I remember Eva going through those with you."

"This is her here, I recognize her. But I don't know that tall man or who these kids are. Were they renters? Or what?"

She shook her head. "I don't know. That

man . . . I think he was connected to Warren's family. Some of the kids might belong to him. Kids or grandkids. I never knew them, but I have a vague recollection of Eva speaking of Warren's family visiting." She nodded. "These folks must've had some particular meaning whether family or friends for her to have kept the photo for you."

She talked a little longer, but I'd stopped listening. I was staring at the photo now, something stirring in my brain. Something familiar, but something that also gave me a cold, sick feeling in the pit of my stomach.

Mom was unaware. She was walking toward the door, saying, "I'm leaving the shoebox with the dress and baby shoes with you, Emma. It's yours and should've been in your care long ago."

Her voice stopped and then she said, "Are you okay? I know this has been a difficult discussion, sweetheart. Do you want me to stay with you a while? Ross won't mind, I promise."

I shook myself. "I'm good, Mom. We'll talk, okay? I have a headache. I think I'm going to lie down."

She walked over to me and put her hand on

my shoulder and kissed me on the cheek. She spoke softly and warmly, "I'll be back very soon, dear. We're going to work some magic in this place. We're going to make it your own. Here or wherever you choose. A fresh start. We all need those, Emma, and I'm going to help you make this the best one ever."

"Thanks, Mom."

We hugged and she went to the front door and left, but I was still standing there holding that photo. And yes, I did have a headache, but I didn't lie down. I went out to the porch and sat there, alone and staring at the photo. Among the kids was a boy. He was standing a few kids away from me. A boy who was about my age and who had a certain kind of smile. In this faded photograph, I couldn't be sure of the color of his hair, but those curls and that grin? I was pretty sure I recognized them.

How did Jake happen to be present in a photo that also included Aunt Eva and Uncle Warren's relative, and *me*.

I understood that I wasn't finished yet with lies and betrayal.

Chapter Sixteen

After Mom left, I sat in a rocker on the porch, the cigar box on my lap, waiting. Foolishly. As if my presence here would somehow attract Jake and Starfish. The afternoon was passing and despite all the craziness, the heartbreak, the drama—I was hungry. My phone was on the table beside me. If Jake had texted me his number as he'd said he'd do, I could call him. Or text him.

I glared at my phone. No way I could text him and tell him to come over with the intent of hurling accusations at him. That felt wrong. Dishonest. I wasn't perfect, but apparently that's where I drew my personal line at ugliness.

But neither did I want to discuss it with him over the phone. This had to be done face-to-face so I could read his expression, hear the subtext in his words through his eyes and observe his body language.

So, in person, then.

But he was involved, for sure. He was connected to Charles Grimes and Beach Heart in some way—and he'd known . . .something. I didn't know exactly what he knew, but he'd befriended me, asking questions as if he didn't already have the answers. And he'd kept those answers to himself.

More secrets and lies.

But this time, I was gonna know. One way or another.

Jake and I must have this conversation. If my suspicions were right, then he and I were finished. I couldn't be friends with someone who'd wormed their way into my life and abuse my trust.

Jake and Starfish always took their evening walk during the late afternoon or early evening. I'd watch for them. I'd grill him and hope I was mistaken about him being in the photograph.

But adding in the caginess of Mr. Smithson, and his failure to return my calls, I wasn't hopeful about a simple explanation solving the problem.

I practiced what I'd say to Jake. I ate supper. I paced a lot. And somewhere in the midst of all that my phone rang. And I knew it was him.

But it wasn't. It was Maia.

She said, "I haven't felt easy in my mind since I left you this morning. Are you okay?"

My first impulse was to start blurting out

everything that was wrong, but Maia wouldn't understand the issue with Jake, not without explanations, and I didn't want to go through all that in response to her simple, kind question. I answered as if we were only discussing what she knew about—the birth certificate and my mom.

"I'm okay, Maia. Mom came and we talked it through. I think my family made questionable choices, but what was done was done with love and good intent. So not great, but understandable, and it did help talking to my mother about it."

"I'm so glad. Goodness, you've had quite a day today and it's still afternoon."

"Thank you, Maia, for your thoughtfulness in coming here this morning to share the information with me. I appreciate that." I laughed softly. "Risky though. You took a chance with involving yourself in something potentially unpleasant."

"I disagree. In the short time that we've known each other I've had the chance to see your strength. Even from the little you've shared of your past troubles, I admire that you're still standing and still trying, and always demonstrate impeccable self-control even when I know you're churning inside. But it does make a difference *where* one hears icky stuff. That should always be in the place where one feels most grounded." After a short pause, she asked, "So I'll see you Monday morning?"

I smiled. "Yes, ma'am. I'll be there."

"Excellent."

We disconnected.

Icky stuff? Yes, indeed. Maia had hit that right on the noggin.

ଓ୫୬ ୨୦

After Maia's call, I went out to the crossover and stood at the end, leaning against the railing. I scanned the beach up and down and saw no sign of Jake and Starfish. Not even Dylan was out. A couple passed by arm-in-arm and ignored me. An older woman with a pail was combing the beach for shells. She caught sight of me and gave a wave, which I returned with a smile, hoping my annoyance with Jake didn't show in my face.

I checked my phone. Jake hadn't texted. I had no number to call even if I wanted to.

As the evening light began to diminish and color was appearing in the sky, I began to feel foolish.

Jake had been here earlier—in that weird, awful space of time between Maia's visit and Mom's arrival—and I'd been quite unpleasant. And *that* was before I'd seen his likeness in the photograph.

Now, when I truly needed to see him and speak with him. Where was he?

ଔଊ

Sunday was a new day and meant new guests. I should've been curious about them, but after what had happened on Friday with my mother, and then seeing the photo of Jake with the older man I believed Aunt Eva had left Beach Heart to….

If that young boy was indeed Jake….

If I was correct about the man….

Still no return call from Smithson either. Smithson, I believed, would be able to answer all my questions if I could just get him to talk.

My head ached. I was all the more suspicious of him since Jake had vanished.

The guy who was always showing up with a smile, had been missing since Saturday morning.

Whoa, Emma. I shook myself. Barely twenty-four hours since he'd been standing here on my porch. I shook myself. *Get real, Emma. Just because you want to hash something out with someone doesn't mean they'll instantly appear.*

In fact, while there was much to be said for a cooler, subtler touch. I wanted the truth. Not to display my hurt, my pain. That thing with my mother and my great-aunt was mine. It had nothing to do with Jake. Jake was only involved because of his connection to Beach Heart and me via him being in that photo with my uncle's relative. Almost certainly the heir.

What did that mean? Did it involve Jake? Coincidence was seldom truly coincidental.

And yet, the big, scary, gnarly thing of my birth certificates had been upsetting and hurtful, but not as ugly as I'd expected. On the other hand, it was likely to be quite inconvenient for me. At some point, I must get it sorted out. All these databases were online now. Processes were stricter in recent years. What if I needed to renew my passport? Register a new car or something? Might not be a problem. But if it might be, I preferred to know ahead of time. In fact, it occurred to me, perhaps I should consult an attorney about this first . . . and while I was musing about all that and trying not to go off the deep end and chase Jake down to demand the truth from him, I heard a car arrive and vague noises coming from next door. The new guests.

There was still no text from Jake on my phone.

Maia had said I always seemed calm on the outside. I wished I could feel that way inside, too.

Finally, with the photo in an envelope and tucked into a book to protect it, I left via my front door, noted several cars now parked in our lot, and walked down the road toward the yellow house. The whole way along, I was speaking aloud, practicing what I'd say to him.

The yellow house was tall, multilevel, but narrower than Beach Heart and not a duplex. There were no cars parked under or around the house. By the time I climbed the steps to the door to knock on it, I knew no one was home. Star must be gone, too, because I knocked and rang the bell repeatedly, and heard not a single bark. I sidled up to the windows I could reach and peeked in. There were furnishings, yes, but the house had a distinctly vacant feel.

Could this be the wrong yellow house? I scanned the street. It was the only yellow house in the direction Jake had indicated.

Might he be out of town? Or could he have gotten wind that I was suspicious and left to avoid me?

He couldn't know about the photo because only I knew that. But he might know that I'd called Mr. Smithson. Especially if both of them were involved . . . in whatever was going on.

So I was back to waiting. One more day. If he didn't show up before I left for work tomorrow morning, I would go to Mr. Smithson's office again in the afternoon. And if Mr. Smithson wasn't in or refused to answer my questions? Well, then . . . I didn't know what I'd do, but I'd figure it out. I wouldn't let this pass. No more secrets.

ଔଓ

On Monday morning Maia arrived at the gallery ahead of me. She greeted me with a smile, and we walked in together.

"All's well?" she asked.

"Yes," I answered, then added half-under my

breath, "At least I think so."

I hung my extra clothing in the coat closet and dropped my tote off in Maia's office. This was feeling nicely routine not having to second guess every little action.

"What's that?"

I turned to face her. "What's what?"

"What might *not* be okay?"

"Nothing that will interfere with work."

Maia pulled out a chair. "Have a seat. Let's chat over morning cocoa."

"Cocoa?"

"Yes, if you don't mind."

"Cocoa's good," I said. "Don't we need to unlock the front door?"

"Thirty minutes late won't hurt anyone."

Okay, I thought, and I sat.

She said, "In fact, thirty minutes of cocoa might do us both a world of good."

"It might." I didn't know quite what to think of this.

She had the milk heated in a jiffy, poured it into the mugs and brought a bag of marshmallows with her back to the table. She sat with a soft sigh.

She stirred the cocoa, saying,. "You can tell

me it's none of my business, but when my other friends keep things in, they bottle it up and stew over it and get into knots over things that aren't actually that complicated. Talking things out—airing them out, so to speak, with an objective party, can make all the difference."

Other friends. She'd said *other* to me. *Other friends*. She considered me a friend. That's why she'd come to my home to speak with me on Saturday morning. Not just feeling an obligation as an employer. Or a way to prevent unpleasant emotional scenes from happening in the workplace. Friend. My heart warmed.

I was tempted to blurt it all out. She'd never discussed other people with me. She wasn't a gossip. I didn't want her to see me that way either.

She waited while I sorted out my thoughts.

"Something we haven't talked about . . . I didn't tell you how I came to be here—rather *back* in Emerald Isle—did I?"

"You said it was your great aunt's house and it was given to you."

"Yes, but she passed about ten years ago. When she died, she left the beach house to a distant relative, a man related to her deceased husband." I shrugged. “None of us knew those folks, but as far as I was concerned, it was her right to leave it where she would.”

“Of course.”

“At the time, I was married—happily—and busy with my husband and stepson. Back then, before everything went wrong . . .” I went silent for a moment and breathed. “He passed three months ago after a long illness—a form of dementia—and I had to sell our home to cover the bills. I was moving out on the very day that I was notified that the owner of Beach Heart was transferring ownership to me. A stranger. To me.” I fell silent again.

“Wow,” Maia said. “Just out of the blue?”

“Yes. Exactly. When I met with the attorney—the same attorney who’d handled my aunt’s business—he said that the owner was in poor health and resolving estate issues and wanted to divest himself of the property.”

“Wow, again.”

“I wanted to thank him. To ask why. But the attorney said the owner didn’t want to talk to anyone outside of his immediate family due to his health. I should respect that, right?” I shrugged.

"So I tried. But then yesterday, after the discussion with my mom—the discussion driven by the birth certificate you brought me—she saw an old photo among the others my great-aunt had kept for me, and recognized the man in the photo as a relative of my uncle's and . . . I'm sorry. This feels ridiculously convoluted to explain aloud."

"Convoluted maybe, but I think I get it. Go on."

"I was maybe four years old in the photograph and there were other children in it. One of them looked familiar. You see, there's a very friendly man, a neighbor I met after coming home to Beach Heart. I think he's one of those kids."

"You suspect that the neighbor who befriended you is in that photo as a child and possibly connected to the deceased uncle's relative who initially inherited Beach Heart? That he knows about you and Beach Heart—the backstory, so to speak?"

"Yes." I shook my head. "And he hasn't said a word about it. He asks questions as if we're just meeting. As if he's a friend."

"And what's his purpose? To do what?"

I gave a grateful sigh. "Yes. That's the

question. Aside from the secrecy and befriending me under false pretenses, he's been watching me . . . That sounds strange, doesn't it? What if this is some kind of scheme?"

"Which upsets you more?"

"Pardon?"

"The possible loss of trust in someone—this man you thought was a friend. Or that someone might try to take Beach Heart from you?"

"Oh." I tried to gather my words. "So maybe he's trying to get Beach Heart back?" My voice was rising along with a sense of horror. "No, that would be truly evil. I don't believe Jake is evil."

"Why else would he be spying on you?"

"Spying?" I grimaced. "Watching, maybe. He shows up outside my house every day. Usually twice a day. Walking his dog on the beach." My voice trailed off. "That said, when he first started showing up, I wondered if he was stalking me." I shook my head. "No. He and his dog aren't like that. As for his intention, I don't know, do I? I tried to contact him. He wasn't home."

She shrugged. "Have you called him?"

"I don't have his number. He was supposed to text it to me, but he hasn't."

"Then don't worry about it for now. You need to ask him. See what he says. There might be a simple explanation."

Perhaps I looked doubtful because she added, "Talking to your mom helped with the other problem, right?"

I nodded.

"Then don't look for trouble before it arrives. Stay ready for an on-point talk with your neighbor but getting worked up ahead of time without all the info is a waste of life and breath and energy. You seem to want to trust this man. Give him the benefit of the doubt until you know more. There may be a reasonable explanation. Either a misunderstanding or more secrets. No one deserves to be lied to, and I'd be very concerned about that. But remember, Emma, not all secrets are evil. Some are meant to be helpful."

☙❧

Maia was right. I knew it. Don't assume trouble. Don't make assumptions without the facts. That said, I disagreed about the secrets part.

Secrets could harm. *Had* harmed. One might

hope that the risk of harm was less than the potential good done by withholding information, but since the information was usually being withheld from the person who had a right to hear it. Well, it was hard for me to justify how one person could make that kind of huge decision for the person who wasn't in the know.

I tried to put my anxiety aside and focused on what Maia was teaching me about the gallery business. She'd handed me a notebook full of pages in thin plastic sheet protectors.

"There's a section for general vendors, a section for the local and regional artists who do business with us, and also information about our sister gallery in Charleston. Some time back, the Charleston group was sold and operated independently, but this past year, we brought them back into the fold. It gives us extra inventory opportunities, and more customer reach, without physically expanding the stores." She gestured toward the breakroom. "Make yourself comfortable and take some time to go through the book and just listen for the bell."

"Delighted," I said. And meant it.

Maia smiled, adding, "If you need me, raise

your voice and I'll come out immediately. Seriously. It doesn't have to be an actual emergency. Just if you feel uncomfortable or aren't sure of an answer, start speaking more loudly and I'll come."

"Got it."

Actually, I was eager to start going through the vendor book. I knew much of it would be dry and routine, but I was very interested in the artwork and the regional artists who contributed to what was displayed on the walls here, as well as the sculptures and pottery on the shelves, and the floor displays like my heron family.

I wanted that added color of history and description. Almost like a hunger.

Maia left the office door slightly cracked open, maybe to reduce distraction and give her some privacy, but enough space for her to hear me if I did need help.

Twice the bell clanged above the door. Each time it was someone who said they were *just looking*. After greeting them and encouraging them to take their time and saying I'd be happy to help if they had questions, I stayed at the counter and brought the book I was studying *to* the counter and sat on a stool to read it so I wouldn't seem odd hanging back in the breakroom while the customer browsed.

The second customer ended up purchasing a ceramic vase with shells imprinted in the clay. The glaze was a swirly green and blue.

"It's lovely," I said.

She smiled. "A housewarming gift for my friend."

"A fortunate friend," I said as she handed me her credit card.

Some of the items in the shop were owned by the shop, and others were sold much like a consignment. I remembered to check the sticker on the base of the vase and record the numbers printed there. So far, so good.

I followed what I'd seen Maia do with credit card sales, then wrapped the vase carefully. I'd had plenty of experience with that from the shopper's side of the sales counter. When we were done, I thanked her and she thanked me, and she left.

Whew. An easy one. I hadn't had to bother Maia.

I was reading now about Anna Barbour, a local painter who specialized in beach scenes. It said she taught classes, too. I glanced up at the colorful set hanging on these very walls and wondered how it felt to be able to apply paint to canvas and yield these beautiful results. Long, long ago, I'd tried drawing and painting before deciding my talents didn't reside there, and I shifted my focus solely to the historical study of art. If I ever met Anna Barbour, which I supposed I might since she was local and her artwork was for sale here, I'd look forward to asking her.

"Emma?"

I jumped a mile.

"It's after twelve."

"Already?" I glanced at the time on my phone. *12:15*.

"I'm happy to stay while you get lunch?"

"I brought today. Ate it in the office. You're probably hungry and ready to get some lunch yourself."

I slipped off the high stool and closed the binder. "I guess I got lost in a good book." I smiled and offered it back to her.

"You did well today. When those customers stopped by, I listened in case you needed assistance, and clearly you didn't. We should chat soon about some of the more challenging opportunities customers can surprise us with and how we've dealt with them in the past. Are you able to come in mornings again this week?"

I nodded. "I can also stay later if you need me to."

She handed me an envelope.

"No more birth certificates, right?" It was a weak jest, but I was trying.

She shook her head. "No, ma'am. This is your paycheck for last week. We pay every other Monday for the prior two weeks."

"Oh." I held the envelope in my hand, but didn't open it.

Maia smiled. "For now, though, go find yourself some lunch. And don't be discouraged that the check isn't all that much yet. If this keeps going well, I foresee a pay raise in the near future."

I took my check, the envelope still unopened, and gathered my tote bag and went out the back door. I put them in the car, but I needed somehow to experience this feeling of goodness. The check would be small. I already had an idea of how much the take-home would be, but—oh, my, suddenly it felt so real. Like a tremendous step forward.

I felt rather floaty. Like I was walking on clouds, some might say. Instead of getting into the car, I headed for the boardwalk, not yet ready to relinquish this feeling to the practicality of dealing with the drive home.

Later, I'd call Mom and we could talk. I'd stick to telling her about the job and not mention my worries about Jake and all that. Not until I knew more. For now, I wished there was someone near that I trusted enough to share this kind of personal triumph with. And that made me think of Jake again.

We'd already discussed so much about this job and my fears and my hopes, and all the while he'd been . . . He'd been doing what? In some way, he'd been deceiving me.

It hurt, and my anger tried to return. I pushed it back.

I leaned against the railing and looked across the water at the view, including the large pristine-looking boats. *Hmm*. Was *boats* the right word? Or *watercraft*? Or? I didn't know, but that would be one more fun thing to learn. Gregory felt nearby. My eyes stung. He hadn't been much for the beach, but for boats like those? Yeah, I could see him wanting to go aboard and check them out. He'd been a traveler at heart, and he enjoyed nice things, including fine art and sculpture, but we shared a curiosity about all sorts of things. Until it had gone wrong. Until my instincts *told* me, warned me *something* was *wrong*. It always came back to Gregory being sick and I should've recognized it sooner. I should've insisted, should've acted. The *should'ves* abounded, but I couldn't fix any of them.

As the soft breeze brushed my hair, I closed my eyes and sent him one more silent *I'm sorry*. I knew Gregory forgave me. I knew that if he was once again the man I married and here to tell me, he would take the blame on himself and ask *me* to forgive *him*.

But Macon. The problem between us was still out there undealt with.

It bothered me. I had to believe it bothered him, too. And my instincts about Jake and the return of Beach Heart, my suspicions… Were they the real thing? Or just unnecessary angst born of this habit of anxiety I now carried around with me everywhere? It tainted things, including my judgment. But if I dismissed it without looking into it, was that the same as what I'd done before? Like when I'd wasted all that time spying on Gregory without confronting him and forcing the issue?

My phone rang. When I saw the name on the screen, I fumbled to answer it.

"Mr. Smithson?"

"Yes. I got your message. Sorry I was unable to return your call."

"I would very much like to meet my benefactor. You already know that, of course. I need to speak with him, to thank him." I wouldn't mention that I also had questions for him.

"Ms. Dance . . ."

"Please call me Emma."

"Emma, then. That would be Charles Grimes, as you know, but he is very old and very frail and now . . . I don't believe that meeting him is possible. His daughter has been making the decisions about his properties in recent months. It was decided between them to transfer Beach Heart to you."

"Can I thank his daughter, then?"

"I am very sorry to say that she lost her son Saturday evening. His health was poor, but no one expected it to happen quite so soon. It has been a shock."

"I am . . .so sorry. Very sorry."

"Yes, it was a blow to the family. He was only forty and always looked so healthy. Some illnesses don't show." There was a pause, and then he added, "They knew he was ill but weren't prepared to lose him so quickly. Very sad."

"I appreciate you telling me this."

"His mother, his family, is grieving now, but if you'd like me to pass your condolences on to her, I'd be happy to do that."

I was stunned. Saddened. Death, unexpected or otherwise . . .

"Yes, please give her my regards and condolences. If you'll pass my information on to her, I promise I won't trouble her further. Let her know that I'd love the opportunity to thank her in person someday. For now, I'd like to send a card. After all, we're almost family, right? Would that be okay?"

After a pause, he said, "Yes, I think so. But send it to my PO box and I'll deliver it to her. Her name is Connie Harris. She lost her husband, John, a couple of years ago, so losing her son, John Jr., is especially hard for her. It's best to contact her via the PO box."

While he was talking, I fumbled in my tote bag, seeking paper and a pen.

I repeated after him, "Harris. Connie. Got it, and thank you," as I wrote *Connie Harris* and the box number. Son about forty . . . Realization hit me with the force of all things ugly and heartbreaking.

"Did they call him John? Or did he go by Jake?"

Mr. Smithson said, "Yes, he did. How'd you know?"

Chapter Seventeen

Mr. Smithson must've hung up. I may have said goodbye, but I remembered nothing after he said the words, *Yes, he did. How'd you know?*

Suddenly, I was on my knees, bent over with my hands against the rough wood of the boardwalk. Someone was touching me. Their hand was on my shoulder, and a voice was asking, "Are you okay? Are you sick?"

The hand was within reach, and I grasped it, nearly blind to the person offering it, but just knowing that I needed to be up and moving. There was something I had to do. But what? My brain was disconnected somehow. The rest of me seemed to be operating without the thinking, reasoning part. I rose to my feet.

The hand tugged me toward a bench. "Sit. I'll call for help."

I grabbed the person's wrist with my own claw. That's how my hand felt. Almost inhuman. Grasping for understanding as my lungs gasped for air.

"No," I said. "No. I'm okay. Better. When I

get my breath, I'll be good."

The face of the hand's owner swam into view. A boy. A teenage boy.

"Want something to drink? Maybe a cup of water?"

Water. It was as if I didn't know the word. Like a word I'd heard but had never experienced and didn't comprehend its meaning.

"Water?" I repeated after him.

"Yes, ma'am. I'll be right back. Stay here."

He dashed into a nearby restaurant.

I stood uneasily, still shaky, but my legs supported me and I felt no pain. Whatever it was that had driven me to my knees a short time before had passed. I was without pain. Or maybe I was numb. Maybe they could be the same thing sometimes.

No car struck me as I crossed the street. No one ran after me to offer further assistance, so I thought I must be looking better and relatively rational even though the world around me looked and felt fuzzy. I walked on wooden legs to the end of the block and then turned and kept going until I reached the small alley where my car was parked. I was surprised to realize I was carrying my tote bag. My keys, too. I climbed into the car, found a partial bottle of water I'd left behind that morning and drank deeply of it. I closed my eyes and breathed, keeping my brain blissfully silent. No thinking allowed. If I allowed myself to consider what had happened, the crash would be inevitable. I needed to get home.

I held the functioning part of myself together because I had to, either by force of will or driven by desperation, much as I had when Gregory was dying. I backed the car out of the parking space and made my way to the highway. I need to get home . . . to Beach Heart . . . before this rigid veneer of control cracked.

ꕥ

When I reached home, I let myself in, dropped my tote in my chair, and stood there.

Now what?

Jake hadn't texted. Jake hadn't been at the yellow house.

I breathed. My lungs hurt.

Jake hadn't looked sick. He'd made that remark about not knowing what the future held or when any of us would move on. I hadn't taken it as referring to life and death, but just . . . moving away.

Jake was kind and funny. Thoughtful.

And his mother was heartbroken.

Poor Starfish.

All those disjointed thoughts and more swirled in my head, and I was still at Beach Heart, but now there was no Jake.

❧

I wandered aimlessly around the house. I continued wandering without knowing why and found myself outside. At the end of the crossover, I paused out of habit and looked up and down the beach because that's what I always did. Soon I was walking on the sand barefoot. When other people came near, I turned my face away because I had no idea what showed there, but I could guess it was unpleasant.

Gregory had died. Once we—his loved ones—had understood what was happening, we had known it was inevitable. Macon had desperately tried to push reality away as if refusing to give in to it would prevent the disease from running its course. For my part, I would do nothing to keep Gregory with us beyond a certain point because he, himself—though he could not express it—would not have wanted that.

Whatever had been wrong with Jake, apparently his outcome had also been inevitable. But I could never in a million years have guessed that by looking at him, by being around him.

I didn't doubt for a moment that his mother was devastated, and I could respect her privacy. Her grieving time. I would send a card to her . . . but not today. Today, I had to find some way to process this and save my sanity.

After Jake and I had walked on the beach beneath the moon and stars, I'd wondered how it would be to kiss him. It was too soon for that. But I'd never even offered him a hug. Even friends could hug.

I wanted to cry, but I didn't know how. I'd lost the knack of tears over the last few years, yet I felt the force of them pushing almost painfully at the backs of my eyes.

When I returned to the house, I told myself I would look for his obituary online.

But I didn't. Instead, I went to the end of the balcony, and regardless of any passersby, I faced the ocean, my eyes fixed on the horizon, and cried. Did I cry as if I hadn't cried for years? Did I cry for Gregory or for Jake? Maybe for Macon and myself. Did it matter? Grief is grief. Some is sharp, some less so, but it all hurts and we all share the pain of it.

I cried on and off the rest of the evening and even woke a few times during the night with tears on my cheeks. Too many years of tears were trying to fall in too few hours.

And it felt long overdue.

ca&so

By morning, I'd mostly stopped crying, but I looked ghastly. Crying jags in one's late thirties left marks that were hard to hide. It was Tuesday, a workday, but I was tempted to call Maia and beg the day off. Instead, I tried to buy myself a little time to right myself by texting her, *Something sad happened. I'll be in but a little late. Will explain when I see you.* If I called her and had to speak the words aloud, I knew the tears would start again—

not good. As for my current state, I could work on the inventory upstairs by myself, and stay away from the public.

Maia responded, *Take the day off if you need to.*

I answered, *No, I'll come in. I'll just be a little delayed.*

❧

I took my time, moving methodically, telling myself to stay calm, that I was in control and that grief was a natural, normal state that should be honored . . . all that usual stuff well-meaning people say in times of loss . . . but my eyes were red, and the lids were swollen. I splashed my face and my eyes with cool water numerous times, but there wasn't much improvement, and then I'd start crying again.

The lack of friends, of a sympathetic someone to discuss such things with, made it harder. A few times I picked up my phone to call my mom. She loved me. She'd want to know, and she'd want to empathize and sympathize but she didn't have the details because I hadn't shared them with her before. Telling her now would require much explanation and bring on more tears. Not her fault. Mine. So I'd have to keep my own counsel for now, and that pain stayed in my heart and the grit that the tears left behind stung my eyes.

Finally ready, I picked up my tote and was walking to the front door when I heard a knock. Not on this door, the streetside door, but behind me, facing the ocean.

No one had knocked on that door since I'd been here. A renter, maybe?

I couldn't go without at least checking, but still, I hesitated.

Nonsense, I thought. I turned, rubbing my eyes again and telling myself not to—that I'd make them even redder than they already were. I returned to the living room. The blinds were open as always and there on the other side of the glass, I saw a familiar face.

Disbelieving, I stared at his smile. At his red hair.

A few feet short of the door, stunned, I stumbled, falling to my knees as I'd done on the boardwalk, but this time I landed better and regained my footing as Jake yelled through the door calling my name.

"Emma? Are you okay?"

I raised my hand as I caught my breath and finally reached the door, but when I opened it, I was without breath or words. I could only reach out and touch his shirt. He was solid. The fabric was real beneath my fingers. Not the stuff of air and imaginings.

He put his hand on my arm as if to catch me if needed. "What's wrong? What happened?"

I shook my head, confused. "Mr. Smithson called . . ." I shook my head again and re-sorted my words. "You didn't text. You weren't home." Panic was welling up in me. I slapped his shirt, angry, but reassured that he was solid and warm. I yelled, "You were in that photo, weren't you? That was you." Then I closed my eyes for a long moment before resuming in a more rational voice, saying, "When you didn't text me your phone number, I went to the yellow house. No one was there. No one answered the door."

"No, I wasn't there. After I left you, I got a call and—"

I interrupted. "I got a call too—yesterday afternoon—from my aunt's attorney, Alan

Smithson. The same attorney who conveyed Beach Heart to me. He said you were—" My voice dropped to a whisper, and Jake's expression changed.

He asked, "Alan Smithson?"

"He said . . ." I stopped again and pressed my hand to my forehead. "How did your name happen to come from his lips, Jake? Do you know him? Why did he tell me you'd died?"

"He told you . . ." He shook his head. "I'm sorry. You need to explain."

"No, *you* need to explain, Jake. *You*. I thought you were my friend. Were you spying on me? Was Mr. Smithson participating in some sort of ruse? Why else would he tell me that?"

"Calm down, Emma. Please." He pressed his fingers against his temples, as if his head ached. "I'm not sure how much more I can take today. After yesterday and today . . ."

And I saw in his eyes that he meant it. I saw that same lankness, the drained look I'd seen in the mirror looking back at me when I'd first arrived here.

"Sit down, Jake. I'll get you some tea and then you can explain."

"I can't stay. I'm sorry. I have to get back."

"Get back? Not yet. First, you sit. I don't want secrets, and I don't want lies. Tell me the truth, Jake. This is your only chance. Sit and I'll be right back."

Frustrated, I went to fetch the tea. Frustrated, yes, and angry at myself for being a fool who seemed to harbor hope that this would come out okay, that an explanation would make everything right.

Well, isn't that what it came down to? If I didn't care for what Jake said, then we were done but if Jake collapsed before answering my questions, then I'd never know. And I couldn't abide that.

He was sitting in the rocker. As I handed him his tea, I asked, "Do you want to see the photo?" I crossed my arms and continued standing.

He frowned, saying, "Photo? No. I don't know what photo you're talking about, but it doesn't matter because it's time to clear the air anyway." He shook his head slowly and sighed, setting the glass down on the table between us.

"I was here because I wanted to see if you'd do okay at Beach Heart . . . if you'd settle in. I wanted to know that we'd made the right choice to give it to you."

Give it to you . . . we'd made the right choice . . . At those words, my knees felt weak. I sat. He didn't seem to notice, lost in his own words.

"Part curiosity too, I guess. I didn't plan to stay around, but I've always enjoyed being at the beach, and then I enjoyed getting to know you and seeing that things were working out well." He paused for a breath, before adding, "I intended to be discreet, then leave quietly and go on with my life." He shrugged. "But I kept returning here." He added softly, "Star likes her walks. You know how she is."

"Being my friend, my neighbor —that was a lie."

"No. There were omissions, yes, given the circumstances. But our friendship is real, I hope."

"Do you? Seriously? Why didn't you tell me you were here representing your family?"

"It seemed better not to. You'd feel watched. Not trusted. Your great-aunt always intended for you to have Beach Heart when the time was right. My grandfather understood that and made sure we all did, too. That—and I'm sorry to say this and maybe this is why I truly didn't want to discuss it with you—but your aunt said that until your husband was out of the picture that Beach Heart should stay with Granddad and our family."

He shut his eyes, and I felt the pain in him when he opened them again. "We . . . I . . . All of us were very sorry for your loss and didn't want to cause you more pain."

"Then why would you disappear and have Mr. Smithson tell me you'd died?" My voice ended that on a sharp upward note that shocked me. I breathed in deeply.

"I think there must be a misunderstanding. Alan is trustworthy."

I started to object, but he raised his hand, saying, "Please Emma. Please let me finish."

I shut my mouth and waited.

"My brother. He was a year older than me, but we are . . . were . . . very close. He had a bad heart. We lost him suddenly on Saturday. I got the call soon after I left you." He pressed his index finger to the bridge of his nose, a gesture of trying to control his emotion. I recognized that, so I didn't interrupt.

“He, uh, went. Just like that. Mom was overwhelmed. His name is John, so I don’t know why Smithson—”

“John Harris, Jr.,” I offered. “Named after your father, Mr. Smithson said.”

“My father, John Harris, Sr., was called Jake. Our parents named my brother after him, his legal name, John, and they named me Jake.”

“I asked Mr. Smithson—” I broke off abruptly as understanding came to me. I lifted my hand as if it would help me sort it out. “Let me try to explain. I’d seen that photograph and I suspected a connection between you and Mr. Grimes, so when Mr. Smithson said Mr. Grimes’s daughter, Connie *Harris*, was instrumental in the decision to give Beach Heart to me, he also mentioned that she was still recovering from the loss of her husband, John. He said their son, John, Jr. had just passed suddenly. My brain made the leap. I asked him if the man who’d died was called Jake.” I reached across and touched Jake’s arm. “I was asking about you. Mr. Smithson must’ve thought I was asking about your father.”

I covered my face with my hands, but then dropped them and reached over to take his hand.

“I’m so sorry, Jake.”

“You couldn’t know.”

“I’m sorry all this came up when you were dealing with losing your brother.”

He shook his head. “It would’ve come up either way sooner or later. How could I tell you about my brother without going into all the rest?”

I took my hand down and watched his face. He was staring straight ahead.

Wanting to comfort him, I said, “I’ve been fascinated by the horizon lately. It’s so perfect. So straight and plain and clear. Too bad life can’t be that way.”

He grimaced and squeezed my hand. “Looks that way, but it’s a cheat. You can never reach it. Every time you think you’re getting close, it’s still beyond you and the water where you are is just as rough and choppy as it was before you spent that time and energy chasing it. That perfect line is an illusion. And it’s unachievable, Emma. Life is messy.”

I said, “What can I do to help you and your family? In any way? Just tell me.”

“Nothing. Not a thing. Just be patient. I have to get back to my mother and grandfather. This is devastating to them. And Star . . . well, with the funeral service coming up, I brought Star back to Emerald Isle to take her to the vet for boarding for the next couple of days. They expect to have an opening later today, so after I drop her off this afternoon, I'll head back to Jacksonville."

"I understand why me attending the funeral might not be the best thing, but I'd like to do something to help. When I'm at work in the mornings, would she be okay alone here?"

"Who?"

"Star. Starfish. Unless you think she's better off at the vet."

"She finds the vet's office stressful, but she'll be okay."

"Then bring her here. She likes me, and being separated from you will be less stressful for her here."

"Are you serious?"

"I am."

"You've never had a dog in your care before, have you?"

I shrugged. "How hard could it be? If you're sure she'll be okay alone here for a few hours each day while I'm a work . . ."

"Absolutely. Put her bed in the sunniest spot and she'll be fine. I recommend you keep her on the leash when you take walks, though." Jake offered a small grin. "After all, you don't have the training I do, and Star does get caught up in her enthusiasms."

His eyes were still sad, but his overall expression seemed a little less strained.

"No worries. We'll manage fine."

He nodded before going on to say, "By the way, Emma, I want to make sure we're all on the same page regarding Beach Heart. I want to be open and upfront about it."

I frowned. "Go ahead."

"We've used the word *give* pretty freely here, but we didn't give Beach Heart to you. Your aunt made it clear that she wanted you to have it when—"

I interrupted, "She didn't like Gregory. She was afraid he'd convince me to sell Beach Heart."

Jake nodded. "I didn't know all the details until recently. But once I did, I knew the house had to come back to you as soon as possible. We all agreed—Mom, John, myself—that it was time to make it right. So, when it comes down to the basic truth, we didn't *give* Beach Heart to you—we just kept it safe for you. I hope you'll believe us and see it that way, too."

Chapter Eighteen

Jake brought Star over from the yellow house, along with her dishes, bed, and assorted toys and treats. He tried to give me quick instructions, but I interrupted. "Give me the name and number of her vet, just in case. Otherwise, we'll be fine for two nights."

He hugged me, and I returned it, enjoying the warmth and sincerity that emanated from him. The timing of the hug felt good, if slightly overdue. Overdue? Maybe, but certainly worth the wait.

He said, "I didn't ask before, but...are you okay? You sound okay but your eyes—" He gestured toward his own eyes. "They look painful."

"I'm fine. *Now.* I was upset over something that ended up not being a thing, and then on top of that I thought you'd died, and I'm more grateful than I can begin to express, truly, that you didn't, but I'm so sorry about your brother and for your family . . ." I made myself stop. I drew in a deep ragged breath and gave him a reassuring smile.

He nodded. "If you're sure."

"I'm sure. Please give my regards to your mother and let her know that when she's ready, I'd love to meet her."

He smiled. "Will do." With a last quick hug, he left.

Star sat at the door. Waiting. Expectant. When the door didn't reopen, she stayed put in front of it, but turned her face toward me, panting, asking a question.

"You'll be visiting me for a few days, Star." I knelt, and she trotted slowly over to let me scratch her ears and neck. "We'll do okay, right?" I smiled, added, "Yes, we're going to do great."

I made it into work several hours late.

When I entered the gallery via the back door and walked inside, Maia was alone and at the counter doing some paperwork.

"Sorry. I'll explain, and I'll stay all afternoon."

"Your eyes . . ."

"Yes, I know. But I'm okay." I rolled my eyes dramatically. "Believe me, it's quite a story. But would you like to get your lunch first? You've been alone here all morning, I can see that."

Maia's expression didn't change much, but I

was good at reading minutia and body language, so I waited while she reached whatever decision she was reaching for. When her decision was made, she smiled and I was relieved.

She said, "I *am* ready for lunch and a break, but I also want to hear this story."

"If it stays quiet," I said, "maybe you can have both at the same time?" I sighed. "I could use some chocolate. Mind if I fix a cup of cocoa?"

"A gal after my own heart."

We talked over lunch in the breakroom. The relief that I felt at being able to share, at how speaking things aloud helped clear my head, encouraged me.

That evening, back home and after Star had been greeted, walked, fed, and then walked again, the two of us settled on the porch and I took out my phone.

I owed Mom a phone call. No, scratch that. I owed us both a long, chewing-over-the-details sort of conversation. And this time, I had *lots* of details to share.

Ꙭ

Star and I did fine that first night. She seemed at home, in fact, and I found an unexpected comfort in having her around. We carried her bed upstairs. *We* because she kept her jaws clamped on one side of it while I gripped the other. It was awkward going up the stairs together like that, but we made it.

The next morning, we started the day extra early in order to get her breakfast in and a quick morning walk done before I left for work. As I picked up my tote and the keys jangled in my hand, she gave me the pity look. I pointed to her bed and said, "Stay." I tried to keep my message clear, but while I was capable of filling food dishes and poop scooping, that was a far cry from knowing how to properly manage a dog.

She looked sad, but she went.

I kept my expression firm as I said, "Good dog." And almost made it to the front door before calling out, "I'll be back as soon as I can."

Her ears perked up and hope lit her eyes. The look in her eyes spoke her feelings, her hope, and they hurt my heart.

Baby steps, I told myself. *You'll learn. And she'll be okay.*

When I made it to Beaufort, and on time, I gave a huge sigh of relief.

It was a good morning at home and at work. Maia laughed when I told her about Star helping me carry her bed up, and during the quiet times, we walked around the gallery as Maia told me all sorts of things about inventory, and ordering product. It was a you-name-it-we-discussed-it kind of time. I felt valued and trusted.

As soon as I returned home in the early afternoon, Star took me out for our walk. She had so much energy stored up from her morning alone, and the absolute thrill that radiated from her, that I'd actually returned and she wouldn't be alone forever and ever, and wouldn't starve. She was very social, and I was pretty sure she didn't have a clear idea about which—loneliness versus starvation—would be worse. For her, neither was acceptable.

Star dashed around, and I struggled to keep up and finally *gave* up and just focused on not getting tangled in her leash. A woman coming our way was also walking her dog, which intrigued not only Star but also the other dog. The woman gave us a wide berth, conspicuously, and with disapproving glares. It was clear that I needed to attend Star's obedience classes, too.

We were wet and sandy. I stopped at the water hose on the crossover to rinse her paws while she tried to capture the errant streams of water in her mouth. I couldn't help laughing, and I don't know which of us was wetter by the time I gave up. I was still laughing as I unleashed her and she ran ahead of me toward the house because it was, after all, suppertime. Star cared about punctuality. When she began barking, I assumed she was telling me to hurry and catch up. And then I saw the man sitting in a rocker in the shade on Aunt Eva's porch.

A grown man. But my stepson for thirteen years. Important years during which he survived teenagerhood and college and started his first job. In a flash of memories, I saw his father's pride in him with each accomplishment, how his father had worried over him during the difficult times—and through it all, I'd been there with them, giving them the best I had to offer. But my best hadn't been enough to help Gregory—not enough to save him and not even to comfort him, especially after he no longer knew me. And my best hadn't been good enough for Macon either. He'd made me feel that failure every day of the past three years, especially during that last, dreadful one.

But here he was. I'd known he'd come to me one day. What I didn't know was whether it would be for healing or to cause more pain.

"Macon."

"Emma."

I said nothing, but stood there waiting. Star had doubled back to me, brushing my legs, and then she approached Macon tentatively, first sniffing around his shoes.

"Your mother told me where you were. She was worried you'd be angry that she did. Don't be, okay?"

"Of course not. I hoped she'd have the opportunity *to* tell you."

"She said you were staying at the beach for a while."

"Did she?"

"Yes, something about a distant relative offering you a place to stay."

Close enough. I nodded.

"It's beautiful out here."

"What about you, Macon? How are you

doing? I've gotten badly needed rest here. I've even found a job."

"And a dog," he said. For the first time, he smiled.

It was a small smile, but I was encouraged.

"Her name is Star. She belongs to a neighbor who needed a place to leave her for a couple of days."

"Nice." He shrugged. "I'm fine. I couldn't rest, you know. Or maybe you didn't know, but I couldn't sleep. Dad did his best to protect his family—especially me—and yet when he needed me, I failed him." He looked aside for a long moment before adding, "I did something, though. It couldn't bring him back, but it helped me not to feel so . . . useless."

That's when I saw he was holding an envelope, a white business envelope like the one Maia had brought me. That old companion, panic, tried to rush in. I breathed deeply to force it away. But seeing the envelope spurred me to say, "You can't know this, but I wrote you. Over and over. In my head and on my computer. But I didn't send them on to you. I hoped that one day, when we were rested and feeling better about things, that we'd have this chance to talk, but I need to know, Macon, are you at peace now? Because honestly, I don't plan to go back to the arguments and blame."

He dropped his head for a moment, looking away from me, and then he faced me again. "Me either. I was never really angry at you . . . or not much, but I did feel helpless. I was frustrated. I wanted you to keep fighting for him. To help me fight for him. But you gave up."

I shook my head. "I understand that you felt that way, but it wasn't how I saw it. Your father deserved better than to have his last months disrupted when nothing could help him. He deserved peace."

Macon nodded and he stood, offering me the envelope.

"What's that?"

"It's for you."

I didn't move to take it from him.

He must've understood that I wasn't ready yet because his hand dropped back to his side.

"I couldn't help Dad, but I did my best to find the people who took advantage of him, cheating him and taking his money when he was clearly unable to make decisions or protect himself."

"How on earth did you . . . How?"

"Without the pressure of taking care of Dad, of worrying over him and whether we were doing the right things, I had time to comb through records and ask questions. I noticed certain patterns, and I confronted those people. For the most part, what they did wasn't strictly illegal, but I had enough proof that making it public would certainly have harmed their reputations in the community. Dad was well loved and respected."

"He was."

"I couldn't get it all back. Will never be able to. I won't tell you who the names of the parties involved because we both need to move on and knowing those names will make that harder for you."

He waited. I realized he was wanting a response.

"If you think it's best not to know, then I'm fine with that." I sighed. "Your father must've known something was wrong before we did because he hid it well. I've often wondered if he may have made some of those bad financial decisions out of a wish to make sure we were provided for . . . and got lost in it."

He nodded. "I wouldn't be surprised. He was that way."

"Yes, he was."

Macon offered the envelope again, saying, "I split what I recovered fifty-fifty. I'm not sure of the legalities, but I think Dad would approve of that. This is your share."

I couldn't bring myself to touch the envelope yet. "Would you like to come in? Maybe have a glass of tea? Tell me what else is going on in your life?"

He smiled again. His eyes were wet. "Sure. That'd be great."

When we walked inside, I said, "Have a seat. Forgive me, but I have must feed Star first. She's been very patient."

From the corner of my eye, I saw Macon place the envelope on the dining room table. I didn't acknowledge it but neither did I tell him to take it back. Maybe telling me what he'd done and sharing what he'd recovered was part of *his* healing.

Star went immediately to eating. The food was gone in the time it took me to pour our glasses of iced tea. To the tune of Star nosing her empty metal food bowl around the kitchen floor like a hockey puck, I carried the glasses over to where Macon was still standing by the sofa.

"Have a seat, Macon, please."

But he didn't. As he accepted the glass from me, he pointed across the room. "Is that the chair from the house?"

"Yes, indeed."

"You brought it here with you?" He frowned slightly, looking a bit uneasy. "Not because of me or our arguments?"

I smiled. "As in holding a grudge? No. But that chair . . . It earned a change of scene, just like we did. We did our best, Macon. Imperfectly, yes, but our best is all anyone can expect of us, including ourselves."

Macon nodded and sat on the beachy sofa.

"Excuse me for just one moment more while I go fetch some cookies? They'll go well with tea, don't you think?"

"Oatmeal raisin?"

"Just like the ones we enjoyed together in better times."

"And will again," he said, "in even better times to come."

ೞ

Jake returned Thursday afternoon. I sat with him on the bench, and noted he looked tired but less stressed.

"Tell me," I said. "I suppose in the greater context of life, this doesn't matter as much as some things, but not knowing . . . well, it bugs me."

We were sitting on our bench on the crossover. This time there was less space between us now, and there would likely be even less in the near future.

I held the group photo so that Jake could see it.

"That's the photo you mentioned?"

"Yes." I pointed at the small boy. "Is this you?"

He held the photograph close, examining it, and then smiled.

"No, that's John." He pointed at the littler kid standing a couple of children away from the one he'd just identified as his older brother. "That's me." He moved his finger along the row of children. "And that's you, right? How old? I'm guessing John was five or six. You and I were maybe four?"

"Probably."

"The man . . . that's my grandfather."

"Charles Grimes?"

"Yes."

"The woman is Eva, my great-aunt." I took the photo back, still examining the faces. "Why don't I remember meeting you when we were children?"

"Because we were so young."

I nodded.

He said, "I have a vague memory of this trip. *Probably* this trip. A bunch of us kids came here with Granddad. Mostly what I remember is that I was afraid of the ocean. The waves were so big and loud, you know? And that's about all I recall of it."

Something nibbled at the back of my mind, and I sat silently, waiting for it to speak. A small boy sitting out of reach of the water. Another boy, bolder, rushing into the water. The other kids, including me, had joined him in playing tag with the waves. If that memory was true . . . then the older boy must've been John. And he was gone now.

"I know I've already said how sorry I am about your brother. I wish I had better words."

“Words often fail, but kindness is always welcome.” He broke off, and again we sat quietly for a minute before he said, “We’ll miss him.”

I took his hand and gave it a squeeze.

“How about a change of subject?”

“Sure.”

“What about that other thing that you don’t want to discuss, Jake? Why the secrecy?”

“The job?” He squinted at the horizon, as if deep in thought. “Anonymity,” he said.

“What?”

“That’s the answer to the question of why.” He turned his face away, but I knew he was watching me from the corner of his eye. “I wanted you to get to know me before you made any judgments based on what I do to earn a living.”

“Okay.” A swift series of job options—jobs that might be questionable—raced through my mind. “I guess I can respect that as neighbor-friends. I think we’re more than that now—after all, I took care of your dog.”

Star glanced up, apparently understanding that last word, and made a snuffling noise before settling back into her nap.

“No more secrets, Jake.”

"Actually," he said, "that reminds me. I think I figured out why Star was so taken with you from the first—beginning with that day on the beach when she greeted you."

"Tackled me."

"She's doing better now, right?"

"She is. The training is paying off."

"For both of us," he said.

I reached down to briefly touch the top of her head. "So why did she greet me so enthusiastically?"

"It's your scent."

I had a moment of *Hmm.* I tried to keep my tone chatty, but I couldn't help a little snark. "I smell good? To a dog? Is that what you're saying? Because that's actually rather —"

He interrupted, laughing. "No. It's because goldens have amazing noses. You were fresh from Beach Heart. Had been here overnight." He smiled. "We've spent a lot of time here at this house over the last few years, and Star's been around for two of them. I think she caught the scent of a place she loved—a smell that said *home* and *family* to her—and when she caught that scent on you as the morning breeze was moving down the strand, you became part of it . . . her home. Her family."

I looked down. Star was watching us. Understanding these words, too? Not likely. Sensing the general feeling of affection that surrounded us? Yes, I thought that was probably true.

He cleared his throat, then continued, sounding a bit more formal. "As for the other question—that of my employment. While I didn't want to just come out and tell you when we were first getting to know each other, it also wasn't much of a secret. It's been right in front of you the whole time you've been here."

This felt like another dodge. I was ready to unleash my annoyance on him in a real way when he stood.

With a certain formality, he said, "Will you come with me, Emma?" And he offered his hand.

I stood, clasping his hand in mine. "Lead the way."

He did. He took my hand and led me toward the house, and Star followed us.

Together, we crossed the threshold into Beach Heart. I couldn't help but think of Jake, of his brother, his mom, and other relations who'd walked this same way, had stayed at Beach Heart during the years that I was with Gregory.

What would Aunt Eva think? Did she have a rule to cover this? I couldn't think of one. But questions? Yes, I had a few. I stopped just inside to ask them.

"Did y'all keep it as a rental? I mean, just using it here and there for vacations and getaways?"

"Yes."

"What about the place you live now? The yellow house?"

"Another rental the family owns. I like the beach. Star likes the beach. But I also wanted to be sure you were comfortable at Beach Heart, so I came for an extended visit." He faced me squarely. "I don't know all that you went through during your husband's illness, but I know some of it and that it was hard. I wanted to be nearby in case you ran into trouble." He flushed a little. "I came acting out of heart . . . or maybe instinct. I didn't think it through, or I would've realized how tricky it was gonna be if I got too close to you."

"If?"

He shrugged. "Yes. I truly didn't want to disturb you. Just to be another person on the beach. Star changed that. There was that one moment on the beach when you looked at me and I had a sudden shock. I thought you might have recognized me from more than thirty years ago. Crazy, right? And when it turned out you hadn't, I knew I should leave, but I didn't. I couldn't."

"I see." I nodded, thinking of what he'd told me, and I realized I was still holding his hand. I squeezed it gently. "Okay, then. What's the big mystery about the job?"

He pulled me past the fireplace, and we stopped at the built-in bookcase next to it. The top of the bookcase was about chest high and had a small stack of books on it, along with puzzles and games. There were more books and puzzles on the lower shelves.

Jake released my hand and reached for a jigsaw puzzle box. I'd seen it, of course, in a general sense, but hadn't paid attention to it.

Jake passed me the box. The picture showed a beach, waves, a boy, and a dog. A golden, in fact.

The two were running together in the edge of the waves. It was more painterly than photographic, and the joy was unmistakable. The puzzle pieces were larger than an adult puzzle, and the box indicated that it was intended for children.

I looked at him, not knowing the right question to ask.

He nodded, "It's mine. My picture."

"It's beautiful." I shook my head. "I still don't understand. Do you create art for jigsaw puzzles?"

I'd been told many times through the years that my face showed everything I was thinking, and I suppose it was showing lots of confusion now because Jake said, "You look puzzled," and he laughed. I felt the goodwill in his laughter as he reached back toward the bookcase, sorting through the stack of books on that top shelf. He chose a thin one that was maybe a foot square. This time, instead of handing it to me, he held it up in front of himself, as if displaying it for me to see.

"A children's book." I took it from his hands and read the text below the title, "Written and Illustrated by Jake Harris." Flashing him another quick glance, I returned my attention to the book, opening the cover and flipping through the pages.

"A picture book." I thumbed through the pages again. "These are beautiful illustrations, Jake."

"I started as an illustrator for children's books—books written by others—and then took the plunge myself. There are several out now. Each book is available in book form, as a puzzle—a version for adults and a version sized for kids—and also as a coloring book for all ages." He sounded so pleased, so proud in a vulnerable, endearing way. "I wanted to offer a product that could be shared across generations, to bring them together in the activities."

I said softly, "In one sense, it's hard to imagine you creating this beautiful art for children . . . and yet, it seems altogether right and not surprising at all." I watched his face and saw he was pleased. "I'm guessing that the book you gave to Dylan's grandmother was one of yours?"

He nodded.

"What are you working on now?"

"A new project," he said. "I'd just started the illustrations when John passed. I'm ready to get back to work. The books thus far have been about a boy and his dog. This time, though—and please give me your honest feedback—I'm thinking the boy and the dog need a friend. Maybe a girl? Maybe one who sometimes twirls on the beach?"

I smiled and nodded. "And don't forget the architect. You can't leave him out. Every good beach book with sand and waves should also have a sandcastle of dreams and a child who, regardless of age, not only dreams up the potential, and maybe even a little magic, and makes it happen."

Epilogue

I'd been living at Beach Heart for over a month and working for Maia at Front Street Gallery in Beaufort for just over two weeks. It seemed longer than that, yet also shorter at the same time. But even if time itself seemed fuzzy, we—including the world, generally—had moved from March into April, and in the northern hemisphere spring was now an actual fact.

The energy of all living things was stirring, with us or without us. The streets of Beaufort, especially on the weekends, were showing it too, in the increase in flowers, birds, and all sorts of visitors. And I loved being part of it.

A month of recovery was behind me. I wasn't perfect—and never would be, of course—but I was better. So much better.

This morning, I left for work early, and when I arrived at the gallery, instead of going inside, I walked from the alley around to Front Street and crossed over to the park. I carried a cup of coffee in one hand and a bag of sweet rolls in the other. It was a mini celebration. I sat on the bench in the waterfront park in Beaufort. The boardwalk and the sparkling water were on one side of me, and Front Street and the gallery were on the other side. No crashing waves here. But Beaufort had its own special charms, and among them was a sense of order and peace. Per Maia, as the weather warmed into summer that peace would become hectic.

I was interested in seeing what a hectic peace was all about, but also, I loved both the magnificence of the ocean and the beauty of Front Street and the harbor, and I'd decided that I didn't have to choose between them. Not yet. If I could manage it, I'd have, and enjoy, them both.

Hearing my name called from across the street, I turned to see Maia standing at the open door to the gallery. She waved, but then stepped out, letting the door shut behind her. The sign was still turned to Closed, though obviously the door was no longer locked. I glanced at my watch. It was almost time to open anyway.

She crossed the street, smiling, and I greeted her. I reached beside me and picked up the bag.

"There's one in here for you," I said. "I'd expected to give it to you inside, so you can eat here or wait. It's time to open the shop, isn't it?"

"It is." She sat and peeked in the bag. "Oh, that smells good. And there's napkins, too. We can watch the door from here just fine." She used the napkin to grab a sweet roll and pull it out and take a bite. She closed her eyes. "Yum. How did you know I needed a little extra something this morning?"

"Can't take any credit for that. For me, it's a celebration."

"Oh? I love celebrations. To what event or triumph do we owe this treat?"

"Life. My neighbor-friend and I are getting friendlier all the time. Not too fast, though. I need time to be me. Does that sound awful?"

"Not at all."

"But he's arranged a dinner with his mom and other family to sort of complete the circle of my aunt entrusting Beach Heart to Charles Grimes and them returning it to me. I'm hoping Mr. Grimes will be well enough for me to meet him."

"Sounds wonderful for all concerned."

I nodded. "And Macon…he gave me a gift. A special gift. He doesn't know how important… what a difference it has made. It helped me clear up the rest of the debt that I was left with when

Gregory died, so that's taken a lot of pressure off me. It has given me some breathing room about other choices I want to make for my future."

She looked alarmed. "You aren't leaving, I hope?"

Smiling, I shook my head. "Not at all. I can stay and enjoy staying for now. Maybe for a long time."

"I'm very glad to hear that."

I heard the note in her voice that told me she wasn't finished speaking. She reminded me of Aunt Eva pausing midsentence to gather her words, so I waited.

"I need someone to train for an assistant manager role. To start training now because we are already into April and the season will be on us in earnest very soon. Would you be interested? It would be a full-time role."

For a moment, I shrank inside. Commitment? Fear of failure?

"I think you could do the job brilliantly, Emma, given a little more training and time. Right from the first, I noted your ability to watch and listen, to anticipate what the speaker is interested in. You are very intuitive. Refine that, and I think you can turn it into a superpower. Perfect for the work we do at the gallery."

Aunt Eva's voice, as whispery as the wind in the eaves, came back to me, telling me to just live and not always try to anticipate. To be myself and trust my gut.

"A superpower?"

"Why not? Superpowers can come in all sorts of talents and skills."

"But is it enough? To be able to take on the responsibilities you have in mind?"

"I'll still be in charge and manage the gallery overall, and between the seasonal part-timers and myself, we'll also cover the gallery so that you aren't working round the clock. I promise you that."

I shook my head, bemused, and almost laughed. Maia noticed and her expression was questioning. I said, "I came to Emerald Isle to be alone. To hide while I recovered. But you think human interaction may be my superpower?" I laughed, but softly. "You think I could be good at managing a retail business."

She nodded. "I do."

"I've been told by people close to me that I

don't hide very well."

"Because you're a people person."

"Am I?"

"Trust me on this for now. Your aunt's house in Emerald Isle got you started on that recovery. I suspect you need people around to help you complete it."

"You truly think I could do this?"

"I've told you I have excellent instincts." She crumpled the napkin. "*But* I am concerned about that drive you make every day. Maybe it's not so bad when you're only working half days and you can still get plenty of beach time, but as a fulltime job?"

"Actually . . ." I breathed. "I'm considering renting out the sunset side of Beach Heart to guests to boost the income I receive from the house. Macon's gift helped, but I need to build up my financial reserves to keep Beach Heart and live a life, too. Maybe I could rent a small apartment in Beaufort for a while? I thought you might have advice about that since you've lived in this area for a while. Nothing expensive, of course. I only need a couple of rooms and a small kitchen." I shrugged. "I've been thinking about it for a couple of days, and after hearing what you've just said—me, being local, would certainly make it all more convenient."

"What about the beach?"

"I love the beach. My heart is in sync with the ocean. But I'm also finding Beaufort a lovely place to be. I'll be honest, Maia. I don't know how it will end up, but for now, if I'm careful about expenses, I may be able to keep Beach Heart and enjoy Beaufort, too."

Maia said, "I'll ask around. Are you needing furnished or not?"

"I can be flexible. I have some furnishings stored over in Raleigh and can bring what I need from there. Other than that…" I grinned and shrugged. "I have a chair."

"A chair?" she asked, with a puzzled look.

Nodding, I said, "Yes, it travels with me, apparently."

Maia shook her head, but laughed. "Well, it's a start."

"Indeed, it is."

"Well, upfront I'll say that everything is expensive and anything that's not, is hard to find or unlivable. But I know people. I'll ask around."

For the briefest of moments, Maia's gaze settled on the gallery. I caught her look and realized she was staring up at the gallery's second floor. Might mean nothing. Maybe it was just where her gaze happened to settle. Besides, that space would need a lot of renovation and updating to make it livable and, more than that, I wasn't sure how I'd feel about living *at* work, so to speak.

Maia looked down at her skirt and brushed away an almost invisible crumb. She said, "In the meantime, none of us can be certain where we'll be a week or a month from now. That's simple reality. All I need to know is whether you are *expecting* to be here through say…September or October."

Expecting…. Intuitive? Was that one of my talents? Was noticing details a superpower? Maybe. But I understood her concern without her saying it out loud. Just because I knew. But I kept my face blank so she could deliver the news.

"Speaking of expecting—that's me." She smiled, her cheeks suddenly flushed. "First time." She waved her hands in the air in a celebratory way.

"Congratulations." I leaned over and hugged

her, careful of my coffee and sugary fingers. "That's absolutely amazing."

"Of course, I'll be fine for many months yet, but pregnancies can be unpredictable, or so I hear. My sister had no issues whatsoever with hers so I hope for the same, *but*"—Maia shrugged— "my sister was younger when she had her babies. My husband is worried that I'll overdo. I've promised him that I'll make sure that doesn't happen. I've been bragging on you—in truth—but also to reassure him." Her tone turned serious. She rested her hand on mine. "But this is *your* life. Your future. Give this serious thought and let me know. If it's not what you want, I'll totally understand, but I need you to be honest with me." She continued softly, "From all that you've said, returning to Beach Heart was a dream you never thought possible. And while Beaufort and town living might have its appeal just now, you've only been coming here for two weeks. Beach Heart was a dream come true for you. It's not an opportunity you should walk away from lightly."

Leaves rustled in the tree branches overhead. The boughs that were so kindly providing us shade were part of the scents and sounds of the harbor and the restaurants around the park. I felt a sense of place—and the gallery gave me a sense of purpose.

"Maia, on a day when I was out of hope—hopeless for the present and for the future—I was given the chance to go back to the place where I was happiest." I watched the dappled shade create patterns on the bricks as the breeze stirred the branches. "The thing is, though—you can't go back. Time doesn't work that way."

I took a breath, then continued. "The people you loved, the person you were—none of those folks are there. It's . . . lonely." I shook my head. "I've learned I don't need to go back to find happiness. The memories, the joys are always with me." I pressed my hand to my chest. "Here in my heart and in my mind." I paused. "Don't get me wrong. I love the ocean. I love Beach Heart. And my new friends? Yes, they are keepers. Including you, Maia, regardless of how the job goes. But I think I've figured out that it isn't just any one thing."

"Pardon?"

"Happiness. Hope. Joy. The things worth having don't come in only one way, or in any one package. We have many parts to our natures. For me, I've decided I don't have to settle for one thing to find happiness. I can reach for both the ocean *and* Beaufort. And somewhere down the road, it may be something else altogether."

I smiled and picked up the bag with the last sweet roll wrapped and waiting for later. "I intend to have my cake and eat it too. And if that doesn't work out? Well, I'm not worried."

Maia looked doubtful. I laughed.

"Well," I shrugged, "I'm not worried at precisely this very moment. I will be again, I'm sure. But in between? In between I won't allow it to distract me from what's important today. I'm going to enjoy my days and my life and be all the more ready to roll with whatever comes my way."

ᴓ

Aunt Eva had given me that advice about not being so distracted by worry. I also remembered when Aunt Eva had said that Beach Heart was, for her, the place she came to when she needed comfort. That it was the place she always wanted to be, and she never really wanted to be anywhere else. It hadn't been one of Aunt Eva's rules, but it had surely been her truth.

It was true for me, too, in that when I'd needed comfort and recovery, I'd received it at Beach Heart. As for the rest, I wasn't exactly sure where my forever place would be. And really…did I have to choose one single place? Was that a rule of some kind? I thought not.

This morning I was returning to a job I enjoyed, had received the offer of a fulltime job—if I chose to accept it. Plus, I had dinner plans with Jake. Not sure where we were going or whether that would include Starfish, but I was okay either way.

And I'd call Mom this evening because I had *more* to tell her.

A family passed along the sidewalk, laughing and eager to reach the marina. An umbrella was tucked into the side of the stroller. Given the blue sky overhead, I guessed they might be intending to sail over to Shackelford Banks where the only shade to be had was via an umbrella. One of these days, soon, I was going to make that trip.

Maybe I'd suggest it to Jake. We could hunt for shells or see the wild horses. Could be fun.

Maia had left me here at the bench and was already at the gallery, no doubt wondering what was taking me so long to cross Front Street and join her at the gallery. I was on my way.

And it was all good. I might not know precisely where my future lay, but I was a work in progress, and I was blessed with friends and with options—and that was *my* truth.

The End

Thank you for reading *Beach Heart*

I hope you enjoyed it.

Author's Note

Beach Heart was the story I was working on when 2019 started going crazy. I'd just finished writing *A Light Last Seen* in late 2019 (published in early 2020) and had started work on the story that would become *Beach Heart.* But when I lost my mom and then Covid came into our lives right after, I continued trying to write it for several months and found I'd lost the heart to write this story. And then Lilliane Moore, in *A Barefoot Tide* and *A Dancing,* stepped up. Writing her stories gave me comfort, so I put *Beach Heart* aside. That said, I still wanted to write about Emma Dance and her return to a place she loved—a place that however loved it may be in her memory may need to be left behind in order to open her life to the future. This is often true of things we cling to—be they objects or past hurts that we need to leave behind, or triumphs we wish to relive and relinquish.

Beach Heart started as the story I intended to publish in 2020, but now, in 2022, I'm delighted to bring it to readers. I hope readers will enjoy it.

I did not intend to include Maia Donovan, a primary character in *Beach Rental, Beach Winds* and *Beach Wedding,* in *Beach Heart.* But Maia had other ideas, just as she did in the Barefoot Tides series. Reading *Beach Heart* won't spoil The Emerald Isle, NC Stories Series or the Barefoot Tides Series for readers—I was careful to make sure that didn't happen when I finally gave in and let Maia join in on the fun. Now I can't imagine this book without her. I hope readers will enjoy seeing Maia again too.

June 2022 ~ Grace Greene

Discussion Questions

1. *The joy and comfort to be found in simple ways and ordinary days* . . . Sometimes we undervalue everyday tasks and simple pleasures. What are ordinary tasks and activities you find comfort in?

2. Is comfort *in simple ways and ordinary days* more likely to be found if the person has the health or financial ability to live their daily life within a stable environment? Does stability in the present make it easier to trust in or take a chance on the future? Or does comfort make it harder to move forward?

3. No right choice or one perfect moment can yield lasting happiness. We are the sum of our parts, many of which are moving and changing as we live our lives. For her future, Emma is determined to make her own path to happiness by *not* limiting her choices. Is it better to focus on one goal or to leave our options open?

4. Prolonged stress has created an automatic alarm response in Emma such that when

something surprises her, she overreacts or shuts down. She recognizes that responding with alarm or panic is pointless, but how do you change those automatic responses?

5. Emma says that preserving the past isn't always the right choice, that sometimes the choice to let the past go—to let it be the past—is the more reasonable option, and perhaps the healthiest one. But to keep or not to keep something is a personal decision and could apply to many things, not all of them physical items. Some items/emotions give us joy. Some items/emotions weigh us down like anchors and hold us back. Family memorabilia, treasured items, grief, resentment, or regret—how do we decide what to keep and what to release?

Acknowledgments

My sincere thanks to everyone who contributed to making *Beach Heart* the best story it could be.

About the Author

Photo © 2018 Amy G Photography

Grace Greene is an award-winning and USA Today bestselling author of women's fiction and contemporary romance with suspense set in the countryside of her native Virginia *(The Happiness In Between, The Memory of Butterflies, the Cub Creek Series, and The Wildflower House Series)* and on the breezy beaches of Emerald Isle, North Carolina *(The Emerald Isle, NC Stories Series, and Barefoot Tides Series)*. Her debut novel, *Beach Rental*, and the sequel, *Beach Winds*, were both Top Picks by RT Book Reviews magazine.

The release of *A Barefoot Tide*, represented the merging of two worlds—that of Cub Creek and Emerald Isle, through the eyes of a new character, and continues in the sequel, *A Dancing Tide* released in October 2021. *Wildflower Wedding* joins *The Wildflower House Series* lineup in February 2022.

Visit www.gracegreene.com for more information, and to connect with Grace.

Books by Grace Greene

Emerald Isle, North Carolina Series
Beach Rental *(Book 1)*
Beach Winds *(Book 2)*
Beach Wedding *(Book 3)*
"Beach Towel" (A Short Story)
Beach Walk *(Christmas Novella)*

Barefoot Tides Two-Book Series
A Barefoot Tide *(Book 1)*
A Dancing Tide *(Book 2)*

Beach Single-Title Novellas
Beach Christmas *(Christmas Novella)*
Clair *(Beach Brides Novella Series)*

Cub Creek Novels ~ Series and Single Titles
Cub Creek *(Cub Creek Series, Book 1)*
Leaving Cub Creek *(Cub Creek Series, Book 2)*
The Happiness In Between
The Memory of Butterflies
A Light Last Seen

The Wildflower House Novels
Wildflower Heart *(Book 1)*
Wildflower Hope *(Book 2)*
Wildflower Christmas *(A Wildflower House Novella Bk 3)*
Wildflower Wedding *(A Wildflower House Novella Bk 4)*

Virginia Country Roads
Kincaid's Hope
A Stranger in Wynnedower

www.GraceGreene.com

Made in the USA
Middletown, DE
10 June 2022

66953524R00230